Rockapocalypse

Disharmony of Justice

A novel by

Byron Suggs

Written World
Communications

ROCKAPOCALYPSE by Byron Suggs
Published by Starsongs, an imprint of Written World Communications
PO Box 26677
Colorado Springs, CO 80936

Lyrics to "White Lightning" are by author Byron Suggs, and not Buddy Holly as they were credited in the book.

Cover designer: Lynda K. Arndt
Creative Team: Patti Shene, Kristine Pratt
Images courtesy of Wikimedia Commons & iStockphoto
Author Photo by Allison Earnest Photography

Library of Congress Control Number: 2012948499
International Standard Book Number 978-1-938679-01-8

Printed in the United States of America

Dedication

To Beth, my wife, soulmate and biggest fan for the last thirty years. To my children, Jessica and Brandon, because I want them to know that life is full of breath-taking possibilities if only they open their eyes and look beyond the stars. To my parents, for bringing me into this world during an era of cultural revolution that spawned my imagination and set fire to my soul; and for their timeless support. And lastly, to the child in every one of us, no matter the age— may your dreams and imaginings live long and vividly in your soul.

Acknowledgements

The roads taken to get this book to print were long, winding and sometimes painful. I learned a lot about my dreams, my desires, and the craft of writing along those roads. I would still be wandering that landscape had it not been for the support and determination of the following people: Kristine Pratt, a wonderfully talented publisher, editor, and all around lover of the written word. She saw promise in a scatter-brained author and his bizarre manuscript, and committed her talents to this book far beyond my wildest dreams. Patti Sheen, Executive Editor of the Starsongs imprint at Written World Communications. She worked tirelessly in our collaboration to put "Rockapocalypse" into print, and I think we both learned a few things along the way. Lynda Arndt, who designed the cover for "Rockapocalypse." She found the essence of this story and delivered a stunning visual. Freelance editors, beta readers and all others who supported me down those roads, I thank you from the bottom of my heart. You know who you are. Also, in my own twisted way, I'd like to thank the agents that turned down my manuscript and the publishers that didn't feel it fit their needs. I learned a great deal from you. Yes, I did. I would also be amiss not to bow with gratitude to the fabulous years of the 60's and 70's that made up my childhood. I couldn't have written a better script in the Book of Life if I'd tried. You rock! And finally, my Creator. I will put it down here, but I give thanks to God every day for giving me the support, drive, focus, and talent to pursue my dreams.

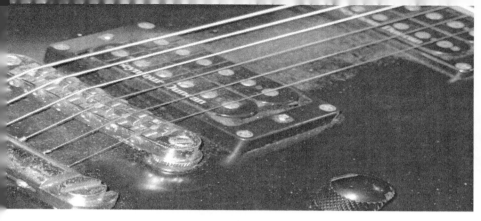

PROLOGUE

1959

BLOODY TEARS RAN FROM the corners of Buddy Holly's ruptured eyes, traveled down smooth temples, brushed the bottoms of his sideburns, downward, downward until they found the hollows of each ear, where they glided smoothly into the ear canals and came to rest against his eardrums. The silence of heaven.

God was calling.

"Buddy," God said.

A string of synapses fired through wet brain matter, seeking refuge in His voice, obeying the instinct that drives all life, the instinct of survival. Nerves and tissue sought out and energized the remaining life force that was Buddy Holly, former rock and roll star.

"Yes, God?"

"I'm sorry about this, Buddy." The voice carried, deep and resounding, like the roar of a tornado. "I know it was all so abrupt, but some things cannot be avoided. Do you have a minute?"

Buddy's hand involuntarily squeezed shut against a jagged guitar pick embedded in his bloody palm. *This is a joke, right?*

"No, no, Buddy. This is serious, in case you haven't noticed."

His irritation apparent, it disappeared as quickly as it had come. "I have a quandary, Buddy. It seems our Dark Angel has upped the ante while I was busy. The rules, you see, were quite simple."

I'm dying here, God. What—

"I know you're dying, Buddy. After all, I am God. But you must pay attention." His voice grew quiet, hovering in Buddy's damaged head before it suddenly roared forth again. "The fight for souls was the goal of the Endgame. A personal endeavor with singular purpose. Now, it seems he may have expanded his reach into another realm. The Dark Angel is playing in my backyard and I don't like it."

Synapses weakening, memories trapped in gray matter seeped from the energy, crowding out God's voice. Girls screamed, drums pounded in rhythm, amplifiers sent walls of sound into the air that was once Buddy's world.

The Dark Angel would never rest. Every second a human soul was up for grabs, and Buddy still had a few seconds for the taking.

But God was persistent.

"Buddy, are you listening?"

"Yes." His cracked, bloody lips mouthed the word in the darkness.

"You have a new purpose, Buddy. If you make it here, I'll tell you about it. I know it's cliché, but just follow my light."

The noise of the crowd, the music, grew in his head again, refusing to let him give up on this life he was now leaving, the one that had created a void in his soul and laid promise at his feet. With the last of his strength, resisting the Dark Angel's pull on his tethered soul, he raised his arm, his bloody hand stretched toward a single point of light in the darkness above, index finger striving upward, the word *wait* forming on his lips.

Oh God, no, he thought. *I'm not going to make it!*

And the finger of God, like a lightning bolt, reached down from all eternity and touched his, retrieving his soul, leaving his empty shell among the plane wreckage as snowflakes began to blanket the earth.

As his arm fell, still smoking, the pick broke free, tumbled toward the ground, and vanished.

PART I

When the Dreams of the Dead...

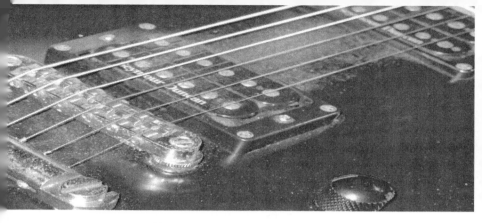

CHAPTER ONE

1959

1200 MILES SOUTHEAST AS the crow flies, the power grid for a map dot called Swift's Cross, North Carolina went down, sending Singleton Baptist Hospital into total darkness, and most of the staff into a panic. Madge Thorsten, Head RN of the Maternity Ward, was sipping coffee and reading *Dr. Zhivago* when the emergency lights kicked on. At fifty-two, she'd been around the block a few times, seen all kinds of things to get upset about, but this wasn't one of them, at least not in her department, on her shift. She placed the book and coffee by the scheduling board and stood.

"Nurse Bledsoe?"

She didn't look at the student nurse, nor wait for her. The request was implicit, Madge was efficient. The young intern was already on her heels as she rounded the nurses' station in the weak lighting and set off for the Nursery. The ward was mostly quiet, a few coughs from groggy mothers, someone called out a name, perhaps waking from a dream. Doors opening, closing somewhere. A louder, busier sound coming from the elevators as they passed.

No preemies, no respiratory cases, Madge ticked off in her head as she walked. *One in delivery.* She knew her floor well. As long as the power came back on soon, all would be fine. They passed the dark viewing window without so much as a glance and stopped at the Nursery door. The sound coming from the other side caused Madge to pause, hand on the doorknob.

"Nurse Thorsten?" The intern hovered behind her, curious.

"Shhh!" Madge waved her hand back at the young nurse, signaling for quiet. She pressed her ear closer to the door, perplexed, holding her breath as she strained to make sense of what she heard. The intern leaned in, chin accidently touching Madge's shoulder. The lights suddenly flickered back to life, and a bulb on a nearby wall went out with a *pop!* Madge jumped a little, then felt embarrassed by her jittery reaction.

"Go check on the mothers, Nurse Bledsoe."

The intern gave her a funny look and hurried away down the hall.

Gaining her composure, Madge opened the door, took two steps into the room…and stopped. There were seven babies in the nursery that morning; fourteen tiny arms and fourteen tiny hands stretched toward the ceiling, seven tiny throats crying in perfect unison, perfect pitch, a chorus to something unseen, some with open eyes, some not. It wasn't an angry cry, but a forlorn, sad cry. A break your heart cry.

Madge stared, mouth open. Goosebumps ran up her arms, belying the sadness those tiny cries should have elicited from her heart. In thirty-two years of nursing she'd never seen such a thing. She looked over at the duty nurse who was sitting in a rocking chair by the window. Nurse Greyford rocked slowly, a swaddling blanket clutched to her chest, tears streaming down both cheeks as she looked up at Madge.

"Isn't that the most beautiful thing you've ever heard? Isn't it?" She smiled, as if listening to angels strum harps.

Abruptly, all the babies went silent, little arms still raised, as if listening for something. Seconds passed.

A shrieking wail from newborn lungs drifted down the hallway from Delivery, punctuating the moment. The hair stood up on the back of Madge's neck. She glanced at the clock on the wall.

2:10 a.m.

Now this is something to get upset about. I've never seen anything like this. Never, ever.

"Congratulations, Mrs. Travers. It's a boy."

The doctor handed the baby to the attending nurse, who cleaned and swaddled him, tiny arms and feet flailing in protest against his abrupt departure from the womb. One little hand grabbed at her scrubs while the other, clinched shut, waved with indignation.

Clarice Travers couldn't restrain the tidal wave of joy that welled up inside her. She looked up at the doctor with exhausted eyes, a smile tugging at the corners of her trembling mouth. "A boy?" It wasn't a question of disappointment. Only awe. Boy or girl, it was still a tiny miracle, and her heart embraced it with all the love she had.

He nodded and stepped away as two nurses moved in to clean up.

The nurse holding the baby returned to the bedside. "Here, you can hold him a minute." She bent and laid the baby in Clarice's arms. The crying had all but stopped now.

Clarice stared at him, overwhelmed with a mother's love. "Peter," she said softly, the name coming to her like fragrance on a breeze. "My little miracle."

Peter squirmed in his blanket, fist still clinched, then fell still.

Perfectly still. His little fist opened and something fell out, landing in Clarice's lap. An angry red mark was visible on his palm, but he wasn't crying.

"What's that?" She stared down at the object, surprise, revulsion and curiosity all fighting for control of her emotions.

The nurse walked over and picked it up. She turned it over in her hand and held it up to the light. Her brow furrowed. "I don't know, Mrs. Travers. It has blood on it, but…"

The doctor came over, held out his hand. "Let me see." She placed it in his hand. He studied it for a few seconds, uttered "Gibs" under his breath and gazed across the room, a puzzled look on his face.

"Well?" Clarice pulled the baby tighter against her breast. "What is it, doctor?"

He pushed up his glasses and rubbed his eyelids hard. "It's a piece of guitar pick, Mrs. Travers." Shaking his head, he pulled his glasses back down, weary face passive when he finally looked Clarice in the eyes. It was obvious that any reasonable explanation eluded him at the moment.

"How do you know that?" asked the nurse as she moved in for a second look.

"Because… I play guitar." He broke eye contact and hung his head. Overhead lights reflected off the pomade in his crew cut as he twirled the pick in his fingers.

With baby Peter clasped snugly against her breast, Clarice Travers fainted.

Beyond the walls of Singleton Baptist hospital, a black cat moved like shadowy silk through the back alley. Feral senses acute, tail twitching with anticipation of tonight's hunt, it approached the service door with caution. The dumpsters sat off to the side, lit from both directions with a harsh glare from the utility lights. The cat took one step at a time, as it did every night, wary of others like him. Ten feet from the containers, it stopped. Ears flat, head down, it crouched low to the ground, all senses alert. The darkness between these two things that held its nightly food was impenetrable. Even with nocturnal eyes, the cat could see nothing in the void. But it felt it. Yes it did.

And it didn't like it.

It dashed away into the night, never stopping, never looking back.

The shadows stirred like liquid in that dark place. The Singing Man sat there on his bedroll, his guitar across his legs, a smile on his broad, black face. He'd heard the baby cry out only moments before. Heard him spill into this world, his lungs ablaze and an imminent responsibility on his soft, pink shoulders. Heard that bloody pick drop with a roar. It was his cue.

Now, as the Singing Man sat in the shadows, strumming his guitar, swaying, softly humming, he spoke to the newborn. Spoke with his mind in soft, soothing words. Important words.

You like music, little man? Music. Yes'um, she's some pow'ful stuff, she is. He could see it behind his coal-black eyes, that baby boy cuddled on his mother's breast, cooing with innocence, mind attentive to the Singing Man's words as he nurtured in the warmth of her embrace. *You do well to 'member that, Pete. Real well to 'member that at the gig.*

He laughed to himself. A low, soft laugh that didn't resonate in this world.

The stage had been set. The countdown had begun....

JOURNAL

| 8¢ | TUESDAY F |

TRAGIC

Plane Crash Kills Four Rising Stars

February 3 - Four persons, three identified as well-known singers of Rock n' Roll early Tues-

Coroner's Investigation
Air crash, Feb. 3, 1959
SW 1/4, Section 18, Lincoln Twp.
Cerro Gordo County, Iowa

Jiles P. Richardson, Charles Hardin Holley, Richard Valenzuela and Roger A. Peterson, pilot of the plane, were killed in the crash of a chartered airplane when it fell within minutes of takeoff from Mason City Airport. The three passengers were members of a troupe of entertainers who appeared at the Surf Ballroom at Clear Lake, Iowa, the evening of Feb. 3, 1959, bound for Fargo, N.D. and was headed northwest from the airport at the time of the crash in a stubble field, 5 1/2 miles north of Clear Lake, Iowa.

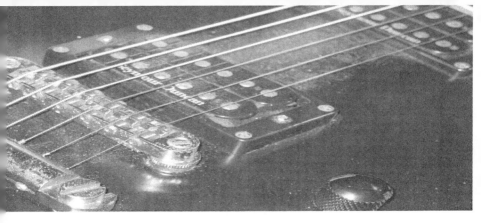

CHAPTER TWO

2011

PETER TRAVERS ROLLED OVER and slammed a hand down on the alarm clock button. He'd been slamming that button, or one like it, for the last fifteen years at precisely 7:30 a.m. without fail. The smell of fresh brewed coffee and pancakes lured him from the sheets. He stumbled into the bathroom and turned on the water. Looking in the mirror, he ran his finger across the bags under his eyes, let out a sigh.

"You're looking mighty attractive today, Mr. Travers," he mocked his reflection.

At 52, he was founder and president of Global Records, the third largest record company in the world. Which was funny to him, since he hadn't seen an actual record in forever.

He showered and shaved, his attitude and energy level picking up by the minute, whistling old music hits from his youth. He loved his job and had good reasons to. About 250 million reasons, to be exact. That was the number of sales Global had pulled in last year.

He slapped on his aftershave, dressed and made it downstairs by 8:00. Margie bent over, kissed him on the head and poured his coffee.

"Big day today?" she asked, placing the pancakes and sausage links on the table.

He watched her for a second as she glided around the kitchen in her housecoat. *She's still as gorgeous as the day I married her.*

"Just some agents pitching, a few video conferences across the water, a board meeting and—"

"And pick up a bottle of wine for this evening," she said, leaning against his arm.

Anniversary! He'd almost forgotten.

"What delicious dish will we be dining on tonight? Besides yourself, I mean." He gave her a wolfish look.

She grabbed a dish towel and snapped it at his arm playfully. "You'll see when you get here, big boy! Just don't forget that wine." She laughed and leaned back against the counter.

"Got it." He wiped his mouth and looked at his watch. "Crap! I'm running late."

With that, he stood up and kissed her a little longer than usual. She blushed and followed him to the door as he hurried out with his briefcase and jacket in hand.

Backing out of the driveway, he noticed she was still standing at the door. He waved as he put the car in gear. She waved back, rubbing her stomach with her free hand. It wasn't until he was at the end of the street that he realized how odd that gesture was.

And somehow, familiar.

He pulled onto Bentley Drive, shifting into second, and decided he would ask her about it when he got home.

Peter adjusted the radio dial to his favorite classic rock station as he cruised down Freemont Boulevard in his Mercedes. He was making good time in the right lane when he noticed the light change up ahead. Before he could come to a complete stop, a vagrant stepped into the road with a bottle of windshield fluid and a squeegee. Peter slammed on brakes to avoid him.

Bev Anderson didn't like being told what to do, especially by her husband. She thought she'd strangle him if he told her not to drive and talk on her cell phone one more time. The argument had made her late for work, and she would get fired if she was late again.

The phone went off in her purse as she accelerated down Freemont Boulevard. She couldn't resist picking it up any more than she could resist sleeping with Ted from the office. Reaching for it, she noticed in the rearview mirror that she'd neglected to put on her eyeliner this morning. She flipped the phone open and jammed it between her ear and shoulder while rummaging through her purse for the liner pencil.

"Hello!" she said, finding the liner and uncapping it. "Jenny? Hey girl! Yes, on the way to work." She adjusted the mirror so she could see without leaning over. "He did what? No, no don't tell me that." She began applying the eyeliner, laughing at Jenny's reply, one hand keeping the Audi between the lines. She never saw the stopped Mercedes looming up in front of her. Never had a clue that all things in the universe are connected.

The Audi plowed into Peter's car at fifty-three mph, overriding his brakes and propelling him into the intersection amidst blaring horns and squealing tires. A cement truck, air horn maxed out, clipped the Mercedes, sending it into a sliding spin before a Lincoln Continental t-boned the driver's side door.

It was over in seconds.

The intersection quieted as traffic came to a stop. Concerned citizens rushed up to the mangled Mercedes to peer in. Oil and gas seeped around their shoes, but no one noticed through the steam escaping from the busted radiator. A few of them gasped, most observed in silence.

A hand, pale, bleeding, lay against the dash, one finger twitching upward, falling, twitching, falling again. Blood smeared the passenger's side window, small bits of hair stuck against the glass.

With a reverence usually deferred for the dead or dying, the curious retreated in quiet murmurs, a few pulling out phones, most walking away, shock etched on their faces.

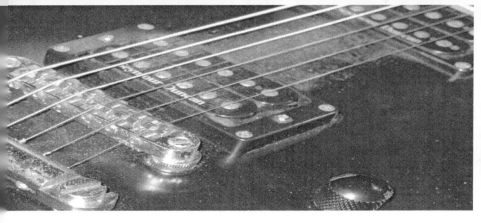

CHAPTER THREE

"WE'VE STOPPED THE BLEEDING, but he suffered massive head trauma." The doctor waited a moment to let that sink in, then, "He's in a coma, Mrs. Travers."

Margie stood on weak legs at Peter's side, puffy eyes scanning the monitors and tubes that kept her husband alive. *Why? Why him?* Despite all the damage now corrected with surgery, despite all the gauze and tubes and machines, he looked as peaceful as a newborn. Her hand wandered down to her stomach and she was overcome with grief again. She'd planned on telling him about the baby at dinner tonight. *Would he ever know now?*

"Will he come out of it?" Her lips trembled as she reached out and clasped his hand under the sheet.

"That's something doctors have been trying to nail down since Hippocrates, Mrs. Travers. I just can't give you an answer to that." He cleared his throat, sliding his glasses up with his finger. "I'll leave you alone for a bit." He started for the door, but paused before he opened it. "Mrs. Travers? What about the press? Should we send them away?"

News traveled fast in the music world, and Margie knew it. But now was not the time, not the place. "Tell them that he's still alive. Tell them to pray for him. Tell them—" she faltered. She wanted to tell them to go to the devil, but that wasn't fair. They were out there because Peter had been instrumental in bringing phenomenal music to the world. She couldn't fault them for wanting to know. "Tell them to get a statement from Global Records. The family would like some peace right now."

"Yes. Of course." He turned and walked out, pulling the door closed behind him.

Margie couldn't stop the tears. They came fast, hard, riding on emotions she had no power to control. Sobs wracked her body. She closed her eyes, laid her head against Peter's mattress, and prayed.

The sun rose and fell, sending light up one wall and down the other. The world existed outside that hospital room, but it was a world that mattered not to Margie. Peter was her life. Peter was the life within her belly. Peter just *was*.

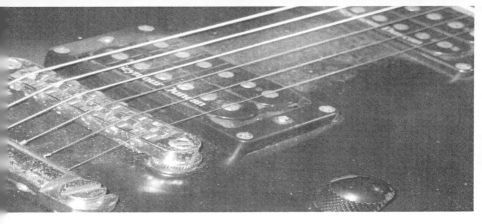

CHAPTER FOUR

Peter

HE DREAMED HE STOOD in the shadows of trees, on a muddy dirt road that ran along the banks of a pond. He was wet, shivering, as a breeze blew off the water, chilling him to the bone. And there was crying, like a thousand people weeping at once. The sound filled his head to near bursting. He turned in the road, once, twice, trying to find the source, the reason for so much despair, when his eyes fell on a figure ambling toward him down that muddy road. It was the Singing Man.

Pete wasn't sure how he knew this. He just did, as if that knowledge was already planted deep in his brain at birth, a whisper impressed on his first conscious thought.

He came now, this Singing Man, strumming his guitar, specks of water reflecting rainbows off the lenses of his sunglasses. Pete stood still, the anguished sounds filling his head, trembling with fear at the unknown.

The Singing Man stepped up to Pete and smiled. "You ready, Pete?" He lifted both arms wide. "Yes'um, Pete, music be some pow'ful stuff. You jus' 'member that and you do fine, yes you will, son." He lowered his arms and patted him on the head, bending down until Pete smelled his dry, sweet breath. "And one day, I's come back fo' you, Pete. Yes'um, I will. I sho' will. Then we sees what's in dat pot, okay? Sees what dat old man gots, yes'um."

Pete felt hot wind on the side of his face, and when he turned toward it, the water was boiling, thick and blood red. He opened his mouth and his cry of terror became one with the multitudes in his head....

I woke from a dream, but I didn't wake. At least not in the real world —Margie and the kids' world. Not in the life I'd built with them. I don't remember much about what brought me here, to this dark place. But the pain is fresh in my memory. *Oh God, the pain!* It was unlike anything I'd ever felt, instant and merciless.

I fight the cold fingers of panic, now. I cannot open my eyes, or move my arms and legs. Cannot speak. But I can feel Margie close by. That knowledge keeps me calm, gives me shelter against the terror that threatens my sanity. I know she'll always be there for me even if I'm not there for her, and it breaks my heart because we've been intertwined for as long as I can remember.

The dream, though, was real to me. As real as the first time I had it. Only fifteen, I didn't expect the wonderment and tragedy that lay before me. But this time, it's opened doors to my past. Doors that I'd closed for good, and I don't think I can stop it.

No. I was warned, but I wished it away like young men full of idealism and bravado think they can.

I never told Margie of that warning. Never prepared her.

And now I can't.

All I can do now is remember. All I can do is lie here in this shell of a body and remember those things that took my youth from me, stained me. It started then. Started when the world was magical and love was just a belief away. Started when my father took me to visit Lath Edwards.

The world never seemed the same after that.

In the Spring of '74, Dad surprised me with a bit of news when I came home from school Friday afternoon. He'd just come in from mowing the grass with our old push mower, wiping his brow with a white hanky. The day was unusually warm for mid-April.

"You wanna ride out to see your Uncle Lath today, Pete?"

"Who?"

"Lath Edwards. He lives about two miles north, out toward Mule Creek Crossroads. I got a call from your Grandma Travers today, said we should look him up." Dad said this like I should know as much about Lath Edwards as I know about my own left hand.

"I guess," I muttered in uncertain tones, remembering I'd been thinking about asking Arlo if he wanted to go salamander hunting down at the Cotton Mill creek.

We took off about four that afternoon and drove out toward Mule Creek. The sun was waning but warm, with promise of an early summer. The Young Rascals were singing *"Groovin'"* on the radio. I tapped along with the tune, my Keds keeping beat on the floorboard.

"So," I said, turning to face Dad, "tell me again how we're related to Uncle Lath?" I didn't recall any mention of Lath from my grandparents over the years.

"Well, he's not exactly blood kin," Dad said, glancing over at me with a crooked smile on his face. "He was a friend of your

Grandfather's brother, Roy, who was my uncle. Roy died a few years back, when you were little." He slowed down behind a tractor, put on his blinker and passed it, eventually easing back into the right lane. "From what I can remember, Lath is a decorated war hero."

That piqued my interest. "War hero? What did he do?" I asked, envisioning John Wayne in the Sands of Iwo Jima, bloodied and grime-streaked, a grenade clinched in his hand as he charged over the beachhead.

"I don't know, exactly, but I imagine he risked his own life to save other soldiers in WWII. That's the way it usually works. I think he was a Prisoner of War in Korea, too."

"Really?"

"Yeah. Captured and held by the enemy. I think someone once said he spent a year in that camp." Dad shook his head at the thought. "Nasty business. I hear it really changes a man."

I started to ask how, but his brow furrowed up deep so I decided to keep quiet.

We turned onto a dirt road, made our way down through a stand of oak trees, and rounded a curve that emptied in front of a little modified Streamline travel trailer. It sat with blocks shoring up both ends, and starting from the side doorway, a crazy maze of canvas covers attached to poles stretched out in all directions, creating a great shady area. Perched atop the tallest pole was a U.S. flag. Beneath that was the pride of the South, a confederate flag.

Dad pulled up next to a rusty El Camino parked out front and killed the motor. We both sat still a minute, soaking it in. Two mangy chickens clucked and pecked hard dirt around the base of an old burn barrel, smoke curling skyward, vanishing in the breeze, shuffling the leaves of the trees.

Just then, the metal screen door on the Streamline shot open, slamming against the frame, and out rolled Lath Edwards in a "glorified" wheelchair, complete with little flags, bells, whistles, reflectors, and various other unidentifiable gadgets. He bolted down a series of ramps and sailed to a stop just a foot or two away from our front bumper. Smiling, he exposed a perfect gap of smooth, toothless gums, top and bottom, in the middle of his mouth as he honked a greeting with a bicycle horn.

"Hey, fellers! What can I do fer ya?" Sun glinted off eyeglass lenses so thick, his eyes looked like the cue balls I'd seen down at Stampy's Billiards.

Lath was a stocky man, his bulk taking up the total width and depth of his wheelchair. Hair cut in a butch crew, his multi-colored suspenders competed for attention with war medals, campaign buttons, lodge pins, and at least one odd looking, half dollar-sized patch in red, black and white colors that looked like a wheel or something. Large, flabby arms, so thick with hair they looked like long sleeves, protruded from his sweat-stained tee shirt.

I was wary and a little nervous, all at once. I'd never seen anything like him. Dad and I got out and walked to the front of the car where he sat.

"I'm Bill Travers. Claudette's son?" He extended his hand. "This is my son Pete."

A look of recognition crossed Lath's grizzled face. "Lawd have mercy! Claudette's boy? I haven't seen ya since you were a snot-nosed little shat running around in durdy drawers!" He shook Dad's hand. "And this is yer boy?" He ran sausage-like fingers through my hair, much like you'd rub a dog's head to make his tail wag. I winced, pulling away as polite as I could.

"Yes, that's Peter, but we call him Pete." Dad ran his hand through my hair, but I didn't move this time on account it was him. I was beginning to feel like a lap dog.

"Well, it's mighty nice of y'all to come way out here ta' see me.

Don't get much dust stirred up on that road these days. Y'all have a seat!" He motioned to several old aluminum folding chairs under the canopy. The seat webbing was almost torn through on them all, but me and Dad, being polite, sank slowly down into two of them. I think we were both praying the bottoms wouldn't burst out and wedge our butts into the frames.

Lath wheeled his chair over to face us. "So, y'all been around these here parts very long? It's been a coon's age since I spoke to Claudette. Don't think she mentioned you all movin' 'round here."

"We moved up to Harper's Mill a few years ago, Lath. Use to do some police work down in Bentonberg, but some bad luck made me rethink that." Dad paused, rubbing his chin as if pondering his words.

"Got shot, did ya?" Lath stared at Dad. His eyes had a way of fixin' on you and just floating there.

"Well, yeah…yeah, I did. Just a flesh wound, but Clarice wanted me out of policin' and into something that didn't worry her to death. I guess it was for the best." Just for a second, Dad looked like he regretted the whole thing. I kept my mouth shut.

"Well, I've taken a slug 'er two in my day. Nothin' more'n beatin' the devil to the draw. Seen many who didn't beat 'em, though." Lath licked his dry lips, stared just past us with a scowl on his face. "Them dern gooks sure did us mean. Rascals broke both my dang legs and left me in a hole to die!" He turned and looked at me, *glared* at me. A moment later a look of surprise crossed his face.

"Sorry 'bout that, son. Get a bit ugly when I think 'bout those days…didn't mean to get worked up an' all."

I glanced down at my shoes. Dad cleared his throat and spoke.

"No apology needed, Lath."

Lath nodded. "You boys ever do any fishin'? You might want to give my old mud hole a try one day…come on, I'll show ya."

Lath wheeled past us and sped up a ramp, his meaty arms working the wheels like pistons. I suspect he was a right strong feller despite his bad legs. We followed him on the plank walk which led behind his place, then curved off into the woods. The sunlight was almost filtered out above us as we walked.

About a hundred yards in, the trees parted and the plank walk ended on a muddy bank. Stretched before us, like Lath said, was a mud hole. Actually, it looked like it had once been a pretty good little pond, stretching a few hundred yards out in any direction. Now, the water didn't look too deep and a green scum covered the entire surface. Green, mossy stumps jutted up here and there, and it generally looked like a breeding ground for snakes. Off to our right, tied to an oak sapling, sat a weathered old rowboat. My eyes drifted to the opposite side.

"What's that place there, Mr. Lath?" I pointed across the water to an opening on the far bank.

"Oh, that. That's just another path that comes from the state road out there. Have me a heck of a time keepin' the..." He paused. "...them coloreds out in the summer time." His gaze stayed on the spot at the far side. "But they's ways to take care of that." He glanced back at us and winked. "You boys can come he'ah anytime you want to fish. Some the best catfish I ever tasted come right outta here." Lath eyed the pond favorably. "Jus' come up here anytime. Don't even hav'ta knock on my door."

"Well, thanks Lath. I'm sure me and Pete will get out this way again and take you up on that offer." Dad was being polite. I wasn't so sure he wanted to do much of anything around this place, and I was with him on that one.

"And you might catch Spike." Lath looked at both of us with a jubilant, almost boyish grin on his face.

"Who's Spike, Mr. Lath?"

"Well, son, it's not s'much who it is as what it is, which just happens to be the biggest catfish in this he'ah south, deep or otherwise." He spread his hands about a yard apart. My jaw dropped. "And blacker'n midnight to boot!" he added.

"You sure that's not just another tall fish tale, Lath?" Dad was grinning at me, but lost it when he looked back at Lath. The old man wasn't smiling.

"I'm a tellin' the truth, Bill!" He seemed a bit riled. "I'll also tell you this. That ain't narry everyday catfish, big 'er not! I seen some things I'm still not sure about." He thoughtfully scratched at his stubble and gazed at us from behind his coke-bottle lenses. "I had this dog once."

He let that sit there between us. Didn't hurry a bit, just stared at us while the statement swelled up like a pregnant lady. I waited for Dad to ask, but he was way too slow.

"What dog, Mr. Lath?" I watched him raise his head and scratch a spot behind his ear. Still, he let the question continue to swell almost to bursting.

Finally, he stared back down at his feet and began in a low, almost remorseful voice. "I had a little dog named Tweezers. Just a puff of fur and a behind that smelled real bad… no matter what I washed him with." He wiped under his eyes with a thick, meaty hand. "He was real happy when I'd give him poke rinds. His little tail would wag like it was ready to fall off." A sad smile pulled slightly at the corners of Lath's mouth. "Then one day, I made me a mistake I'll never fo'get." He grew real quiet.

I grew impatient.

"So what happened. Mr. Lath?"

"We was down there on the bank by the boat tie-offs. Just sitting there, eating a bag of poke rinds. I tossed a few to Tweezers. He had a way of crunchin' down on them with his lips drawn back, almost like he was a'smilin' and sayin' thanks. I tossed a big 'ol han'ful of 'em in his direction and the wind caught 'em, sent 'em out across the edge of the water. Did ya know poke rinds float? I didn't… never gave it that much thought." His brow furrowed, as if pondering this revelation anew. "Lil' Tweezers ran right into that pond, dog-paddled out a few feet into those reeds yonder and snatched the first poke rind wid his little teeth.

"I heard this gawd awful screamin', and seen Tweezers go down under the water. They was nothing left but a few bobbing poke rinds swirling around in that spot. I found lil' Tweezers that evenin' on the bank by the creek feed. He was punctured all over like a pin cushin', most of the life bled outta him. He died in my arms."

Lath removed his glasses and wiped at his eyes again. He cleaned his lenses with his dirty shirt tail. For a big man, he certainly had a soft side, I thought. I looked at Dad, who had his head down. Lath regained his composure. "I'll tell ya one thing, though. I'm gonna ketch that black rascal one day an' mount his sorry butt on the wall." His eyes turned steely, like gun metal. So much for his soft side.

"We're sorry to hear about all that, Lath," Dad offered. I was stunned by the story, and Dad's face read the same. Lath nodded solemnly, then smiled and reached around behind his chair, fidgeting with something for a second. Without warning the clang-clang-clang of an old alarm clock broke the silence, causing me and Dad to jump. It seemed Lath had a multitude of noisy contraptions on that wheelchair.

Suddenly, all heck broke loose. Along the bank, a few feet down from us, a great screeching and caterwauling noise pierced the stagnant air. The branches shook and thrashed about like a bull elephant was charging through them. I backed up a step. Dad looked at Lath. Lath looked at the bushes with a smile on his face.

"Well, 'nough of that sad stuff. Boys, meet my second in co-mand, Lucifer." He waved his arms in a grand flourish, and there on the bank appeared the ugliest ape I'd ever seen. My jaw dropped. It was about my height with reddish brown fur all over, and wore an old Army fatigue shirt with the cuffs rolled up. Powerful looking arms hung low to the ground. A piece of white cloth was flapping from his khaki pocket. Some kinda' weird black squiggly marks covered the fabric with a patch of blue peaking over the pocket edge. I had seen pictures of orangutans in Mrs. Johnson's class, but this was my first *live* one and definitely my first one in clothes.

Dad just stood there, unsure of what to do. I had no doubts of what I wanted to do, and that was run. Lucifer seemed agitated, but I wasn't sure since I don't own one myself. He let out a low, guttural sound and pounded his chest.

"Just don't move too fast, Bill," Lath said under his breath. Dad backed up a few feet, about as fast as grass grows, and stopped next to Lath.

"Lath, is that thing riled up about something?" Dad asked.

"Naw, he just gets that way when strangers shows up around this pond. Should be fine once he puts our smells togetha'." Lath pondered. "Had a feller come through here a few years ago sayin' he needed to find Lucifer a home. I didn't have no hankering fer a monkey 'round here. Told him no thanks, but after he drove off, Lucifer wandered out of those bushes by the porch. Been he'ah ever since. I lets him sleep under the trailer and gets him a bushel of apples when I can. Guess he lives off a whatever else he can find."

Lucifer had stopped his hootin' and hollerin', and was walking circles in the mud bank. He kept snatchin' at something in the air, kinda crazy-like. Then, like his fur was afire, he grunted and dove for the nearest hangin' branch, jumpin' and swingin' his way into the camouflage of the trees. A big pile of poop splattered back down through the leaves and made a quiet plop on the ground a few feet away.

"I'll be doggone," Dad said. He stared at the poop for a second, then turned to Lath. "Lath, I guess we best be getting along. You sure have an interesting place here."

With Lath leading the way, we headed back up the plank walk to his trailer. Clouds were gathering overhead and that breeze was growing stronger. We reached Lath's driveway and stopped in front of our car.

"You boys don't be strangers, y'hear?" Lath gave us a smile, but to me it didn't look comfortable on his big face.

"We'll stop by in a few weeks and I'll bring the missus. Maybe we'll check out that pond when we do."

I glanced at Dad. *Was he crazy?* He could be funny sometimes. But truth be known, I was intrigued with this Spike creature.

We climbed into our Rambler and were soon headed down the dusty drive leading away from Lath's paradise. I twisted around in my seat and watched Lath as we drove away. He just sat there, the smile gone from his face. And I could have swore I saw Lucifer perched on that trailer top, waving his clenched fists in the air, teeth gnashing away at an imaginary throat. I turned back around, that image stuck in my head. Dad was quiet. I'd come to realize that this was one of his ways, and it seemed to me that he did it most when he confronted something odd, or out of the ordinary.

We drove back toward Harper's Mill down Open Bridge Road, my mind whirling and my mouth eager to catch up.

"Dad, why does Mr. Lath live way out there by his self like that?"

"Don't know, Son. Some people just don't feel comfortable around other people. Maybe Lath is like that." He kept his eyes on the road.

"Do you think Lucifer would hurt someone?" I was going to say *hurt boys that came around to do some fishing?* but I suppressed that.

He shot me a glance and stayed silent for a few seconds, a frown working on his face.

"I think he could hurt someone, if that's what you're asking. Could hurt them pretty bad, too. I don't care what Lath said, Pete. If you go back there to fish, you let Lath know you're there. I think he can handle Lucifer. I hope so, anyway. Understand?"

"Yes sir."

"And let's keep this little trip between me and you, okay?"

"Okay." I knew what he meant. Mom would have a fit if she heard about that ape.

About two miles outside of town, we approached close to a dozen cars pulled over in the grass and Dad eased up on the accelerator. A few people were milling around the fence that ran along the road, rubber-necking off toward the field. He pulled over and stepped out of the car, motioning for me to join him as he made his way across the ditch to the fence edge. There were people in white robes wandering around in the field, at least a hundred or more. Pointy, white hoods with the eyes cut out. It was a little spooky, like a Halloween party where everyone came as a ghost. There was someone with one of those bullhorns standing on the back of a flatbed truck. He was speakin' and wavin' his arms like a preacher full of the Holy Spirit. I couldn't hear what he was sayin' too well, but I noticed Dad cringe every now and then.

A big hand fell on Dad's shoulder. "Why don'tcha' join us, Bill?"

It was Ed Sessom. Mr. Sessom was a big man, six foot five, if an inch. He had a barrel chest and shoulders like an ox. His skin was fair and tinged an angry pink from the sun; crewcut, a sandy blond, no doubt by the same means. I knew he owned the busiest gas station in town, and there was only two. He had a swagger about him. I noticed how his form cast a shadow over Dad as he spoke.

"We could use another hand to get this job done. It pays to watch out for each other, right Bill?" He squeezed Dad's shoulder. Dad never turned his head.

What job?

"I think I'll pass on that, Ed. I have enough to keep me busy." That's all Dad said and you could tell by his tone, it was all that would be said on the subject. Ed pulled his hand back and chuckled.

"All right. Fair enough. Y'all have a good day." He touched the brim of his John Deere hat and strolled away.

I watched him walk up to a VW van and climb inside, shutting the door behind him. The crackle of the bull horn turned my attention back to the sea of white. To my surprise, they had erected a large cross of timbers just a ways past the flatbed. I wasn't sure what that was for, but I was straining to hear that bullhorn feller better. The wind must have shifted a bit because I started to catch some of his preachin'.

"...and we can't sit here and do...while them ni'gers and Jews... our jobs and our..." The bullhorn crackled and a rowdy roar rose up from the crowd. Ol' Bullhorn was pumpin' his fist at the crowd, surely a sign that he was pleased with their reaction. "...if we hav'ta rope...and hang 'em by...we will! And if the rope do...we'll burn...."

He had 'em going now. Dad looked down at me, his eyes hard.

The sun was setting, orange sky giving way to a few stars overhead.

39

I turned my attention back to the commotion, mesmerized. Someone lit a homemade torch down by the flatbed. Black smoke billowed toward the twilight sky as the faintest of shadows flicked off the cross in the background. The smell of kerosene filled the air.

That was Dad's cue. I felt his hands grab me by the shoulders and he led me roughly back to our car. I looked over at the van as the side door slid open and out popped another robed man, only his robe looked dark in the twilight. He stepped down and I could barely make out a large design on his robe front and something similar on his pointy hood. And he was tall...real tall, like...like....

I lost my train of thought as Dad opened my door and gently pushed me inside. I craned my neck to see the tall man makin' tracks toward the flatbed. Dad cranked our car and wasted no time in pulling away from that ditch and out onto the road.

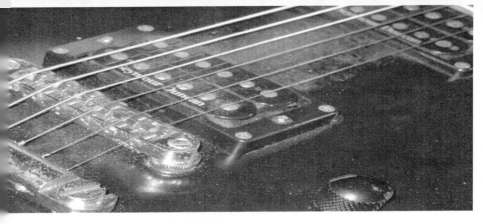

CHAPTER FIVE

2011

"MARGIE?" CLARICE TRAVERS STOOD in the partially open doorway and gazed at her son on the bed. Eyes red, lips trembling, she was frozen in place at the sight of Peter bandaged and hooked to so many machines.

"Clarice!" Margie stood and ran over to Peter's mother, embracing her in a warm, but desperate embrace. "Oh, Clarice."

They leaned on each other, silently crying for the man they both loved. Bill Travers stepped around them and walked over to Peter's side. His stooped shoulders added to his broken look. With a slightly palsied hand, he reached out and laid it lightly on his son's shoulder, careful not to put pressure on it. Both women moved to the opposite side of the bed.

"God, this is awful," Bill said, barely above a whisper. "How is he, Margie?" He looked up at her with haunted eyes.

"The doctor says he's comatose." Clarice Travers grabbed the bedrail, her knees going weak, and Margie grabbed her tightly under one arm for support before she continued. "His vital signs are stabilized and they've stopped the bleeding."

Clarice was silently crying. She broke from Margie's grip and moved slowly to one of the chairs to sit down. Bill pulled the other chair closer to the bed and collapsed into it.

"What are his chances?" He looked up at Margie, hope in his eyes.

"They don't know at this point. He's alive...and he's stable."

"Peter was always a tough boy," Bill said as he gazed at the far wall. "A lot tougher than I was at that age." A smile played at the corners of his mouth. His words hung over the room as the monitors beeped, lights blinked. "He's a tough man, too. He'll come through, Margie. We just have to believe that."

Margie looked at Bill, but saw no certainty in his features. He was scared. They were all scared.

"Why don't you go down and get yourself some coffee...maybe a bite to eat, honey," Clarice said, still dabbing at her eyes.

Margie considered this for a moment as she looked at them both. They had always been strong people in her eyes. Always stood up in the face of tragedy with dignity. She was glad they were here.

She bent down close to her husband's ear. "I'm going outside for a bit, Peter. I won't be long," she said softly, knowing...no, *hoping* he heard her.

Margie was almost to the door when she heard Bill Travers speak to himself in the dying light of the room.

"Where are you, Peter?"

She paused, looked back. From the side, his face was overcome with grief, fragile in the glow of the monitors. He gently stroked Peter's forehead with a tremulous hand, but it was more than she could bear to watch. She knew what he was referring to, and the same question was on the forefront of her mind as she opened the door and walked out.

PART II

A Dark Destiny Unfolds

CHAPTER SIX

Peter

WE WERE ALL THROWN TOGETHER back then, the same way I imagined God threw the stars out in heaven. Randomly. But we were a shining constellation to the eyes of those who dared to look. Dared to dream. Dared to believe.

It's empty here, wherever *here* is, but I can hear something in the distance. The soft strum of strings on a cheap acoustic guitar. I can hear *My Sweet Lord* vibrate softly from my memory and I have to wonder…but only for a fleeting moment. The face of one that gravitated to me, that balanced me during the dark time, looms up from memory. One with an arm like Don Drysdale, with spiky red hair and a beacon in his smile. I can see him jumping and prancing, slashing at the guitar strings with the recklessness of youth, and I am laughing. I am laughing, then crying, but I'm not.

Can you laugh, but not laugh? Cry, but not cry? I think so, lying here in this dark void. Lying here thinking about leaving God's hand and landing in the grass at Harper's Mill Middle School thirty-seven years ago.

I'd seen Arlo around school as the years went by, but we never seemed to cross paths until that fateful February day in '74. I pulled the collar up on my winter coat and tugged my toboggan cap down over my ears, making my way from the gym across the south lawn of Harper's Mill Middle School. At first I didn't notice the large group of kids at the far corner of the school grounds, but a whooping noise made me look in that direction, and the crowd parted just as I reached the corner of the auditorium building. Somewhere from within the circle of five-and-dime coats I saw two boys running in circles, arms flapping like angry geese. The roar of the crowd's laughter carried across the open yard.

Curious, I veered off course and wandered over to the commotion. Arlo stood off to the side, a big grin plastered across his freckled mug, accented by a silver front tooth. Several of his buddies hovered at his elbow, matching his grin. But the sight that caught my attention was far more disturbing than the Arlo gang. Billy Cray, also known as "stutterboy", and Percy Smith, a black boy with glasses (and unfortunately, the only person in our school with six fingers on his left hand), were running in a circle like two dogs chasing their tails. They had both hands tied behind their backs, sweating profusely under wool caps, each with an Astro Pop dangling from their mouths.

As I stepped to the edge of the crowd, Billy's feet tangled and down he went face first into the frozen winter dirt. I grimaced. A scream erupted from him as he rolled over onto his back, hands still bound. Blood gushed down his face, doing little to obscure the pointed rainbow end of that Astro pop protruding like a fish hook through his skin.

Mom's right…those things are as dangerous as scissors.

Arlo and his buddies quickly disappeared into the crowd. The girls screamed, mittened hands flapping like spooked hens in girlish disgust at the bloody carnage. I ran to Billy and yanked my gloves off. Slipping my Swiss army knife from my pocket, I quickly cut the twine that bound his hands and helped him up. That Astro pop dangled loosely from both his open mouth and pierced cheek, making me slightly squeamish. Billy had reduced his screams to deep sobs, consoled, I guessed, that he was not at death's door. I met his eyes, nodded once, then reached up and pulled the culprit from his mouth with a wet plop. I tossed it aside, where it rolled through the dirt, parting the crowd of horrified spectators.

Percy had spat his on the ground and stood gaping at Billy, eyes ballooned like two golf balls, chest heaving in deep gulps of air. Someone helped him untie his hands and he took off running like his pants were on fire. I sat Billy down on a nearby bench and helped him wipe at his cheek with his coattail.

I'm not sure what made me look up, but when I did, I locked eyes with Margie McMillan. She was in a few of my classes, kind of cute, but I'd never spent too much time thinking about it. Now, she was giving me goo-goo eyes, like I was a hero or something.

Suddenly the crowd dispersed like dandelion petals in the wind, including Margie, and I could see why. Marching across the grass, the tails of his overcoat flapping in the wind, was Principal Taylor. Thick bifocals balanced on his hawk-like nose, arms pumping with determination, he strode up to us and grabbed me by the arm.

"What's going on here, Mr. Travers?" He gave me a little shake.

"I-I-It wus- wus…." Billy stammered out between bloody teeth and swollen cheek.

Mr. Taylor looked around, surveying what was left of the scene. "Good Lord, Son, spit it out! What happened here?" He could see the blood on Billy's cheek and neck, but I don't think he realized there was a pea-sized hole in the middle of that mess.

"A-A-Arlo….Arlo-o-o Hak-k-kshaw…." Billy labored out. "He

had u-us ti-ti-tied up and made u-us run 'round w-w-with those in our m-mu-mouths!" Billy's shaky finger pointed to the nearest Astro pop in the dirt.

Principle Taylor released me and took Billy by the arm. "We'll get to the bottom of this, young man." He led Billy back toward the main building. I made like a bird and flew before Mr. Taylor got any more ideas. Just as I was rounding the corner to the cafeteria, out stepped Arlo and his sidekick, Martin. Arlo's stocky frame blocked my path like a bulldozer. Spiky red hair and pale skin, he appeared kind of cartoonish, but that severe upper lip and silver tooth made him menacing.

"Well, look-y here." Arlo sneered. "If it ain't the helper boy." He sidled up closer to me, fists balled tightly at his sides. Martin's invisible leash dragged him alongside Arlo's elbow.

"That was kinda…sweet…helpin' those two sissies like that." Arlo moved in closer. I could smell sour sweat and Juicy Fruit gum. His lip jerked up at a steep angle. I swallowed hard.

I don't know why I did what I did next. I didn't draw back my arm. It just kinda shot up at a funny angle and connected with Arlo's nose.

I'll give him credit. Arlo did not cry out, just gulped air in through his mouth, made an *ugh-ugh* kinda sound, grabbed his nose and stumbled back. He stared at me, then started smiling as the blood ran over his lip and covered his teeth. That sneer gave me the creeps, but the sight of his bloody silver tooth sent chills up my back.

Martin took a few steps back, waiting for his idol to unleash unholy heck on me, but that didn't happen as we stood there face to face. Confused and a bit disappointed, Martin ran off.

It wouldn't be the last we saw of him.

I ran into Arlo on the path behind the lunchroom a week later. There was nobody else around and I thought *this is it, this is where I get snapped like a pretzel,* but Arlo was all smiles when he approached me.

"Hey Pete, no hard feelings about the other day, okay?" He held out his hand, and I could see something like humbleness in his eyes. For a moment I stood there, wary and a little off balance. *Was this the same Arlo?* I looked him up and down. No red flags went up. I shook his hand.

"No problem, Arlo."

"Let's just forget about it. You throw a mean upper cut, though." He smiled again, sun glinting off metal.

"Just a lucky punch, I guess. You scared me a bit, and well, it just happened."

He laughed at this and started by me, then turned. "Catch you around sometime?"

"Sure."

I watched him continue on down the path and disappear around the corner.

Now, you won't believe this, but Arlo and I became friends that day. His reputation as a bully diminished over time and we pretty much became inseparable.

We took to hanging out at my house after school, mostly watching the Flintstones or Dark Shadows re-runs, until we could catch a few neighborhood kids looking for a game of baseball or whatever. Sometimes, I would try to teach Arlo a few chords on my acoustic guitar.

My folks gave it to me on my 14th birthday and I'd learned to play two songs from the songbook that came with it: *Ol' Joe*

49

Clark and *Jingle Bells*. They were terrible. I was terrible, but I could lumber through them if I went slow. Arlo, on the other hand, couldn't master the two-hand concept.

"No, Arlo. Hold it like this." I took it from him, positioned my fingers on the frets and strummed the strings. Arlo nodded and I handed the guitar back to him. He put his fingers on the frets.

"Strum the strings with your other hand," I told him. He strummed the strings.

"Move this finger here." I moved his finger for him. "Now, strum the strings."

He sat there, studying the strings far too hard, his hand still.

"Strum the strings!" I said, exasperated. He looked at me and grinned. Then he jumped up and danced around the room, slashing at the strings like a maniac, making *waaa-waaa* noises like he was a rock and roll nut. I gave up, like I always did.

One day, we were tossing a baseball behind my house when a thought occurred to me and I held onto the ball.

"Why did you beat up on other kids?" I asked him.

He shrugged, lowered his eyes and kicked at the grass. I could see he was thinking of the right thing to say. When he glanced back up, his somber look didn't waver as he spoke.

"I guess I just got tired of always taking it and never giving it back." He punched his ball glove for emphasis and opened it for the next catch.

I wasn't sure what that meant, but I found out later. Boy, did I ever.

I'd been over to Arlo's house on a few occasions, but his father was always at work. The first Saturday I ever went over there, Arlo had chores to finish and one of them was taking out the trash. When he was done, he grabbed his football and we went out back to toss it around for awhile.

"Go for a long one!" I yelled. Arlo took off for the far corner of the yard and I released the ball with all I had.

"Arlo!" A man yelled through the back door. "You left the lid off the trash can again!"

The screen door slammed against the house and out came Mr. Hankshaw, wide leather belt in hand. Unshaven and barefoot, he made a beeline for Arlo.

Arlo stopped, panting, and looked back toward the house. I could see fear cross his face. The ball, coming down from its high arc like a bullet, smacked him in the side of the head and staggered him.

Mr. Hankshaw whipped that belt through the air quicker than a diarrhea attack. Arlo made a little squealing noise and took off like a baking soda bottle rocket, but Mr. Hankshaw was too quick for him. He snatched Arlo by the waistband of his pants and commenced to stropping his legs with no mercy. I was still frozen in place, unsure what to do. I could see Arlo's face and he was trying hard not to cry, not to make a sound as his father beat him. I felt the heat as my face flushed, embarrassed for Arlo, but the look in his eyes told me he was far more embarrassed than me.

The screen door squealed on its hinges. I turned to see Mrs. Hankshaw standing there with moist eyes and a look of resignation on her face. She waved me toward the carport, a clear sign I should leave. I could still hear that belt landing on Arlo's legs as I took off running toward my bike. *Why did some people have to be so angry about the small things?*

The ride home was long as I thought about Arlo and his father. I finally understood what Arlo said to me that day about taking and no giving. If I'd ever doubted the sincerity of our friendship, there was no doubt now. We were in this together.

Friends till the end.

"Pete, let's get 'er rollin'! Bud's got his clippers waitin' for us!" Dad's voice echoed up the stairway.

I rolled over and looked at the alarm clock. 8:37 a.m. *Clippers? Aw, darn! I forgot about my haircut today.* My brain felt fuzzy from the strange dream I'd had about our visit to Lath's. I rolled out of bed and slipped on my jeans. A quick wash-up would have to do for Mr. Bud Fellows today.

As we arrived at Bud's Barbershop, I felt a sense of resignation. I dreaded this trip. Mr. Fellows was a nice man, but he was blind as a bat. The first time he cut my hair he nearly scalped me. When Mom saw the results of his services, she joked that Bud gave new meaning to the term "crew cut".

Bud's Barbershop sat at the corner of Burbee and Main. The building was a hold-over from the Civil War. Ok, maybe not that old, but it was definitely ancient. The high plastered ceiling fished down at us with long-poled fans that kept the flies to a minimum and a breeze blowin' across your tonic-splashed head. I imagined it had the same effect as being naked in an icehouse in mid-August.

We parked out front and Dad fed the meter. Five minutes later, I was sitting in Bud's chair. He grinned at me with those coke-bottle glasses slightly crooked, and turned to Dad.

"You hear 'bout that Kim feller, Bill? They say he was last seen drivin' north outta town. Had his fishin' poles hangin' out the rear window. I didn't even know he fished." Bud snip, snip, snipped, reducing my hair to stubbly tufts.

"Clarice was goin' on about it last night," Dad said. "Can't say that I knew the man too well. Maybe he's just got a taste for the hard stuff. Probably laid up somewhere sleepin' it off." Dad peered over his newspaper to make his point, then settled further into his

52

seat along the wall, scouring the news clips on President Nixon and the war. I got the feeling he was pulling Bud's strings just to get him worked up. He did that sometimes, I guess, because Bud was so easy to rile. Whatever the reason, Dad seemed to enjoy it. I'd of bet my allowance he was smiling behind that newspaper.

"I don't know. Heard he was a deacon in that there All Saints Church off Claxie road. Don't seem much liked he'd want his mug all over the paper like that." Bud eyed his work in the mirror, which I now faced with renewed bravado.

He was right, though. I could see Mr. Kim's face reflected in the mirror from Dad's paper. LOCAL BUSINESS MAN MISSING! read the headline. Mr. Kim's round, pleasant face peered back at me. I guess there was something a little off about this whole thing. I mean, the Open Air Market had been closed for two days now and that was the first time, except for Sundays, that I could remember that happening. Even in winter, Mr. Kim ran a full grocery store six days a week.

"Well, just give it another day or two," Dad said. "Maybe him and the missus had a spat and he needed to cool off." He made quick to change the conversation. "Hey, Bud...who you with this year, the Sox or the Dodgers? I think the Sox might have a chance this year." Dad knew Bud hated the Boston Red Sox. I was just glad the hair cutting was finally over.

Bud slapped the back of my neck with several harsh swipes of his horsehair brush. "They couldn't find a ball in a paper bag. I think you've been drinkin', Bill Travers!"

Dad laughed.

Just then I saw Arlo and Martin peering through the window, flapping their arms, basically acting like fools to get my attention. I waited until Bud untied the barber's cape and swung it to the side, then paraded around me with his giant mirror. I'm still not sure why he did this. It wasn't as if he could undo the damage. Dad grunted his approval and I hopped down.

"I'm gonna go hang out with the guys, Dad."

He waved his hand dismissively and climbed into Bud's chair. I scrambled out the door, intent on making the best of this Saturday. Arlo and Martin tried to "frog" my arms simultaneously, but I jerked away. I did slap one of Martin's big ear lobes, though. Man, he hated that. Arlo snickered.

"So, what'cha wanna do, Sugar Ray Pete?" Arlo could be so poetic. Martin laughed. I ignored Arlo and slapped at Martin's other ear lobe. Just nicked it, really.

"Hey!" He covered his ears and stepped out of my reach. "Stop that!" His face edged toward scarlet, but for Martin, it was more embarrassment than anger. "It's not my fault your head looks like a lawnmower ran over it!"

Good one. I let it go and turned my attention back to Arlo. "I don't know, Ar-lo. What do you guys want to do?"

"Look..." Martin pointed over my shoulder. "...the girls are comin'!" I looked down Main toward the blinking traffic light. Sure enough, here come Percy Smith and Billy Cray. Now, in case you're wondering, things had improved considerably since the Astro Pop incident. After Arlo and I became friends, and Martin humbly found his way back into our new bully-free gang, Arlo and Martin made amends with Billy and Percy. Heck, they had even played ball a few times together at the high school diamond. But a fair amount of ribbin' was still dished out, much to the disdain of Billy and Percy. I waved for them to join us. They seemed excited, Billy panting when they reached us in front of Bud's.

"Y-y-you guys s-s-seen what's c-com-comin' down M-main?" Billy gulped in huge amounts of air. We all shook our heads no. Percy, being the talkative one as usual, turned and pointed down

Main. I squinted my eyes and focused on the rise that crested just beyond the town's only flashing light. Frankly, it looked like marshmallows bouncing down the street, but they were growing bigger and taller as they crested Main and Eldridge. Arlo waved us on and took off in the direction of the commotion.

We all caught up in front of Tidwell's Skating Rink as the procession was coming through the light. The sheet men were back, only this time there was no empty field, no flatbed truck, and no burning cross. But there was a bullhorn, and about a hundred sheets bobbin' in an organized march through Harper's Mill. Close behind them, a car covered in white billowing material crept down the asphalt two-lane. It floated like a ghost, only the bottoms of the tires showing. A white-robed man with the bullhorn stood in the passenger's side floorboard, shouting at the sidewalk crowd. Another one steered the car, hooded eyes straight ahead. Standing in the rear end, waving like Napoleon, was the dark-robed figure I'd seen that night with Dad, only now I could see the robe was green.

Me and the boys worked our way down further, almost abreast of the procession, stopping short of the flashing light. Russell's Drugstore loomed behind us and several people had moved to the big glass storefront to gawk out at the white wave that flowed down Main. Percy, I noticed, had moved quietly to the rear of our group. I swear, in that instant that I glanced at him, he looked as white as me. I expected to see freckles appear across his nose any second. Looking around at the crowd milling along the street, I realized how white they seemed, too. Not a drop of color. I suddenly knew what Percy was feeling.

The ghostly apparition made its way by us, a throng of sheeted men, shoes pounding in unison, and I thought of the witch's guards in *The Wizard of Oz*. Their dark eyeholes showed very little in the way of eyes, as if there was really nothing at all under those hoods. One carried a confederate flag, a few more hoisted signs above their heads that said things like "coons git out!" and "gooks go home." Some said things worse than that. You could feel the hatred radiating out from that sea of sheets.

Arlo nudged me with his meaty elbow and broke my concentration. "What?" I looked along the street in the direction of Bud's shop. In all of his mangled, proud glory came my dog, Fang, loping down the sidewalk with his grizzled snout held high. He carried an air of canine nobility, even with bald patches of mange in his brown coat and a decaying incisor jutting proudly over his lip. Edging up next to me, it was clear he wasn't too happy with the whole scene. He plopped down on his haunches and laid his ears back against his skull, a low, growling disapproval coming from his throat.

The sheets were almost past us when I had the strangest feeling of being watched. I glanced around to scan the crowd, then turned back… and made eye-to-eyehole contact with the green robed man. He was literally twisting around to keep his attention on me, or at least that's the way it felt. Then he waved right at me. Ice water ran down my spine. Fang growled more forcibly now, rising slightly on his haunches, his eyes going all squinty, head lowered a few inches. Green robe turned back around and resumed waving to the crowd.

I eyed Percy working his way back to the curb. Arlo looked bored. He play-punched Martin on his arm, causing him to wince and curse under his breath.

"Come on," I said, turning to make for the drugstore. I needed something to shake the willies I'd just been handed.

The gang followed, clowning their way into the store behind me. We scraped together enough change to get one shake, a fountain-mix cherry cola, and small lemonade. Miss Cindy, decked out in her best soda-jerk apron and sporting a red bow in her long brown hair, served up our drinks and went back to cleaning the shake machine. Percy hated cherry and had a problem with milk, so he took the lemonade. Arlo and I split the shake, Martin and Billy shared the cherry coke. There was real diplomacy involved in sharing. Be polite, no backwash, halves to the ounce. It wasn't easy.

Anyway, we settled in, each of us entrenched in our own favorite magazine. From where I sat, I could see Mr. Russell Beecham behind the pharmacy counter. He was talking rather intently on the phone, keeping his voice low. His occasional rise in volume kept me looking up from my magazine, only to have a souped-up Mustang draw me back again.

Now, for a man in his fifties, Russell Beecham was quite the playboy-about-town. At least that's what Mom heard through the grapevine. He had a pompadour hairdo speckled with gray and stood about five eleven. From what I could see now, he also had this vein that stuck out real big on his forehead when he was angry. And he looked real angry behind that pharmacy counter. I nudged Arlo and made the motion for us to leave. We had to thump Martin on the ear to get his attention before he reluctantly put the *Beach Beauties* magazine back on the rack. Fang was waiting for us when we stepped out into the sunshine. There was no sign of the sheeted parade as far as I could see, in either direction. Things seemed a bit more normal on the streets of Harper's Mill.

"Whatchu' guys wanna do now?" Percy spoke up, a rarity for him.

"M-m-my d-d-dad just p-put up our tramp-p-line yesterdday…" Billy spat out. His stuttering didn't bother us too much. We'd all gotten quite used to it by now.

"Naw," said Arlo. "We always get our heads cracked when we jump on that thing. My dad said I should stay off of trampolines… and, uh, wild bulls." I rolled my eyes at Arlo. Only *I* knew he was afraid of heights.

"Hey…." It suddenly dawned on me. "Let's go fishing!" I remembered Lath's invitation, and even though he'd only made that offer yesterday, I didn't think he'd mind. I doubted we'd catch much of anything in that mud hole anyway, *except maybe a harpoon-headed catfish the size of a whale.* Besides, standing here on the sidewalk, the thought of that monkey didn't seem so ominous now.

"Let's meet at the cotton mill in one hour."

We needed time to get our bikes, poles and worms, anyhow. The mill sat on the edge of town along O'Reilly Street, which turned into Open Bridge Road as you headed toward Mule Creek Crossing.

"I-I can't go-go guys," Billy said. "G-g-gotta cut m-my g-g-grass." We all nodded, understanding the inconvenience of chores, and bade Billy farewell.

I took off for home with Fang at my side. There's something to be said about a loyal dog. He walked about five paces in front of me, head held up firmly, surveying the surroundings for any danger that may approach.

We walked past the Kim house, which sat back a ways from the road. Finely painted and well-kept, the clapboard structure dated back to the 1920's and was on the Harper's Mill Historical Society preservation list. The Kims were modest people, but Mrs. Kim was known to keep her planters filled with beautiful flowers. The yard was full of fruit trees and saplings.

Today, that house looked gloomy from the street. Sad even, like the sun wasn't reaching it at full force. A small flagpole stood like a silent sentry on the neglected lawn, topped by an American flag and a small, white flag with strange markings just beneath it. *Must be their Korean flag.* Fang's ears twitched up a bit as we strode past. I couldn't help but think that a whole lot of sadness must be *inside* that house as well.

Fang and I made quick to get by, hoping Mr. Kim would be found soon.

CHAPTER SEVEN

2011

MARGIE SIPPED BITTER COFFEE as she sat in the hospital cafeteria. She felt alone and afraid among the family members and patients who were well enough to venture from their rooms. Her phone jingled its ringtone somewhere down in her purse and she snatched it out in haste. She'd left messages with Millie and Peter Jr. earlier. They must have been in classes at the university. She hoped this call would be one of them.

"Hello?"

"Mom!" It was Millie. "What's wrong with Dad? I just got your message. I was in class." Her voice was full of apprehension.

"He was in an accident, Millie." She felt her throat seize up with emotion, but continued. "It doesn't look good, sweetheart. We're at Mercy General."

Millie drew in a sharp breath. "I'm on my way, Mom. I'll throw a few things in the car and be there in an hour. Don't worry—"

"He's in a…in a coma, Millie." Margie felt the tears rise in her again and covered the mouthpiece.

"Oh my God, Mom…I'll be there as soon as I can."

Margie listened as her daughter hung up, put her phone back

in her purse, and pulled out a wad of tissues to dab at her eyes. Silverware tinkled, someone laughed out loud at a joke, a line cook shouted "order up!", but she might as well have been a thousand miles away from all of it.

The hand on her shoulder startled her and she jumped a little before she turned around and peered up.

"Percy?" Her eyes grew wide. It was Percy Smith. She hadn't seen him in years.

"Margie, how are you holding out? The nurse told me I'd find you here." He pulled out a chair and sat across from her. "I was doing chaplain duties when I heard about Pete. I came as fast as I could." He reached across the table, took both her hands in his.

She hadn't seen Percy since their tenth high school reunion. He looked well for his years. There was just a hint of gray starting at his temples. An old school friend of both her and Peter, Percy had graduated and followed an evangelical path in life. It seemed his calling had been good to him.

"Oh, Percy, he's alive…but he's in a coma. They don't know when…*if*…he'll wake up."

He squeezed her hands gently. "He'll pull through, Margie. Just have faith."

His hands were warm, his voice confident, and it calmed her. She glanced down, more to hide her teary eyes than anything else. The sixth finger, a pinkie, on his smooth, dark hand surprised her. She'd forgotten that little detail over the years, and now it brought back a flood of memories of a group of friends bound by something special. Memories from a lifetime ago, when the world dropped out from under them.

"Do you think so, Percy? Do you really think so?"

He nodded.

They sat like that, in silence, for a long time. Two from before, brought back together by tragedy once again, as the world turned quietly on its axis in the vast universe.

A nurse was reading the monitors, marking Peter's data on a chart when Margie and Percy entered the room. Bill and Clarice stood off in the corner, faces expectant, full of the hope that parents must always have for their children.

"How is he?" Margie whispered.

"You don't have to whisper, Mrs. Travers. In fact, the more you talk the better. It may get a response from your husband. If you'll hold on just a minute, I'll go get the doctor." She patted Margie's arm as she left the room.

Percy had moved over to Bill and Clarice to speak to them and offer support. Now he was at Margie's side, looking down at Peter.

"It's hard to see him like this, Marge," he said. "He...he was always so big in my mind, the glue for all of us, really." He reached out and caressed Peter's cheek with his extra finger.

Margie smiled. That gesture spoke a thousand words. So much had happened back then, so much they couldn't control. But she remembered his gift, and it made her feel warm inside to know that this man, this friend, could drop all he'd become just to be that friend they had all known long ago. Blessed with that gift, he'd answered his first calling and stood beside them that fateful day.

"I know, Percy. He led us into the inevitable with so much heart, so much courage."

Margie watched as a single tear left Peter's eye and rolled down his cheek. Her heart skipped a beat. "Percy! Did you see that?"

The door opened and the doctor strolled in, checking his watch. "Mrs. Travers—"

"Doctor! Peter…a tear! See?" She grabbed his arm and pulled him toward the bed.

He examined Peter, using his thumb and forefinger to pry his eyelids open and shine a small pen light across them. He straightened up and shot Percy a sorrowful glance before he turned back to Margie.

"Mrs. Travers…." He cleared his throat. "What you saw is not uncommon in comatose patients. It's more of a physical reaction. Something the body does naturally without conscious thought."

Margie's smile faded along with her hope. "Oh," she managed to say. "I just thought…."

"I know. It's not uncommon for friends and relatives to misinterpret such an occurrence. I will tell you that as of right now, his vital signs are holding up. That's encouraging at this point." He smiled at her. "If his condition changes, we'll let you know immediately. In the meantime, if you have any more questions, please feel free to ask a nurse to page me." He turned and left the room.

Percy grabbed her arm and led her to the closest chair. "Sit down," he said, gently but firmly as he lowered her into it.

"Percy, I—"

He was already on one knee in front of her. "Margie, do you think for one minute that God wasn't there with us that day?" His eyes were leveled on hers.

She shook her head, a little taken aback at his sudden change.

"Do think this was an accident, some freak of nature that came upon me out of the blue?" He held up his left hand. The extra finger turned translucent and burst into a brilliant light that painted the walls. Clarice, standing beside her husband, covered her mouth, unable to hide the surprise in her eyes.

Margie gasped and drew back, caught off guard more than

anything. She'd seen the power behind it, the purpose, many years ago.

"He gave me that gift for a reason." The finger dimmed, returned to normal. He dropped it from her sight. "The second gift he gave me was you. All of you. Peter, Arlo, Martin…"

"Percy—"

"I'm not through," he said, laying his hand on hers. "He gave Peter a gift, too, Margie. He gave him strength to face what none of us believed to be true. He gave him courage. He made him a leader." Percy's face softened. "Do you really think God will abandon him now?"

She looked at him, mouth agape. His words rang true.

He stood up, walked over to the bed and knelt down. When he was through praying, he stood up and walked to the door. "I'm going to get a coffee. Do any of you need anything," he asked, turning to them as he pulled the door open.

They all shook their heads no. Percy walked out. They watched the door close behind him.

Margie didn't move. Bill Travers walked over and placed his hand on her back.

"Margie, maybe we will step out for a minute and join Percy for that coffee. You need some time. Are you okay with that?"

She looked up at Bill's face and saw nothing but compassion there.

"Sure. I'll be okay. You both go on." She mustered the best smile she could and watched as they left, Bill's arm tight around Clarice's waist.

Time crawled by as she sat there thinking of everything Percy had said. Shadows grew in the room, but she didn't bother to get up and turn on the light. She felt tired, stinky, and out of sync.

All she could do was wait…and pray.

CHAPTER EIGHT

Peter

IF YOU'D HAVE ASKED any of us that warm spring day so long ago what we expected to find at Edwards Pond, we would have looked at you the way awkward young men tend to look at the world: with confusion and excitement, yet full of blind hope. Then we would've shrugged, uncertain.

We simply did not know.

What we did know, what I sensed the moment I set foot there with my father, what I tried to instill in the others through camaraderie and sheer determination, was that there existed an adventure somewhere down Open Bridge Road. And I could no more resist it than I could explain it. Had I known that day what would eventually unfold, I would have spent a considerable amount of time on my knees in prayer to a God with which I had, up to that point, an unfamiliar relationship.

But we went at it anyway, completely blind to the things we should have seen, to the signs God laid at our feet.

I was the first there. The old oak tree, rumored to have been planted somewhere around 1857, spread its arms a considerable distance and provided a shady lunch spot for the people working at the mill. Fang and I lay stretched out beneath those leafy arms now, contemplating Charlie Russ.

Charlie was the town's only vagrant by choice and spent a considerable amount of his "downtime" in this little park area in front of the mill office. He was enjoying some of that "downtime" now, stretched out on his back across a weathered bench, old food rotting in his beard. Flies swarmed around his head in a cloud.

I slowly laid out one peanut at a time down the length of my leg. Fang methodically licked each one up with his tongue, chewing the crunchy nuts with an exaggerated grimace, tail wagging.

Charlie, however, was not so content.

Back in 1971, Charlie had been a senior at Harper's Mill High, Class President, Captain of the Harper's Mill Cavaliers football team, a MENSA inductee, and the Little League Baseball coach. He'd even been accepted to a prestigious state college.

His girlfriend, Jenny Lee Beecham, had been the definition of perfection to anyone of the opposite sex. Somewhere during her junior year she exploded into womanhood. At five foot three, one hundred and ten pounds, with long blond hair, hazel-blue eyes, a chest that was stolen off of Jane Mansfield, and a strut that warped asphalt, Jenny Lee was a walking hormonal agitator. Head cheerleader, active in all her church functions, a big sister to no less than two local handicapped children, and Miss Teen Harper's Mill twice, Jenny Lee rocked.

Enter the Black Cats. They were not a local bunch, but they'd breeze into Harper's Mill at least once a year, revving their motorcycles up and down Main to the horror of the townsfolk. Many people were prone to be uncomfortable when they rolled into the predominately white community of Harper's Mill, probably as much for their wildness as the color of their skin.

The Cats rolled into town one day that spring raising Cain, and there was somebody new at the head of the pack this time. He was large and lanky, and had the name *J. Marshall* stitched across the back of his leather jacket. His afro was enormous, strangled midway with a colorful bandana, a cross between hot pink and a hazy purple. Strapped to his back was a guitar case, heavily embellished with stitching that read *E.V.* in foot-tall letters, and smaller ones on the neck that spelled *Stratocaster.*

Two hours after arriving, they came dragging down Main Street…with Jenny Lee. Word spread fast and Charlie showed up with half a dozen of Harper's Mill's finest athletes. By the time the police arrived, Charlie and the boys lay bloodied and beaten in the street. Oddly, the new guy never left his bike. Jenny Lee was spotted leaving town on the back of his chopper, and that was the last we saw of Russell Beecham's daughter.

Charlie graduated that summer, but hit rock bottom by the time the leaves changed. He became depressed, wandering the streets, waking up in more alleys than Elvis had hip thrusts. Love had dealt him a crushing blow.

And Russell? Well, he was a proud man. Packed all his emotions inside and was back to his old routine before long. Some speculated he found Jesus, but most were just glad he was being Russell again.

So, that brings me back to present Charlie. As I said, Charlie was sleeping, completely oblivious to the dozen or so flies now landing in his beard, feasting on the foul morsels trapped there. Fang just sat, looking at Charlie with his ears perked up. Even *he* thought better of getting too close, and dogs aren't usually too picky about anything. Charlie's mouth hung open, his breath pulling at the flies, then blowing them askew, as he snored in a deep slumber.

He had one leg sprawled across the grass while the other sat rigid across the bench back. The wind must have shifted at that moment because I'm sure I got a whiff of Charlie and had to restrain a gag reflex. I was moving away from the smell when up rode Arlo on his banana bike, sparkly tassels and all. He did a little sissy slide in the grass, laying the bike down. An orange push-up dangled from his mouth.

"You babysittin' Charlie again?" Arlo displayed that award-winning sneer with a milky silver tooth. I could see an orange ring around his lips. Such was the pleasure of a cool push-up on a summer day.

"Just trying to keep my lunch down." And I really was. The thought of two peanut butter and jelly sandwiches and a whole glass of milk coming back up through my nose did not thrill me in the least.

He gave me a quizzical look. "You sure this pond is cool?"

"It's cool enough for the likes of you, trust me," I said, quietly pushing Lucifer to the back of my mind.

Charlie abruptly farted and rolled over on the bench. The smell would not be pleasant if we stuck around too long. I turned my head and spotted Martin and Percy coming down the service road now, cane poles strapped across their handlebars like lances.

The arrangement was simple: Martin and Percy brought the poles, and Arlo and I brought the bait and four bottled soft drinks. Today, Arlo announced he had four slightly chilled RC Colas in his backpack. I had a can full of worms strapped to the handlebars of my bike. As an added surprise, I had brought four little cloth bags of Gold Nugget bubblegum, four bubblegum cigars of various colors that I'd saved up for a rainy day, and two bones for Fang, of course.

So it was that we converged under the grand oak, giddy with

a lack of knowledge and empowered with a sense of adventure that boys seem to revel in. We bid Charlie farewell, for what it was worth, and struck out on our bikes for Edwards Pond, Fang running shotgun. I reached into my Dickies as we peddled and switched on my transistor radio. I'd heard that every moment worth remembering can be defined with a song. I don't know about that, but the thump, thump, ratty-tat-tat of *White Rabbit* spilled forth from my Japanese song box with a seemingly subdued, yet haunting, Grace Slick cooing her way through the words like a runaway train builds momentum. We would truly *feed our heads* today.…

We peddled north out of town for about twenty minutes under a warm sun. Traffic was light as we merged with Open Bridge Road, and we soon found ourselves approaching Mule Creek Crossroads. I don't know about the mule part, but a rather healthy creek ran roughly south by southeast across the surrounding farmland, and even fed Lath's old stump-filled pond. We stopped on a tiny bridge where it ran under the road and watched the water whip the bank grass and weeds as it traveled to points south. I reached deep in my pocket and clicked off Aretha Franklin just as she finished spelling *R-E-S-P-E-C-T*. The quiet of the countryside seemed to swallow up the space in my head where Aretha had been.

"Hey, you guys. I'm up to 8 feet now."

I turned toward Arlo to see what he was talking about. A sizable arc of pee angled off the bridge into the rushing creek below. Fang found this somewhat entertaining and barked, his tail wagging with vigor.

"That's about eight feet, right?" He grinned.

His spiky red hair ruffled in the breeze, and for the briefest moment I felt this may be the best of times for all of us, past, present and future. A strong breeze blew up, buffeting his geyser and severely lowering his range.

"Naw, Arlo." I grinned back. "That's about three inches...and that pee stream is about four feet when the breeze stops."

Percy hee-hawed out loud. Martin stepped up to the rail. I was so busy razzing Arlo and listening to Percy cackle, I didn't realize Martin had launched his own minnow through the bridge couplings until he yelled out.

"This is how a man does it, Arlo!"

He let it go and it whipped several feet past Arlo's, even with the breeze. Percy was in tears now, down on both knees. I was trying not to laugh, but it was hard.

I heard a car engine and looked down the road toward Harper's Mill. A VW van was coming up the road. Not fast, but fast enough. Directly behind it, like a shadow, was a rusty baby blue El Camino. I realized the boys were still parading around like roosters.

"Put those tadpoles away! Here comes some traffic!" I shouted.

Arlo took one look at the approaching van and did an about-face, yanking at his zipper. Martin ran down the creek bank to do his up. I suspect he had some problems, judging by the sharp yelp I heard from below. The van and Camino cruised by at a fairly good speed, and I couldn't exactly make out who was driving. They sat in shadows, but I think I saw their heads turn as each passed, noticing us noticing them. I didn't like that attention. It felt like a glass of ice water had been poured down my backside. Arlo came up beside me with Percy in tow. Martin was apparently still struggling with his zipper by the creek, with Fang sitting on his haunches, staring down at him in rapt fascination.

"What's the matter, Pete?" Percy asked, pushing his glasses up on his nose.

I shrugged my shoulders. "Nothing. Just got the willies, I guess."

I eyed the tail end of those vehicles, certain I knew them both. Just then I saw another car approaching from the opposite direction. Martin had joined us now. It took about five seconds, shielding my eyes from the sun's glare, before I realized it was Dad's Rambler. I felt a moment of relief.

Our car approached, but it was going pretty fast. Too fast, in fact. I squared my shoulders and waved as Dad passed not ten feet from our unruly gang. But he didn't see us. It's not like we were hidden. A few steps further and we would've been hood ornaments. Dad was staring straight ahead. It felt weird. I watched as the rear of our Rambler disappeared down the black top, bound for Harper's Mill.

"That was your dad, right?" Arlo asked.

I nodded. "He must be in a hurry to get somewhere."

I was closer to the truth than I knew. As I would find out much later, my dad was on his way to the police station. And he wasn't going there for a social call.

Our silly mood became solemn as we gathered our bikes and struck out for Edwards Pond. The afternoon was waning and we wanted to get in enough fishing before we lost the light. Spike was still my secret, for now anyway. Twenty minutes later, we stopped at the head of Lath's dirt drive. The sun was dipping to the tree line and I noticed that the late day midges and flies were getting thicker across the fields. Seemed the best feeding time on any pond was early morning and over toward dusk.

"Where's the pond?" Martin looked around, gathering his bearings.

I pointed to a clump of woods off to the right. "It's out in there. We can go up Lath's drive…" I paused, remembering Lath's comment about the path from the road. "…or we can go up there a little ways and go in through that mud path off the road there." I pumped my chin in that direction.

Percy picked up a rock and tossed it across the blacktop into a wild blackberry bush growing up the opposite ditch bank. He studied Lath's drive and shook his head as he spoke.

"Y'all go on up that drive, but I'm takin' the path."

It was odd for Percy to say that much at once. I looked at Arlo and Martin, and they gave me that *don't ask me* look. So I didn't. I asked Percy instead.

"Something wrong, Percy?" I studied the sudden hardness on his face.

He shrugged his shoulders. "Naw, I just ain't going up that drive, that's all."

I knew I would get nothing more from him. The path it was. I waved them on as I grabbed my bike and set off in that direction, Fang trotting alongside. Arlo fell in behind me with Percy on his heels and Martin bringing up the rear. We stayed close to the road and could hear the loony birds calling out from the direction of the pond. *At least that's what I hoped it was.*

Arlo pulled up beside me and I looked over at him. Big streaks of sweat ran down his neck and pooled in brown salty spots around his collar. We reached the path, which we almost missed in the growth of sour weed that crowded the road edge. I decided a foot approach was probably best, judging by the drop of the bank and the slick sheen on the mud. I jumped off my bike.

"Come on." I led the way as the others dismounted and fell in line, bikes by their sides. Fang took scout and ran ahead of me. The tree line loomed in front of us maybe twenty or thirty feet. Beyond that, it looked dark and cool. I entered among the thick branches and felt an immediate change in temperature. The gang followed closely, too close in fact, as Arlo almost went up my leg with his bike wheel. Fang barked once, but he was lost in the shadows somewhere up ahead.

"Maybe we should leave our bikes here," I offered. A quick check of nodding heads confirmed this was a good idea. We all found a place to lay our bikes, then gathered our fishing gear and grouped back in the middle of the path.

"Where now?" Percy asked.

I looked around, unsure of my sense of direction. The growth was considerable and I concluded that the path, even though not always obvious to the eye, was our best bet.

"Let's just follow this in a bit. The pond has to be right up ahead."

We trudged along the footpath, fighting sweat flies, no-see-ums and mosquitoes that threatened to lift us by our collars and fly away. The air became thick with a moldy, rotten smell and Martin was the first to comment, his nose scrunched up. "That smells like your butt, Arlo."

Arlo, who was sweating profusely now, just ignored him. He was too busy eyeing the foliage that surrounded our little fishing party. I heard a growl somewhere up ahead and held out my hand for everyone to stop.

"Hear that?" I whispered. No nods this time, just wide eyes and flushed faces.

I moved a few feet further until I saw Fang in the path up ahead, back in a half-haunch, ears back against his head, crooked tail stiff. The growl came again, deep from Fang's scrawny chest. I couldn't see anything, but I heard it all right. From somewhere off to our left came the slam of a car door. I motioned for everyone to squat down, fast. Arlo stood there like a babbling lump.

"What was that?"

I reached up and jerked him down by a handful of shirt. He started to yak again so I put my hand over his mouth.

The sound of an approaching car caught my attention. *Car, car...was there a road in here? I don't remember Lath mentioning one.* The engine died and a second door slammed. We all looked at each other, except Arlo. He looked down at my hand. I removed it.

"Sorry."

I rose up a little and slowly parted the branches of a wild blueberry bush. I could see the tail end of a van, but not clearly. Two men, one dwarfing the other, stood with their backs to me and they were not singing church hymns. The short one, who seemed the most agitated, was gesturing further into the woods and heatedly telling the big one a great deal about *whateveritwas*. The large man kept shaking his head in disagreement. I'd grabbed Fang and was stroking his back, hoping he wouldn't get too worked up. Fortunately, the most coming from him was low growls and some barely audible whimpers.

Percy spoke in a hushed tone. "What's he sayin'?"

I turned to shush him and heard a large *smack!* that drew my attention back to the situation. I felt Fang tense, but I held him tight. Short man was bent over, hands clasped defensively against his face. Big man was partially turned. I drew in a breath of surprise. Fred Sessom grinned at short man, spit on the ground by short man's feet and walked off, heading somewhere down the dirt road. Short man stood back up, rubbing the side of his head and walked around to the opposite side of that van. By the sound of the door slamming, I was certain he climbed inside.

I looked at Arlo, who looked at Martin looking at Percy, who was looking at me. I shrugged my shoulders. The van's engine roared to life and when I looked back through the bush, it was gone. A quiet settled over the woods again.

"Come on, guys. I don't know what that was about, but we better get down to the water if we want to wet a hook today." They fell in behind me, Martin and Arlo swatting at gnats, Percy bringing up the rear. Fang would settle for nothing less than point dog, and he did just that.

We pushed our way through the overgrowth that threatened to choke the well-worn path. At last we heard a loud swooshing as a crane lifted off, spooked by our approach. The bushes gave way to a mossy, snaky-looking mud bank as we emerged. Something large made a splash in a stand of reeds off to our left.

"What we gonna catch in this place?" Percy eyed the pond skeptically.

"Well, you never know," I said. But I knew of at least one thing. I gazed out at the hazy bug-covered surface.

Martin and Percy divvied out the poles and Arlo passed out the bait. We were tending to our baiting when a gut-knotting scream ripped out across the water. Arlo jerked around, eyes like saucers, and his hook and bait landed squarely in the middle of Percy's short afro. Martin broke into a laugh, but I ignored them as *my* eyes settled on the bank almost opposite ours. I saw an orange flash but it was gone in an instant. Then I spotted Lath's boat ramp. I wasn't sure, but I could have sworn that I saw something metal-like reflecting back at me along with that flash. I knew what the orange was and I suspected Lath was watchin' us through those woods over there.

"What the Sam-hill was that?" Arlo didn't look too well. Percy and Martin were busy getting the night crawler out of Percy's hair, but you could tell they were nervous. We glanced at one another, but no one spoke. Finally, I shrugged and waved my hand toward the pond.

"Aw, probably ain't nothing," I said. They all looked at me and nodded, relief on their faces.

I finished my baiting and tossed my line into the water. My cork floated prone for a second, then bobbed back up as the weights pulled the line taut. Soon, all lines were out and we settled back, each finding a rock, log or stump to sit on. I passed out the RC's and tossed Fang his dog bones. The Gold Nugget gum came last, and I smacked Arlo beside the head with his. He gave me a goofy grin and dumped the whole bag into his maw.

For a while, the only sound you could hear was Fang crunching those milk bones. A few mosquitoes were busy making a feast of my neck as humidity stuck my clothes against my skin, making me feel too hot. Without so much as a cork bob, my line suddenly went tight and my pole started to bend. Since it was propped in the fork of a tree branch I'd pushed into the mud, this was not a good thing. I went to grab it and the line snapped, causing my pole to whip back and out of the branch and land halfway in the water. Martin made a muffled whistling sound and Percy uttered "damb!" Before anyone else could comment, the water broke about thirty feet out and the biggest fish any of us had ever seen made an arc in mid-air, rolling in the sunlight like a miniature version of a leaping dolphin. We all scrambled to our feet, knocking RC's over and nearly choking on the juice that a full bag of Gold Nugget gum can produce.

The fish seemed to hang there in slow motion, reflecting rainbows of shimmer across Edwards Pond. But what made four jaws drop simultaneously, what we would never forget, was the red-breasted robin that came out of nowhere just as that fish was approaching his pinnacle. We were stunned as the robin, speared through by the six inch dorsal fin of that behemoth catfish, wings flapping wildly, tried to escape. The descent was a flurry of feathers and shimmering grey skin, the splash sending a spray of water that touched us all as we stood there slack-jawed on that muddy bank.

No one said a word. No one moved. Not the slightest flinch of muscle or skin. Even Fang just sat there with his ears pinned back, stony. In a few seconds, the pond's surface had settled back to a calm, mossy tranquility. Fang whimpered and sniffed at the edge of the water. I noticed he kept his distance, though. Arlo, Martin and Percy all turned to look at me in unison.

"Whad?" Suddenly filled with indignation, it was all I could mutter at that moment.

"Whad? Whad? Is thad all you can thay?" Arlo was angry, frightened and a bit shaken. "You bwought us ouwt here, Peth! You tellin' us you didn't nowd aboud thad…thad…ting?"

He looked to Martin and Percy for backup. They scowled and jutted their chins toward me. Arlo's slurred words filled my head, but just for a second. My hackles went up in attack mode.

"Utay! So I nowd…..so whas? Ast freaky ast it is, dat's still the bigdest dang cathfist I ever seen. An'…an' you gonna thand there an' thell me you dond wanna cath it? None of you?"

I was livid with defense now. Gold Nugget sugar juice leaked from the corners of my mouth and spittle flew with every word. I could see the stuff oozing from Arlo's mouth as well. There was no argument in the world worth spitting that sweet goodness out. We sounded like we had golf balls in our cheeks. It felt like I had a softball in mine.

Martin and Percy stood off to the side, chewing their nugget wads and watching the argument. At a stand-off, Arlo and I both looked over simultaneously at Martin and Percy to get support, turn things in our own favor. Both stood side by side, gazes transfixed on us. Both had nugget juice running down their chins. But it was the fly that landed on Percy's chin that broke the mood. He didn't flinch. As a matter of fact, all he did was gently swat his six-fingered hand at his chin with a dazed look behind his glasses and that wad of gum puffing his cheek out.

We lost it. We howled with laughter, spit and juice running from our mouths, cheeks stretched to bursting, knee slappin' and trying to catch our breaths without choking to death. I turned to Arlo and grabbed his shoulder to steady myself.

That's when the gun went off and that gosh-awful animal cry pierced the air again…at least *I think* it was an animal. We quickly sobered up from the laughing, and I'm certain I wasn't the only one who had swallowed his gum. Birds flew from the trees with a rush. The commotion had brought Percy around, and it certainly had our full attention now.

Big, whooping noises came from the trees about two hundred feet away. We could hear car noises again, someone revving an engine, and what sounded like a motorcycle. I broke the spell.

"What the heck was that?" I retreated into the bushes. Without much persuasion (or maybe they'd had a lot by now), the rest dropped their gear and followed me back into the overgrowth.

"Where you goin' Pete?" Martin whispered.

"I'm goin' to see what that was. Just seems like there's a lot of weird stuff going on, don't you think?" I whispered. My eyes squinted with suspicion. Martin nodded in agreement.

We crouched down and followed the path a few dozen yards along the ponds edge until I saw a walkabout almost concealed off to our left. I knew we were further in, but wasn't certain if we were still hugging that road.

"We can cut through here and get close enough to see what it is…."

I was almost afraid of 'what it is'. Especially with bullets flying.

The barely trodden path snaked its way around several old oaks and through a mucky depression before cresting just shy of a wild honeysuckle hedge. The noise was louder now. I shushed everyone down and eased closer to the honeysuckle. The smell was heavy, rich with that dewy-smelling sweetness. Arlo and Martin were pressed around behind me. I could feel them breathing hot air on the back of my neck. Curiosity can be a powerful thing.

I heard a muffled *humfff!* and turned to see Percy on the ground clutching his chin. *Shhhh!* I motioned to him to be quiet. He stood up and kicked at a metal pipe protruding from the ground about ten inches, then caught up to us.

Reaching out, I carefully parted the bushy vines. It was hard to see much of anything, for standing partially in my view were two old outhouses, side by side. The doors hung part way off and the sides were nearly collapsed. Just to the north side of them, I could see the edge of an old lodgepole cabin.

Two men suddenly walked into view, not ten feet from the far side of that left outhouse. I jumped, and felt three nervous jumps behind me. Arlo had gripped my arm while trying to lean into the honeysuckle, but now he practically tore it off.

"What you boys doin' there?"

It came out of nowhere. As God is my witness, I think we all left a track in our underpants. We let out a strangled "ahhhhggg!!!" in unison and the others all fell over on top of me. As soon as they were on me, they were off, scrambling backwards to escape the thing behind them. Lath squeezed that bicycle horn, *whaaanka, whaaanka,* and pulled to a stop just a few feet from us.

"I sez', what you boys a'doin over here?" He peered at us through those optical abominations he called glasses, eyes floating, jittering back and forth, assessing the situation. It was obvious we were snooping on somebody or something, and I almost stuttered as the words caught in my throat.

"Mr. Lath, me and the guys just came down here for a bit a fishin', and…and we got distracted cause we heard a noise over there that sounded funny…so we were just lookin' for it…we—"

Lath bleeped that darn horn again and cut me off in mid-sentence.

"I don't mind ya boys a' fishin' up in here…just keep your min' to the job et hand. What goes on through them trees ain't none of yer business, you hear me?" He shot a glance over my shoulder.

"But Mr. Lath…." I couldn't help myself. "I thought you said you had a'time keepin' folks out of here that weren't invited."

Lath gave me a look that said *smartypants*.

"I know what I said, Petey. How I run my o'ffairs ain't nobody's business!" He was getting agitated with me and the rest of the boys picked up on it.

"Pete…." Arlo spoke up first. "Let's just get out of here. It's gonna be dark soon and I gotta get back." He looked at me and I could see what he was trying to do.

I took a good look at Lath and the pond, then swung around to eye that honeysuckle bush one more time. "Okay. Sorry to bother you, Mr. Lath. We need to be going, I guess."

I said this with my back to him. But when I turned around, I made straight eye contact with him. He flinched behind those glasses. None of this felt right, but this was not the time or the place to make more of it. After all, I'd been taught not to argue with grown-ups.

"You boys are a'welcome to keep fishin' if you like. Might lan' that devil Spike." He grinned and turned his wheelchair around on the path. "Hav'a good'un!"

His big arms pumped furiously and he disappeared through the trees, chunky wheels grabbing and slinging moss and dirt behind him. I turned to the boys.

"Y'all wanna stay and figure this out, or go home?"

"Pete, Mr. Lath said...." Percy threw his arms up exasperated-like.

"I don't care what Mr. Lath said. Something's going on here and I don't think it's good." I was a little surprised at my brash mouth.

Percy dropped his arms, frowned.

Martin took a step toward me and laid out his point of view. I listened.

"Pete, we seen some strange things in these woods, heard cars comin' and goin', seen something...." He looked down, shaking his head for a brief moment. "Something killed a bird flying over this pond, and Mr. Lath just made it clear that short of dippin' our hooks in his water, we don't have much business here. Besides, there ain't nothing normal biting here today, no ways. Now I'm for votin' to go back to Harper's Mill."

He stood there, eyes fixed on me. I glanced at Arlo and Percy. They both shrugged and I felt the air go out of my sails.

"Okay, you're right." I waved Martin aside and made my way down the path in the direction we came in. I didn't care if they followed or not. I don't know why I was so mad. Mom always said I was stubborn, but I didn't see it that way. Lath was hiding something.

I stopped and looked back. Arlo, Martin and Percy had gathered the fishing poles and were making their way back up the path. I stood beside the bikes and waited. I don't know if it was my imagination or what, but I could still hear something wailing and mawing like a cat in heat...or someone in pain. Just barely, but it was there.

Arlo and gang caught up to me and we grabbed our bikes and

started the hike out to fresh air. The gnats and skeeters were getting as thick as molasses in the trees around us and our walk out was a lesson in patience as we swatted about our heads to keep them at bay.

I was about fifteen feet from the clearing when my swat brought my eyes to a place just twenty yards away through the bushes on my left. I won't tell you I *thought* I saw something. I won't even tell you that those bushes may have been playing tricks on me. I saw the eyes, and maybe a hint of orange, but not much else. Just two eyes peering out from a lot of leaves. I knew whose they were, too. But I just kept walking, and I don't think the rest were none the wiser.

We cleared the woods and mounted our bikes in silence. I think the whole thing had thrown us all for a loop—out of whack you might say. The ride home was quiet and moody. I flipped on my transistor and caught the last minutes of *Soul Man* groovin' through the airwaves, as I broke from the guys and made my way home. Fang, as usual, led the way. Twilight descended on Harper's Mill.

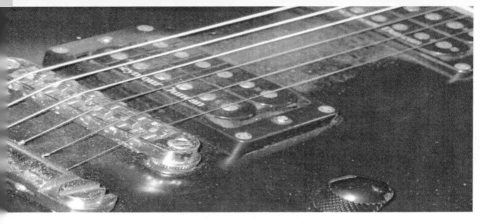

CHAPTER NINE

2011

MARGIE HAD TO GET out of Peter's room. The walls were closing in on her amid the beeps, lights and constant hissing of his respirator. She kissed his forehead and slipped into the hallway. Several nurses were reviewing charts and bustling around the nurses' station when she approached.

"Excuse me," she said to one that was placing a clipboard back in a wall tray. "I'm stepping out for a minute. Can I give you my cell phone number in case you need to reach me?"

The nurse nodded in that quiet way nurses have, removed a pen from her smock pocket, and started writing as Margie read the number aloud to her.

Taking the elevator to the first floor, she walked toward the entrance but noticed a few news reporters mulling around the lobby. She veered into the nearest hallway and left by a side door, taking the sidewalk toward the parking lot. The sun was dropping to the west, cooling the air as she walked briskly with no particular destination in mind. The sweat pants and shirt she'd thrown on that morning now felt comfortable as she moved through shadows created by the dying light.

She had just stepped off the curb, intent on taking a shortcut through the parked cars in visitor parking, when Millie's yellow Volkswagen pulled into the entrance a bit too fast and zipped into an empty space thirty feet away.

"Mom!" she called, jumping out of the car and running to Margie. Peter Jr. climbed from the passenger's side and joined them. There was silence as they group hugged, clinging to each other for support, tears trailing down cheeks. Margie pulled back, appraising her two grown children. She could see Peter in Millie's eyes, the way she held her mouth, in Peter Jr.'s cheekbones, his hair so similar to Peter's at that age, and she almost broke down again.

"Take the side entrance," she told them. "Your grandparents are in the cafeteria with Mr. Smith."

"Mr. Smith?" Peter Jr. asked.

"An old friend of ours. Just go in and introduce yourselves. I'll be back in a few minutes."

The kids turned and made for the hospital as Margie struck out across the well-manicured grass for the street. She walked fast at first, trying to think of anything but her husband lying in that bed, poked and probed, his life in the balance. Three blocks up, she felt the effects of her power walk and stopped in front of a church. She sat down on the steps and took several deep breaths, watching the traffic move busily along Abbott Street.

Feeling a little rejuvenated after a few minutes, she was about to get up and leave when her phone jingled. She jumped, her nerves right back to square one.

"Hello?" she said, fumbling with the palm-sized gadget.

"Margie? It's Martin," the man's voice said from the other end.

"Martin?" He sounded familiar. "Martin Sanders? My gosh, how are you? How did you get this number?"

"I was at RDU waiting on a connecting flight when I saw the

news report on the TV in the sports bar. I came over to the hospital as soon as I could change my flight. The nurse said she could reach you and dialed this number for me. Where are you?"

"Oh, Martin, that was sweet of you. I just took a walk to clear my head. I'm at….Hold on a second." Margie looked around, spotting a brick-encased sign with the church name across the top. Underneath, in small letters, were the words 'Pastor Percival Smith'. *Percy? I didn't know he had a church this close by.* A glance at the sign post on the corner told her the cross street was Thorn.

"I'm three blocks up at Abbott and Thorn…in front of the Salvation Baptist Church," she said.

"I'll be there in a few minutes." Martin hung up.

She put her phone back in the pouch on her sweatshirt and studied the church sign again. Percy's call had been such a natural progression. Of the five of them, he had been the one gifted by God during those dark days. At least that's the way she saw it.

God.

Margie felt a pang of guilt fill her up like bitter water. She and Peter had always believed, but had they believed enough? Had they done enough in their lives to show that? She placed her hand on her stomach and closed her eyes. With Peter in a coma and a new life inside her, it was all so confusing. *Were we designed to feel immense pain and joy at the same time?*

"Margie!" Martin walked up the few steps to her and helped her up before giving her a big hug. "Look at you," he said. "You haven't aged a day since high school."

"Well, no need to tell a lie after such a long time, Martin," she said, feeling some relief with their banter.

He shook his head and smiled at her. "If I'm lyin', I'm dyin'," he said, chuckling a little.

They both sat down. She glanced over at Martin. She marveled at how gracefully he'd aged, how fit and healthy he seemed. She noticed he wore no wedding band.

"So, how is he, Margie?" Deep furrows creased his forehead.

"He's in a coma." She didn't elaborate. What was there to elaborate on?

Martin drew a deep breath and let it out slowly. He took Margie's hand in his and turned toward her. "You have to believe he will come out of it, Margie. We all have to believe."

His words rang true and she briefly flashed back in her mind to a time when she stood with four childhood friends, hand in hand, and they believed. Believed with all their hearts that things would work out. That they would find their way out of the darkness.

"Do you believe in miracles, Martin?" she asked suddenly, pressing her hand to her stomach as she spoke.

Martin broke eye contact and gazed across the street, clearly thinking his answer through. Two boys came down the sidewalk on bicycles, laughing and shouting silly things at one another as they rounded the curb and disappeared from view. Martin kept his eyes fixed ahead.

"When I was young, I believed in what was before me. My mother told all her friends that I was the most sensible young man in Harper's Mill. But that all changed the day Peter, Arlo, Percy and I went to Edwards Pond. That day something opened in me that went beyond the black and white of the world." He paused, lowering his head before he continued. "That day, I believed there were things we couldn't put our hands on, things we couldn't see with our eyes…things that live in a realm that's alien to us." He let out a long sigh as if he'd just bared his soul. "When it all came to an end, I wasn't sure any of us could deny a world beyond ours, or the possibilities that we couldn't imagine." He squeezed her hand. "To answer your question, yes. I believe in miracles."

They both sat there on the steps as darkness dropped around them, each lost in thought, until Margie suddenly realized how long she'd been gone. She stood up and brushed the seat of her sweatpants as Martin rose to join her.

"Is that brother Percy's name on the sign?" He pointed to the church marquee.

"I'm sure it is, but we'll ask him when we get back," she said, taking Martin's arm as they both descended the steps.

They walked in silence toward the hospital as evening drew a veil over Raleigh, streetlights flickering on at random to drive away the darkness. Margie hugged her arms together, the heat of the day lessening with each step. They were a block from the hospital when a distinct chill ran up her back as if something icy bore into her. She turned around quickly, but the sidewalk was deserted.

"You okay?" Martin asked, stopping with her.

"Yes." She shook it off and started walking, Martin falling back in step with her. But she wasn't as certain about that as she'd pretended. The feeling left her violated in a way she couldn't comprehend.

Not again... please... not again.

CHAPTER TEN

Peter

I WONDER, LYING HERE in this darkness—this nothingness—if I am closer to God than I was that day in Jim's Grill. That day I saw things that nobody else saw. That day I met a dead man in a vinyl booth, a *very* dead man, with a bag of hot dogs clutched in my hand and Van Morrison rocking the jukebox for the lunch crowd.

I knew who God was then. I went to church and fell asleep like most dreamy-headed young men, too busy mapping out their future to pay attention. But I heard the Word, sometimes. I just never heard anything about dead people that come back to do good things. Except maybe Jesus. It was all straight out of a comic book for me when I shook Hardin Holley's hand that day in '74.

It was like a dream.

But I was closer to God that day than I could have ever imagined I would be at fifteen. Closer than I dared to be, had I known the truth. Closer to good and evil, but not necessarily in that order. The preacher said you had to walk through darkness to see the light, and I soon found out how true those words were.

Five weeks passed, all too slow for me. School was officially over and we had the whole summer ahead of us. The antics at Edwards Pond with Lath and his mysterious goings-on had just about been forgotten. Just about. The whole thing, while paling in the heat of summer, was never far from my thoughts.

Mr. Kim had never been found and the whole town was going about its business with a shadow looming over it. Martin and Percy had both accumulated additional chores, and Arlo's old man had secured him a summer job down at Daughtry's Lumberyard stacking lumber. I didn't know what that was supposed to entail, so I went by there one day and watched Arlo from the road. He'd told me he was making one dollar and twenty cents an hour, and that he was supposed to get a raise in a few weeks if he did good. I sat there watching him move one pile of lumber from this spot to that spot, turning the boards so they wouldn't warp from the rain. It looked like hard work and I noticed Arlo was getting that shirtless, Charles Atlas-look about him as the summer wore on. (This was confirmed later when I referenced the Charles Atlas ad on the back of my latest edition of *Creepy* magazine.) I also noticed that Arlo had burnt that fair skin so many times he was starting to look like a splotch of red leather.

I took a job making deliveries for Taylor's IGA Supermarket in the afternoons and usually had a grass mowing job lined up for the mornings. My guitar playing was improving somewhat, and I was getting my share of romance with Margie. Remember Margie with the goo-goo eyes? Her father was the town veterinarian and she was fine in my eyes…real fine. The miles of road peddled and yards of grass mowed were going to payoff down at Rawlin's Jewelers by summer's end. I had my eye on the coolest friendship bracelet in the place. A sweet gold, bejeweled marvel with enough engraving space to profess my deepest affections for Margie. I'd carried her books the last few weeks of school and was certain I would eventually marry her and have a dozen children.

But this isn't about my love life, is it? Those days of peddling groceries all over town and keeping the lawns of Harper's Mill well groomed gave me considerable time to mull over the whole mystery of Edwards Pond. The one thing that seemed to dig at me night and day was how human that last ear-splitting sound was that shook us up so bad. The whole thing was eating at me like a bad case of jock itch, and I was determined to get to the bottom of it before the next schoolbell rang.

Meanwhile, Mom took a part-time secretarial job down at Ethan's Old World Emporium. "Ethan" was really Fred Sessom's wife, Naomi, who bought it a few years earlier when all her kids had flown the coop and she needed something to do. The name just stayed the same. Mom was also spending a great deal of time with Mrs. Kim, providing some level of community comfort and helping her get the family affairs in order. Mrs. Kim never did close the Market after her husband's disappearance. Mom said it helped keep her busy, so as not to go crazy through the whole thing.

Dad was still flat-footing insurance in the tri-county area. He wasn't home much, but when he was, we tossed some ball and worked on my soapbox project, which was going nowhere fast. Our conversations lent truth to that fact.

"Pete, you need to tighten the screws on the pedal base." He handed me a wrench.

"I can't tighten them with a wrench, Dad."

"Oh, I guess you can't." He fumbled around a second and handed me a hammer. He seemed a bit distant, and I chalked it up to his workload.

The effects of the disappearance on the town were as real and plausible as a rock in your shoe. I could even feel it in my family. Mom and Dad seldom talked, and silence was nothing less than a stranger in the Travers' house. But our family had its moments of fleeting normalcy, and one came on a sweltering evening around the dinner table. The three of us had silently competed in food picking and shuffling for at least thirty minutes when Mom broke the silence.

"How was your day, Bill?"

Dad looked up from his plate like he hadn't understood the question. He nodded slowly. "Okay, I guess. I might have two more full life policies by the week's end." He poked his meat loaf with his fork. Mom chased a few peas across the Wedgwood plate, raised her head and cleared her throat.

"Soon-yi is thinking about selling the market. She doesn't think she can run it any more. We got a lot of her husband's..." Mom's eyes dropped to her plate. "...things stored away this week. I just wish her relatives could afford to come and spend time with her." Back to the peas as the silence threatened to creep back in.

Dad chewed his meat loaf and stared into space for a few beats. "She could always sell out part of it for a co-ownership." This came out in a mechanical drone around the meat loaf. He swallowed.

"Bill, I think she'll have more problems than she knows. I didn't know this, but she told me that when they came here, they had papers made for them and Mr. Kim's family paid a lot of money for them." She waited for a response. "Bill, I don't think they were legally married. I'm worried for her." There was definitely anguish in her voice. "I mentioned it to Naomi, but she said I shouldn't get too involved in their personal affairs."

Dad laid down his fork. It was brief, but I swear I saw just a moment of complete surprise on his face before that glazed look came over his features again. "That could be trouble, Clarice. That means the state could get everything if it was all in his name." Now, picking his fork back up, he ran *his* peas across the Wedgwood surface.

I'd made a nice little slide on the side of my mashed potatoes and poised two peas at the top to race down when the silence took over and remained for the rest of dinner. Both peas stuck and never finished their journey, much like the current state of the Travers family.

Martin took to riding his old man's dairy route with him daily at five a.m. It was a long route that covered Harper's Mill and most of the outlying rural areas. Sunday was the only day it didn't run. He didn't like it, but his dad believed boys shouldn't be idle.

It was after one of his early route runs that Martin came to my bedroom window around nine-thirty one Saturday morning. I was standing in front of my mirror in my underwear, holding my guitar and trying to play the chords to George Harrison's *My Sweet Lord* when a sharp *piff!* on the window pane nearly scared the doo-doo out of me. There was some comfort in knowing that had that happened, my Fruit of the Looms would have graciously captured it all. I put my guitar down and walked to the window, almost tripping on my old Batman helmet, and threw open the sash. Martin still had his Paola Dairy shirt on, and the morning dew had soaked his pants legs up to the knees. *Note to self: cut my own grass for a change.*

"Pete!" Martin moved closer to the window, his voice low, but strained with excitement. "Pete, I saw 'em!"

"Saw who?"

"The guys from the parade!" He looked at me like he'd just shared the Meaning of Life. I became impatient.

"Martin, what the heck are you talking about?" I glared at him, hands on hips, a very serious look on my face. My underwear was drooping at the crotch, but I stood there like a rooster, my skinny arms flexing for action.

"Geez! The guys in the sheets…you know…from the parade? I saw them down at Lath's place. I was puttin' Mr. Lath's milk on his stoop when I looked down through the trees at the pond and saw 'em. They were going down the opposite side in a line, like. I don't think Dad noticed from the truck, though." He glanced over his shoulder, fidgeting there in the dewy grass.

"They didn't see you, did they?" The idea of Martin being spotted bothered me, but I wasn't sure why.

"I don't think so. What do you think they were doin' down there, Pete?"

"I don't know. But it can't be anything good."

My brain felt itchy. The whole thing didn't feel right. People were acting strange, not as friendly. In Harper's Mill, that was not normal. People didn't say hello on the street, the old-timers were never on the drug store bench like was their habit, and there was no lack of short tempers in Harper's Mill. The disappearance of Mr. Kim had become a festering boil, a subject of gossip and unrest over the last two months. His wife, or widow, as some might say, was at the police station every week, but they were giving her no answers. Miller's Reservoir and Finley's Lake, two big recreation areas, had been searched with divers and dredged as much as local resources would allow.

There were even a few ugly rumors floating around that Mr. Kim had sported a gambling problem before his disappearance. Some even said he'd won big money betting on the horses up in

Raleigh and had skipped out with it to start a new life. I don't think most people bought that story. According to Mom, anyone who knew him would think that was hogwash. Yep, there was definitely something rotten in this town, and the stench was getting worse as summer wore on.

"Hey, can you get the guys and meet me at the old mill tree around noon?" I had a plan. I didn't know exactly what it was yet, but it was in there somewhere.

"Sure." Martin grinned. He was always up for a game of 'no good'. He took off through the overgrown grass.

I made quick to get my pants on, get my bed made and my room cleaned up. Dad was on the road this morning and Mom was cleaning house, a Mom Travers routine every Saturday morning. Fang paced outside the screen door to the porch, anxious to run shotgun on any mischief. I only had one pressing errand to run for Mom, and a grass cutting…maybe.

It was a standing tradition in the Travers' household to eat hot dogs on Saturdays from Jim's Grill. This little hole in the wall had a special on that day; three hot dogs with all the fixins' for a dollar fifty. An order of fries was fifty cents and they were hot, greasy and piled high on the plate. We ate lunch on Saturdays for about four bucks, and Mom didn't have to cook. Dad always scheduled his Saturday around his hot dogs.

After doing a double check of my cleaning, I dressed, grabbed the hot dog money and my ball cap, and hit the screen door so hard on my way out that it slammed against the house. I started across our yard, dandelions slapping against my pants bottoms as my feet left impressions in the overgrown grass, and stopped. There was no way I could ignore this jungle another day without a warning from Dad.

Jim's wouldn't be ready for the lunch crowd yet, so I grabbed our lawnmower and proceeded to mow grass for the next half hour. Fang, of course, waited patiently by the steps. When I was finished, I put the mower up and went back inside to cap off my thirst with some chilled Kool-aid. By ten-thirty, Fang and I were on our way to Jim's.

Jim's sat just off the road between the Western Auto and the Texaco Gas station on Main Street. On a warm day the big screen door continuously opened and slammed shut as flies fought against the current of a big, old-fashioned ceiling fan just inside. The smell of dogs and fries drifted through the screen as I parked my bike next to the building and told Fang to stay. Jim was slinging spuds and speed wrapping slaw dogs, chili dogs, foot longs and a special of his, the "Doggone Biggest Dog" (this included everything that would stay on a foot long without falling off), while his wife, Edna, took orders and directed the two waitresses working the lunch crowd.

I got in line at the Order Here sign and surveyed the diners. Local business folks filled most of the booths and side tables as Van Morrison wailed about his sweet brown-eyed girl on the jukebox thumping in the corner. Edna was screaming "order up!" over Van and the smells were intoxicating.

My eyes wandered over by the bathrooms and fell on the last booth along the wall. It was empty, a sign taped to the edge of the table read **closed for repair**. A delirious fly buzzed my face and I swatted at it several times. When I looked at the booth again, there was a man sitting there. *Can't he read the sign?* He seemed fairly young, just old-fashioned looking, like some of the guys in my dad's old high school yearbook. He glanced up, looked directly at me. I looked away, careful not to be rude, like Mom always taught me. When I glanced back that way, he waved me over with a motion of his hand. I ignored him. Not because the whole thing was weird - *it was* - but I couldn't lose my place in line.

Edna whirled around on me.

"What'll it be, sweetie?" She smiled. It was a forced, *I'm-workin'-my-butt-off, so-be-quick-and-don't-waste-my-time*, smile. She smacked her gum with gusto, her over-painted lips a blood-cherry red. I liked Edna, but she could put a hurtin' on the term 'trashy'.

"I'll have two specials, mustard, onions, ketchup and chili on all, and two orders of fries...to go, please."

I glanced back at the man in the booth. He raised his head in my direction and did a little wave of some kind with his hand. Edna broke my gaze with her gum-smacking and order placing, both at great volume. "Two specials, dress 'em, and two orders of spuds!" she yelled, loud enough to make my neck hair prick up. Then I noticed her gaze fall on the booth the man was sitting in. Her forehead scrunched up for a second, then smoothed out. Her eyes kinda went flat-looking before she turned and walked away.

I took a good, long look at that booth and the stranger sitting there. He was dressed in something that looked like a low-end rack suit from Sears. Only it was just a little off from purple, kinda pale like old grape gum. His white shirt was buttoned to the collar. Frosty white socks peaked from under the table before disappearing into what most around here would call western boots. His glasses were big, boxy, giving him an owlish look. A shock of brown wavy hair wrapped around his skull in a stylish way. He caught me looking again and smiled. He was all teeth—mildly distracting from the rest of his face. He sipped his cola through a straw and waved that little wave at me again.

"Here ya go, Pete." Edna slapped the brown bag of goodies down in front of me. The smell of hot dogs and greasy fries enticed me through the paper. I grabbed the bag and started for the door. Rack suit waved at me again and motioned for me to come over. I don't normally have much to do with strangers, but Jim's was pretty crowded and my curiosity got the better of me. I wandered over to his booth. He slid out and stood, extending his hand in greeting. I took it and shook it, noticing a mild tingling in his fingers, like a low current. He spoke first.

"Holley! Hardin Holley! And you must be Pete." His drawl was thick and about as far south as you could get without wading into the Gulf of Mexico.

"That's right, sir. How did you know that?" It was an honest question. He smiled, exposing his pearly whites. He looked genuinely happy to see me. I could see Jim's lights glaring off his sizeable glasses and squinted my eyes.

"I knew ya' mom back in school. We go back a'ways." He held his teeth at attention. "I hear there's some good fishin' to be had in these parts. Know of any places close by?" His question was odd. He could have asked anyone in this town to get that information.

"Well, there's Miller's Reservoir and Finley's Lake. Not too far from here." I hitched my pants up with my left hand. "The fishin's good, but you'll need a boat." He stared at me from behind his glasses. I fidgeted.

"I was lookin' for something to just throw my line in for a few. Someplace quiet, maybe." He continued to stare. His lip twitched a bit. Perhaps holding that smile was beginning to labor him.

"Well, there's Lath Edwards' pond a few miles out off Open Bridge Road. You'd have to ask him, though. May be some good cats and bream in there. You can see his trailer 'bout a quarter mile off the road on your right."

He smiled. Another twitch. *This guy is good. Must sell used cars for a living*, I reasoned.

"Thanks, Pete." He held out his hand and I shook it again. "You get that lunch to ya' mom, now." He adjusted his glasses and turned his attention back to his cola. I was dismissed. Just like that.

I turned and headed for the screen door. People gave me strange looks, but I ignored them. The Stones were *Tumbling Dice* on the jukebox as I risked a glance over my shoulder. The booth was empty. No Mr. Holley. No glass of cola… no bull. It was empty.

Edna yelled over the music to one of the employees, but it sounded miles away. I was off balance. She turned to me.

"Next time you want to spend time staring at one of our tables, let me know. That one…" she pointed to the one I'd just left. "… needs a good sanding down and varnishing. I'll give you ten dollars if you decide you want the job."

I just stared at her.

I pushed through the door and onto the sidewalk with my bag in hand and a sudden desire to be anywhere but here. Fang greeted the bag with an eager wag and we were off. I had just enough time to stop by the house before meeting the guys at the mill. Problem was, my encounter with Hardin had scattered my thoughts to the point that now I really had no idea what my plan was going to be once we converged on Edwards' Pond.

What came into view as I arrived at home put all those thoughts to the back of my mind. I slammed the brakes of my rusty bike and fish-tailed across the road, barely missing the backside of a Harper's Mill police cruiser.

CHAPTER ELEVEN

2011

THEY WERE ALL SEATED AROUND a table in the cafeteria when Margie and Martin entered. Millie and Peter Jr. sat texting the news to friends, their eyes bloodshot and tired. Percy was discussing something of an evangelical nature with Clarice, her worried face concentrating on his every word. Bill Travers simply stared off into space.

"Sorry I was gone so long." Margie stopped in front of them and pulled Martin's arm until he was standing next to her.

Everyone looked up and managed a pained smile at the sight of Martin. Millie and Peter Jr. simply stared at him a second and resumed texting.

"Martin!" Percy jumped up and moved around the table, grabbing Martin's hand and half hugging him. "How have you been? What's it been, twenty years since I ran into you in Charleston?"

Martin laughed. "That's right, six-pack. Twenty long, beautiful years."

Percy waved him off with his six-fingered hand. "You haven't changed a bit."

The kids were taking an interest in the conversation now, eyes averted from their chiming phones. Millie turned hers off, slid it in her purse.

"How are you, Martin?" Bill Travers asked, standing up and shaking Martin's hand across the table. Clarice smiled and nodded her greeting from her husband's side.

"Well, for everybody's sake, I'm doing just fine. I just wish we didn't have to meet under these circumstances."

Everyone nodded.

Margie felt a sudden urge to be with Peter, to check on him. "I'm going up to see Peter. Martin, would you like to come?"

"That's what I'm here for, Marg." He smiled, but she could see a moment of anxiety cross his face.

She grabbed his hand and they took off for the elevators.

"Grandpa," Peter Jr. said, finally putting his phone away. "You ever know anyone who was in a coma?"

Bill Travers stared at his grandson as he ran a hand through his graying hair out of frustration. He'd been shot, seen men do things to other men that was beyond cruelty, and witnessed things that defied explanation, things that he still couldn't talk about to this day. But he'd never known anyone that was in a coma.

"No," he finally said, looking directly at Peter Jr. *But there was something about his son's coma that bothered him. Something he couldn't put his finger on.* After a minute, he stared off into space again.

Everyone looked at each other, gave Bill Travers his moment of quiet reflection, and let it go.

Margie opened the door to Peter's room and motioned for Martin to follow. The doctor was at Peter's bedside conferring with a nurse when they entered. Fear gripped her insides when their chatter stopped and they both looked at her as if caught sharing a secret.

"Is something wrong, doctor?" She grabbed and squeezed Martin's arm, bracing herself for the worst.

"Ah, no Mrs. Travers. Not really." He had a puzzled look on his face. "Nurse Wilson was just telling me that a few minutes ago your husband seemed to be smiling."

Margie's heart fluttered in her chest, hope and relief overcoming the fear. But his earlier words kept her from overreacting.

"And?"

"Well, nothing really. That's a bit more unusual than the crying he was doing earlier. It's still my opinion that it's involuntary muscle movement. Nurse Wilson seems to agree," he said, nodding at the nurse. "But there's still no change in his prognosis, I'm sorry to say."

The wind went out of Margie's sails, again.

"Visiting hours will be over in a few minutes," the doctor said, looking directly at Martin. "Immediate family can stay, of course." He closed his chart and walked out, the nurse on his heels.

"Well, that was another emotional rollercoaster," Margie said, trying to rally a half-hearted smile as she walked over to Peter and stroked his forehead.

Martin stood at the foot of the bed, gripping the rails. Margie looked up and noticed his face was pinched with concentration. Finally, he walked around to the other side of the bed and stared down at Peter.

"I'm going back down to speak with the others, Martin. I guess I'll go home and clean up a little. I didn't bring anything when I ran out this morning." She bent over and kissed Peter on the forehead and whispered next to his ear. "I'll be back later, sweetheart." She wiped the corner of her eye and left the room.

Martin stood still, closed his eyes. Images of the past fluttered up and brushed his cheeks. Something sparkled with the colors of the rainbow for a second and was gone. He felt that place where things can happen just beyond reality, and he felt it deep in his heart in that moment.

He began to talk.

CHAPTER TWELVE

Peter

I HEARD MARGIE'S VOICE, or at least I think I did. Her breath was warm against my face, but she sounded far off, as if the darkness had swallowed her too. It was good to know she was here, somewhere. I've felt a chill growing in me, not something that raises the skin and hair, but something that tries to wrap its tendrils around me and send coldness to the core of me, to my heart.

As I float here, perhaps in God's abyss, I can only wish I had the optimism, the heart and substance, of one I knew long ago. One that laughed in a carefree way and said what she thought. One that spoke to the heart with wisdom and hope. I think of her now, all of her color, bravado, and sass. I think of all that in the spirit of a dead woman, the complexity of it, and I wonder if I will still be me if I can't find my way out of here. Yes, I think of this…and more, as I did back then.

I cleared the curb and came to a halt near the front door. Fossy Smith was pacing around outside, thumbs hooked into his regulation pants. He was a part-time police officer with Harper's Mill, and raised hogs just outside of town the rest of the time. He approached me as I dropped my bike. The smell of hogs preceded him like an odoriferous cloud.

"Pete!" He smiled at me, but I knew butter when I saw it. "Your dad's inside. Go on in." He moved aside and I caught sight of Dad's car by the side of the house. "That sure smells good!" he added, nodding his head toward me.

I glared at him with a piggish look, until I realized I still had the bag of hot dogs in my hand. I ducked into the house before he could start salivating. Dad was sitting on the couch, next to the Chief of Police, J. L. Lewis. Chief Lewis looked somber. His lanky frame barely filled up his uniform and his trademark shades added to his stony composure.

"Pete." He nodded at me, clutching his hat in his hands. I nodded back with a "Sir" for respect. I turned my attention to Dad. He didn't look himself, a bit disheveled to say the least.

"They arrested your mom, Son."

I stood there with my mouth hanging open. What was he talking about?

"Mrs. Sessom accused her of embezzlement," he continued. Chief Lewis dipped his head slightly in agreement.

"Embezzlement? What's that?" I'd heard the word before, but the meaning was a different matter. And I knew if it was something bad, Mom couldn't have done it. Not Mom.

"They've accused her of taking money from the store account...." Dad's voice broke. "Naomi Sessom says she's got evidence. " His eyes darted toward Chief Lewis. "They're gonna hold her for arraignment sometime next week." He rubbed his hands on his pants.

Chief Lewis rose and put on his hat. "Bill, you should be able to see her in a few hours. Just see me or Fossy when you get there and we'll take care of you." He turned to me. "Pete." He nodded again and headed for the door.

"Jerry...." Dad spoke now, stopping the Chief at the door. "You don't believe she did this, do you?"

The Chief just stood there. I'm not sure what passed between them, but I could see a brief look of understanding cross Dad's face. The Chief turned and left. I sat down beside Dad. He ruffled my hair with his big hand. I didn't mind.

"I'll take care of it, Petey. She'll be home soon."

I couldn't remember the last time he called me Petey. He looked away and I could tell he wasn't as sure in his heart as he was with his words.

Fang's bark grabbed my attention, and I remembered what I'd been about to do before all this. I knew Dad wouldn't want me to go see her now, and he probably didn't want me sitting here watching him struggle with this news. I was already late meeting the boys, so I gently set up my exit. I handed him the paper bag and stood.

"Dad, do you want me to stay here?"

"No, Pete. You run along. I'll know more in a few hours. Just be home by dark. And pray for your mom, Son." He sat the bag on the couch and put his head in his hands.

I'd never seen my dad so beat down. Never. I turned and pushed my way outside where Fang seemed all fired up about something. Arlo and the boys would be getting antsy about now, so I hopped on my bike and sped off with Fang in tow and Mom heavy on my mind.

I peddled hard up Frazier Street, trying not to think of our family problems. Fang's tongue was lolling out the side of his mouth, so I guess I was a match for him today. I rounded Frazier and Elm, and was almost in front of the courthouse when a black Bonneville came out of nowhere and cut in front of my bike. I swerved to the right, bounced off a beat-up Chevy truck and came to a wobbly stop a few feet from the curb. I was a little rattled, but otherwise okay.

The driver never slowed down, but I was certain they knew what they'd done. Fang hung back on the sidewalk, eyeing me with reverence from the comfort of his haunches. I suspect he had just witnessed a near fatality, much like he faces daily in the streets of Harper's Mill. A boy and his dog can sure bond in strange ways.

I watched the car work its way slowly up Elm and pull over about a block up the street. Crouching down between two parked cars, I kept my eyes on it. A tall man, lanky, and wearing a brown fedora, stepped from the driver's side and leaned against the hood as he scanned Elm Street, his eyes hidden in the fedora's shadows. There was something familiar about him, but I couldn't put my finger on it.

Just then a '63 Impala cruised by, blocking my view, and when I could see him again, he wasn't alone. Russell Beecham and Fred Sessom greeted the man in front of his car. When Russell gave him a brief hug the gears in my head clicked into place and I remembered where I'd seen him before. Russell had thrown a community picnic together last spring with help of the local rotary club. This man had shown up with much fanfare from Russell and his family. Mom later explained that the man was Russell's brother-in-law, Thelonious Nichols, and he was a big-shot lawyer out of the state capital. But that wasn't the only gear that clicked into place. The second gear caught in my skull and I remembered where else

I'd seen him: climbing out of the van with Fred at that KKK rally. Yes, something was definitely rotten in this town.

I gazed back over at the courthouse, reflecting back on the events of the morning. It suddenly dawned on me that my mom was in there, locked up in a jail cell. Up the street, the three men climbed into Thelonious' car and pulled away from the curb. Several cars behind me, on the opposite side of the street, another car pulled out and cruised by me real slow like. It was a baby blue Cadillac, and behind the wheel was Hardin Holley, big glasses and all, and he did that little wave with his hand. His hair remained a wavy pompadour of perfection, even with all four windows rolled down. The big Caddy was quiet as a mouse as it passed. It was kind of creepy.

I pushed my bike across the street to the courthouse. I had to see if this madness was real, see it with my own eyes. Fang followed me around the side of the two-story red brick building, where thick bushes grew along the side. Small barred windows sat low to the ground, partially hidden. Laying my bike down, I squatted and wiggled between the hedges until I could peer into the first window. The glass pane lay open and I could see Charlie Russ sprawled out on the metal bed attached to the wall. Splayed legs, arms hanging loosely over the side, Charlie appeared to be sleeping. I was not too surprised, and I guessed that Charlie spent a lot of time in the Harper's Mill jail as a guest of the town. I shuffled crab-like under the next hedge until I came to the second window. The odds of finding Mom were with me now, as Harper's Mill only had two jail cells (something I learned studying local history at school.) I peered through the grimy window behind the iron bars. At first, I couldn't see anything.

"Mom!" I kept my voice low, but urgent. There was a rustle.

"Pete?" More rustling. The window opened all the way and I

stared down at her face. "Pete, what are you doing here?" She didn't look too bad for a jailbird. No jail issued clothes, no ball and chain. She just looked pretty. And scared. The relief on her face when she saw me was evident. "Pete, I'm sorry you had to see this...." She looked down, shame etched on her face.

"It's all right, Mom. I know you didn't do it." I smiled at her. She looked up with that calm motherly look on her face and at that moment I understood the strength of this woman. "Dad'll be down in a little bit to see you. You doing okay in there?"

Just then a twig snapped behind me and I whirled around to find Chief Lewis squatting down behind me. He pushed his shades up on his forehead.

"Great balls of fire, Pete...you know I don't allow no window visits at my jail." His face was lean and stern below his wavy hair. I swallowed hard as he put his hand on my shoulder and...smiled? "You can see your mom when your dad gets here. Now run along and don't let me catch you window-prowling around my jail again. Understand?"

I did. I mouthed a goodbye to Mom, scurried from under the bush and pushed my bike back around the building. Fang ambled up beside me and gave me a quizzical look, his head cocked to the side, fang jutting out.

"Come on, boy." I scratched him behind his ear and took off for the mill. Martin and gang would be waiting for me and I already had a change of plans. In the distance, the town fire alarm started its slow-building wail as another disaster came to Harper's Mill.

I never made it to the mill. As I cut through town all heck broke loose. People were running outside from storefronts to see where the smoke was coming from. Fire was a big deal in a little town like Harper's Mill. At first I couldn't tell where it was because smoke was billowing down Main Street, making blind spots on both sides. The Harper's Mill fire truck came roaring by, sending me to the gutter as I jockeyed to safety. When I was sure the fire truck was past me, I fell in behind it, peddling furiously to keep up. It passed through the main intersection and roared down the street until the storefronts were no longer in view. We were in Shantytown by the time the sirens started winding down.

Shantytown was a word-of-mouth name given to the now dilapidated, undesirable structures that had been the pride of Harper's Mill in its boon days. Three saloons, four brothels and various boarding houses comprised its bulk. As the town struggled to keep economically stable with the various cash crops it relied on, more and more transient help took up residence in the aging buildings. Most of them were immigrants, or of the "colored" persuasion. What remained to this day was a claptrap of leaning, weathered buildings that provided little comfort from icy winters and sweltered in the dog days of August.

In 1942, a colored man by the name of Freeman Davis had taken up residence in one of the old saloon structures with his family. He was a shrewd man, and one of only a few of color in the area to have an education of any type. He read and wrote well, but it was his way with money that marked him. He could hold his own with any of the white businessmen in town (although his color kept him out of many local ventures), and in 1945 he somehow purchased a single-level building just twenty feet off of the main road. He called it Butterbean's Fixit Shop (for reasons known only to Freeman).

For two years he labored at turning it into a community store and he did well at it. But it was the two garage bays he built that were his pride and joy. Seems Freeman had a good mechanical mind as well. There weren't many cars in the county back in them days, and Freeman did most of his business by word of mouth. He would take trade for most anything, since most anything was valuable after the salvage years of the war. Between cars, Freeman would tinker with anything that people brought in. White folk, who wouldn't break bread with the likes of a colored man, sure didn't mind him fixin' their possessions. Such was the South.

It's rumored that in the winter of '62, Freeman walked out of his garage one day and found a bus sitting at the side of the road in front of the Butterbean. Five young sharply-dressed black men were standing huddled and shivering by the side arguing about something and occasionally bending down to look under the bus. Their thin tailored suits were little protection against the cold wind. Freeman made small talk and spent the next five hours under that bus fixing a worn tie rod.

Years later, as the story goes, Freeman would speak casually about that encounter, telling everyone that the young men called themselves the "Tem'tations", and that "they's was some kinda singin' group." Said he refused what little money they offered him, and finally agreed to sit for over an hour and listen to them sing a cappella in one of his garage bays. They sounded good, he said, for a bunch of "younguns."

In 1963, Freeman's oldest boy Cecil went missing. The Civil Rights movement was gaining momentum and Cecil was among the many young black men who grew increasingly outspoken for the cause. His disappearance fueled a growing divide between the color lines of Harper's Mill. Accusations flew, local and state law enforcement went through the motions, but Cecil was never found. Freeman grieved and time marched on. That was the last racial flare-up Harper's Mill had seen. Until now.

Smoke billowed above Shantytown, blotting the sky. The fire truck came to a stop about three blocks from Butterbean's. Flames shot out the bay windows, fueled no doubt, by the flammables and combustibles Mr. Davis kept there. Many citizens, some white, most black, lined the side streets to watch the inferno. I pulled up beside a cab parked along the curb. Harper's Mill only had two cabs that I knew of, and this one didn't look familiar. After a cursory glance at the cab, I scanned the gathering crowd. I knew the guys wouldn't wait for me at the mill when they saw the smoke. Fires were like undeniable magnets to boys.

"That's a heckuva fireball...."

The words caught me off guard. I glanced over at the cab. Smoke of a different kind wafted from the driver's window. This astute observation came from the driver. Dressed like a hippie flower child, she looked to be in her twenties, and had a voice like nails on a chalkboard. Reddish, unruly hair went in all directions, held in some kind of cosmic order by handmade flower tie-ins. Large, rose-colored sunglasses seemed a permanent part of her face, as well as the cigarette hanging from her lips. She was freckled on all exposed areas not covered by her loose, homemade cheesecloth dress, at least what I could see from my bike. She was probably well worth a mom-warning for a boy my age. Quite unlike anything I'd ever seen.

She flicked her ash out the window. It scattered and vanished on a breeze.

"Burn, baby, burn." She smiled. It wasn't a malevolent statement, I don't think. Just another 'hip' observation. Her profile seemed to shimmer as cigarette smoke coiled to the roof and slid out the top of the window.

"How did it start, Ma'am?"

"Oh honey, don't call me Ma'am. I ain't nobody's mama." She took another drag from her cigarette, expelling the smoke in a thin, smooth line through the window. The Holding Cab Company sign across the roof became momentarily obscured. "Call me Pearl, or don't call." She laughed, high and wild, broken glass on vocal cords. "But I tell you something, sweet thing…hate started that fire. Pure hate." She winked at me, but there was no smile on her face.

I stared at her for a second more, then turned my attention back to the blazing Butterbean. I noticed Mr. Davis standing down by the fire truck. His head hung low, shoulders slumped. He stood there in his tee shirt and pants, belt unbuckled, feet bare. Some things, and I guess some people, wear their weariness on their bodies like a shawl. The weight of their sorrow pulls their heads low, deflates their pride something awful.

"Pete!" Arlo's voice brought me back to myself. He came peddling up, with Percy and Martin bringing up the rear. They stopped next to the cab, catching their breaths.

"Where were you? We waited at the mill for over an hour…." Arlo's face was skewed in a mask of indignation and pity.

What a lacy-drawers.

"Sorry, guys." I spoke to all of them. "Mom got arrested for something she didn't do. I had to stop and see her over at the jail…" I let the words trail off, suddenly feeling exposed. Three mouths dropped open before me. It would have been four, but Pearl kept her lips locked on her Pall Mall.

"Arrested?" Martin was off his bicycle. He put the kickstand down. "Whada'ya mean arrested?"

I glanced over at the cab. Pearl sat stony-faced, staring at me, her Pall Mall hanging loosely from her lips, effortlessly filling the cab with wisps of tobacco smoke. Rose-tinted glasses reflected billowing clouds from the Butterbean. She could have been a paper cutout, some one-dimensional character from a book. I ignored her and turned back to the guys.

"Lady she works for says she took money from her job…stole it." I glanced around at three indignant faces. Mom's reputation in Harper's Mill was one of pristine morals, hard work and shining Motherhood. Somehow, these faces vindicated me just a bit.

How long is she going to be in there?

The thought…no, the question, filled my head in Pearl's voice. Funny thing is I'm not sure it ever reached my ears. I turned again to look at Pearl. Her lips were pursed tightly as if she anticipated my reply.

"Don't know. Dad thinks she'll be out soon. I think she has a hearing before the judge on Monday. I guess he'll set her bail then." I glanced over my shoulder at the guys. Arlo, Percy and Martin looked at me quizzically.

A cough like crushing gravel drew my attention back to the cab. Pearl gazed out at the inferno that was once a part of Harper's Mill's history. She lit another Pall Mall, put the cab in gear and slowly pulled away from the curb. She stuck her head out of the window. "I'll see you later, Pete!"

And she was gone. No sound of wheels on gravel. No exhaust. Nothing. I wasn't even sure if the ground in front of me had been shadowed for the last twenty minutes. My skin crawled. I looked across the street and saw Fred and Russell standing on the sidewalk opposite. They were both fixated by the fire and commotion, almost a look of awe on their faces.

"Are you okay, Pete?" I didn't answer, wasn't sure who asked the question. My head was swimming.

Percy broke the moment. "I gotta get home, guys."

Martin nodded his head in agreement and mounted his bicycle.

Arlo followed his lead.

"Basketball behind the school tomorrow?" Arlo looked around for confirmation. We all nodded. Tomorrow was Sunday and we made it a habit to offset Sunday's slow pace with a few games of hoop after church. Boys tend to be a bit antsy like that. Arlo looked at me solemnly. "Hope your mom's okay, Pete." Heads shook all the way around. I hoped so, too. I was anxious to see her without bars between us.

We headed our separate ways. I thought about Freeman Davis and Mr. Kim as I peddled home. I hoped they would be all right. That something good would rise out of all this bad. Somehow, in Mr. Kim's case, I doubted that would happen. He'd been missing for sixty-four days, and counting.

CHAPTER THIRTEEN

2011

"PETE," MARTIN SAID, HOPING his friend could hear him. "I don't know if this is the way it should be, or if it's this way for a reason that I can't understand."

He felt odd standing here, the monitors and IV lines quietly working on a level he couldn't comprehend. Odd but natural, as if this moment had been written in the book of life long before he ever met his friend.

"I saw her today, Pete." He stopped and shuddered, a chill so deep it almost took his breath away. "I was leaving the airport, trying to get here...to see you." His hands were shaking. He clasped them together to steady them. "It was the oddest thing, Pete, that old car sitting there in the taxi line. Something pink and feathery was blowing out the driver's window. I could see the ash of her cigarette glowing. I think I could see her teeth, Pete. I think she was smiling at me."

He felt weak and stumbled backward to land in one of the chairs. The image of her, of seeing her, hit home now as he sat in the quiet of Peter's room, the place that held his friend's life in the balance. It all meant something. Peter near death, Pearl rising from somewhere deep in their past. Rising from the dead. Again.

Yes, it all meant something. And it scared him.

He stood up and looked out the window as he spoke. "She's back, Pete. Back for a reason." He hung his head, unable to comprehend such a thought. No, comprehend was too tame a word for what he felt right now. It was ominous, this thing. And it swelled beyond just her image, opening that place inside him that peeled away the black and white. He shook his head, the question forming on his lips. "I wonder if the others are, too?"

A sudden *swoosh* from the respirator startled him out of the past. Out of that place.

He approached Peter's bed and laid a hand on his friend's head. "I don't know what you're doing in there, Pete, but if you see her... see *them*, let them know I'm in for the ride again. I'm in all the way."

The next thing he remembered he was in the elevator with his finger on the lobby button. The ride down was quiet.

CHAPTER FOURTEEN

Peter

I LAUGH NOW, LAUGH with some part of myself that I'm unfamiliar with, laugh at the absurdity of remembering my mother in such a place, in such a time when the world was so big to me, so long ago. I can afford to laugh, now. I have no face exposed to the world. No fear of memories being drudged up for all to see.

But now I'm distracted by lights that twinkle and disappear in this black void. I thought they were the lights of salvation I saw so many years ago. Yes, I thought that. But the coldness inside me grows deeper and the lights are slowly converging, one absorbed by another as they twinkle. I fear the lights now. I fear they are not what I expected, what I once knew them to be. I would run away if I had legs to run with. Can a soul run? The answer to that makes me colder.

So I wait. Wait with fear of the unknown.

Just like I waited that day. Like we all waited.

When I got home, Dad was closing the trunk of the Rambler.

His face was a quandary of emotions: tension, worry, irritation. I could read every one of them like a large print book. Mom's situation was wearing him down.

"Hey Pete, I was just getting ready to go see your mom. You ready?" He forced a smile, opened the driver's door. I threw my bike down and climbed in the passenger's side. We slammed our doors closed in unison.

Our drive was short and silent. I could tell he had a lot weighing on his mind. *Between the two of us, our heads should be flat.* We pulled into the courthouse parking lot and took one of the visitor spaces. That left nine empty ones, a testament to the quaintness of Harper's Mill and the optimism of its citizenry.

Dad and I were just reaching the steps when Thelonious Nichols pushed the front doors wide and stepped out with Charlie, gripping his arm to steady him. They paused on the steps, Charlie's eyes too bloodshot to focus and Thelonious doing his best to ignore us. Dad bristled. I don't know why, because he had no dealings with Thelonious, or Charlie, that I knew of. He pulled me back a foot or two as the two men passed. He didn't say anything, but I could feel his grip tighten on me as Thelonious and Charlie made their way down the courthouse steps. He abruptly turned my shoulders back toward the entrance and practically drug me inside.

The courthouse doors closed, cloaking us in the cool shadows of the main hallway. I craned my neck back to look up at the lofty interior of the ceiling dome. Dust motes formed a hazy, transient cloud that drifted timelessly through the sunbeams penetrating the high-set windows. The place smelled old, and I wasn't really a stranger to it.

The town library was located in the basement of the courthouse, and I was a regular visitor. I lost many rainy days somewhere in the Fiction section, or scouring the magazines for articles on rock stars and other famous people, my butt planted on the aging hardwood floor, cross-legged, leaning against the wall with a baseboard heater cooking my shirt to my backside.

But we weren't headed there today, and it felt odd. We passed the library and took a hallway turn off to the right. The door lay straight ahead with its bold, black lettering proclaiming **Harper's Mill Police Dept.** across the frosted, wire-filled glass. Dad grabbed the door handle and pushed through, me at his heels.

So this was the actual POLICE department.

I was not impressed. The door closed behind us slowly. I was standing in the Mayberry courthouse. No joke. Okay, there were two desks, not one. And Chief Lewis bore no resemblance to Sheriff Andy Taylor. It was really quiet...and, for the most part, empty. I guessed most of the officers were tied up over at Shantytown. Dad shook the Chief's hand and I strolled over to check out the gun rack on the far wall. The firepower had me in awe. Pressure on my shoulder startled me.

"Nice bunch of shoot-em-up, ain't it?"

I turned around. It was Mr. Holley. I was struck with a profound thought at that moment. *This guy came out of thin air.* His pressed suit and hawkish glasses made him look awkward for some reason. And he was still *all* teeth. I looked over his shoulder to see where my dad and Chief Lewis were, and saw them talking quietly over two mugs of coffee. Dad looked over at me.

"Pete, we'll go down in a minute and see your mom. She wanted to freshen up a bit before we go in." He turned and resumed his conversation with the Chief. He didn't even acknowledge Mr. Holley. *Odd.*

"I have a few things to tell you, Pete...things I think you should know." He was somber, almost sad. The teeth-marquee shut off.

"Things like what?" This guy was creeping me out.

"Bad things, Pete. Bad people. And mystical things that aren't what they seem."

"Wait a minute...you mean...who are you, mister?" I stepped back and bumped into the gun case.

"Now, Pete...just bear with me a minute, okay?" He looked around, but not, it seemed, at Dad and the Chief. I hoped it wasn't at another invisible person. I already had one of those, thank you. "I passed you on the way in...." He waited, like that was supposed to mean something to me. "Plane crash?" He waited. I waited. "You were arriving, I was departing this world. We were paired up, kinda."

"Passed...." I looked at him deadpan, then scrunched up my face. "Passed where?" I thought about that for a second while waiting for his answer. The wheels were grinding and crashing about in my head. Quite a mess. *Plane crash? Just arriving? Like being born? I was born in 1959...1959....* Then it hit me. *I'd read about it in the library. It happened on February 3rd, 1959. In the early morning hours...and there were picture...pictures of the four of them.* Something the size of a basketball settled below my rib cage. "You're...you're *the* Buddy Holly?"

"*Was*, Pete. *Was* Buddy Holly. But I've been sent for a reason." He pushed his glasses up the bridge of his nose with his middle finger.

I was still slack jawed. A chill went down my back and disappeared into my pants.

"What reason...?"

He took a deep breath.

"Okay, let me see if I can explain this. Music is universal, Pete. Music means so many things to so many people. When I was growing up, it was a way to express myself. And it had to do with happiness, good times, love...a lot of positive things, see? While there is sad music, it's really not sad at all. It's just another way of expressing something positive. Like loving someone you miss, or celebrating someone's life. Even a negative song is positive because we can express ourselves and we feel better…follow me?"

I slowly shook my head yes.

"Well, since I checked out, music has grown a lot for the good. The entire 60's has been a time of peace, love, happiness and feeling good." He paused. "Except for war. That's never a good thing." A sad smile tugged at the corners of his mouth. "There's a lot of bad things in this world, Pete. War, hunger, death…." He looked me straight in the eyes. "And hatred and ignorance.

"Hatred and ignorance are like gunpowder, Pete. Always set to explode, always willing to take innocent people from this world." He grew silent, contemplating his next words. "You got a problem here in Harper's Mill, Pete. A big problem. And, like I said, you need to know a few things. First, two people are missing—"

"Two?" This was news to me.

"Two. And that's just the here and now. When this all unfolds…." He shook his head. "For now, you need to know that Mr. Kim and Mr. Davis are still alive."

Mr. Davis? Mr. Kim…still alive?

He seemed to read my mind. "Freeman Davis. Not twenty minutes ago. They have both of them." He hesitated. "You need to find them, Pete. Soon."

I digested this for a second. He held up his hand and a white cloth dangled from his long fingers. It was covered in red squiggly lines with something round in the middle. I started to open my mouth and the thing just evaporated in the air, small particles floating away as they faded. He smiled.

"Mr. Kim's prayer cloth. Find it, Pete. You and the boys find it and you'll know you're in the right place." His smile wavered for a

second, then disappeared. He started to fade a bit. That's right...
fade. I took a step back.

"Pete!" Dad called from across the room. I jerked my head in
that direction, shocked back into reality. "You ready?" I nodded my
head up and down, more out of reflex, then turned back to Har...
Buddy.

There wasn't much left. I could barely see his outline, his teeth
white and floating. My head suddenly hurt. I pushed my palms
against my temples, closing my eyes. A small, tinny-sounding
crescendo of drum beats grew to a roar in my ears, joined by a
rhythm and lead guitar, as Buddy's voice steam-rolled through
Peggy Sue in my brain.

"Pete? You all right?" A hand on my shoulder made me jump. I
opened my eyes and looked at Dad. Concern was etched into his
face. Buddy was gone, of course.

"Oh...I'm okay," I stuttered. I felt weird. Dad looked at me, his
eyes all serious-like.

"Let's go see your mom." He guided me toward the back, his
hand on my shoulders. Chief Lewis nodded at our passing and
went back to his paperwork. We walked through a set of heavy
double doors and entered a short, dimly lit hallway. The first cell
was empty, but the door stood open at the second one. Apparently
she was not in maximum security. "She's in here." Dad led the way
to the open door and stopped. Mom was sitting on the bunk bed.
She smiled when she looked up.

"Bill!" She was in Dad's arms just like that. Fast. "Pete...." She
ran her hand through my hair and gently pulled me into a tight
family hug. I could smell her hand lotion—cherry-almond. I took
comfort in that. A tear trickled slowly down her cheek.

"How you holding out, Clarice?" Dad held her back at arm's
length and eyed her appraisingly. I wandered over to the bunk

bed and plopped down on the edge of the lower one. It felt like a concrete slab.

"I'm okay, Bill." Looking up at him, chin set, her face got a little rigid. "I just hate being treated like a criminal...." She pulled away, wiped at her eyes.

"I called Toby Bryson today. He said he'd take your case." He smiled. I imagined he was trying to lift her spirits a bit. "Couldn't believe they would even entertain such a thing. Said he'd be around Monday to talk to you."

"Oh, Bill...is he any good? You know those Taylor boys he defended back in March got jail time, and everyone I know thinks they were innocent!"

"I know, sweetheart, but I heard they lied to Toby from the git-go, and the prosecution had Toby for lunch. He never knew until the last minute. This is different, all right? We know you're innocent."

Mom's eyes were brimming over with tears. "But if this is a setup, Bill, they could get away with it...they...." She pulled away, stepped back a few feet, hugging herself as she tried to get the tears under control. I stared at my feet, uncomfortable with it all.

"I know, sweetheart." Dad wrung his hands. "We'll get this all ironed out real quick. Toby'll figure it out. Your reputation is not as questionable as the Taylor boys'." He stood there with a pleading look on his face. Mom just stared at him and wiped at her eyes again. Finally, he brightened up a bit, changed the subject. "Hey, I got some clothes and stuff out there with Jerry Lee. He said they'd give 'em to you after they check it out. Policy, or something." He glanced at me. I forced a smile, nodded. I figured he needed all the help he could get.

"Thanks." She seemed to find calm for a moment, then that fire came back in her eyes. "I just don't see what would drive Naomi

Sessom to claim such a thing about me. I never stole a thing in my life!" She was pacing now. It was evident that her short time in here had not been wasted worrying about getting out any time soon. "Heck, if it weren't for me, that store would have gone under by now....Naomi just don't have any business sense."

"Clarice," Dad spoke up, I guess with all intentions of quelling the storm he could see brewing in Mom. "Why don't you sit down a second?"

He came over and sat down on the edge of the bunk, patting the empty space next to him. I moved to the window, studying the bars as if they held some great secret. They were having a mom and dad moment, which made me feel a little awkward. Mom hesitated, then joined him. Dad put his arm around her shoulder. It was his way of bringing it down a notch. I knew because I'd seen him do it as long as I can remember.

"Bill...." She paused, gathering herself, "I'll be all right. I'm... I'm just not sure what's going on right now. I mean, why me? And poor Soon-yi! I was supposed to help her sort out the store this week." This brought fresh tears to her eyes. "She thinks he's dead... she gave up...just like that. I can't blame her, but what will she do now?" She looked at Dad like he had the answers.

My attention to the spider web in the corner was broken by her words.

Mr. Kim dead? *No!* I wanted to scream. *He's not dead!* But who would believe me?

Ah, Mom...Dad, Mr. Kim is alive. A dead rock star told me. Which one? Ummm...the one that connected with me the day I was born. What's that? No, it's complicated. You'll just have to believe me. I could see it now.

It was time for drastic measures. "I think I'm gonna go see if Margie's home." I needed an excuse, any excuse, to get out of there and clear my head. I hugged Mom and took off down the hallway. Chief Lewis was at his desk when I came through the holding area door. He nodded at me and I threw my arm up, but never looked at him. I would see the gang again tomorrow, and this time we couldn't get distracted. I had a feeling there was a mess brewing in Harper's Mill.

Sunday came early. Maybe it was the stress of Mom being locked up, or my hallucination of Buddy, or just everything in general, but I didn't want to get out of bed.

"Pete! Get it in gear, Son! Church starts in an hour!" Dad called from the hallway.

I crawled out of bed and stepped on an Incredible Edible treat I'd made the night before. It squished between my toes. The remains looked like a smashed nightcrawler. I flicked it off hastily, leaving the pieces on the floor, and headed for the bathroom. After a quick shower, I brushed my teeth and hurried back to my room to get dressed. When I emerged, Dad was sitting at the table, sipping coffee.

"Morning," he said without glancing up. He looked tired.

"Morning," I replied. Travers men were not big on small talk in the morning.

I grabbed my box of Cap'n Crunch from the cabinet and poured a heaping bowl, topping it off with milk to the brim. I liked to drink the sweet milk after caking my teeth with the golden squares. I ate in silence, Dad nursing his coffee, as we contemplated the events of the past few days.

The First Christian Church of Harper's Mill sat on Elm Street, right next to the elementary school. We parked the car and made our way to the front entrance with its broad granite steps and towering Georgian columns. Pastor Stevens stood at the door greeting the morning crowd in his nicely tailored suit and spit-shined Tom McCanns. Dad had his arm draped across my shoulders as we queued into the greeting line. I could feel all kinds of eyes on us as he guided me along. When we got even with the Pastor, Dad let go of me and gripped his hand, both of them leaning in as they shared hushed words between them. I could have sworn I heard someone behind us say "jail" as we turned and started through the vestibule.

We took a seat on a pew about halfway to the altar. As soon as my butt hit the cushion, my gaze drifted from the preacher to the folks seated around us and my bottom half got fidgety. I spotted Mr. Rogers from the Texaco, and Russell and his family one row back. Naomi and Fred Sessom sat in a back corner kinda to themselves. I saw Arlo and Martin with their families down in the front. Arlo twisted around in his seat and we waved at each other.

Now I have to tell you, I'm a sleepyhead in church. I just can't help it. But the sermon that day was on judging others, or something like that, and between nods and heavy eyelids I heard some things that got my mind to itching. Like when you see or hear something that rings a bell but just can't connect it somehow.

The choir sang like they were gonna sprout wings and fly around over our heads, and the organ seemed extra loud to me. Dad sat dead still during the whole thing, and I suspect he had Mom on his mind, along with some heavy praying.

Me, I had a feeling during all of that nodding and eyelid propping that there was something bad behind me. Something or someone that didn't care too much for me or Dad for that matter.

I could feel their eyes heavy on me through the whole sermon. I turned around once, just a quick glance, but no one appeared to be looking in our direction.

When it was over, we made our way up the aisle. I never wanted to get out of any place as bad as I wanted out of there. The sunlight felt good on my face when we stepped outside, that bad feeling washed away in the warmth. Dad always mingled a few minutes, so I took off for the car to wait for him. When he got in he was agitated to say the least.

"Buckle up," he said abruptly, and I did, no questions asked. We were home quicker than a dog can lick its butt. I was surprised we didn't get a ticket.

I met Arlo, Martin and Percy at the basketball court near school. Arlo was wearing his new tie-dyed tee shirt with Jimi Hendrix on the back. Martin and Percy had been smacking rocks across the playground with a wiffle ball bat, but were currently discussing the possibilities of using a Super Ball, which Martin was tossing absently in the air with his right hand.

"Pete, how's it hangin?" Arlo grinned and leveled his PEZ dispenser at my head. The candy bounced off my ear and landed in the dirt.

"Nice shot, jerko." I picked it up and flicked it back at him. He ducked, laughing. The wiffle bat made a dull *thunk* sound that startled both of us.

"Whoa yeah!" Percy yelled.

The bat dangled at Martin's side as he and Percy stood with their necks craned upward. I shielded the sun from my eyes and followed their gaze. Arlo did the same. I couldn't see the Super Ball, but what I saw made me blink several times. Arlo saw it, too.

"What the heck is that?" Arlo elbowed me as he pointed.

A small cloud formed out of nowhere, moving quickly across the blue sky. A pulsing, white fireball sat at the center. We tracked it for a few seconds, then it disappeared as quickly as it came.

"Look!" Percy shouted. He had Martin by the elbow, pointing at another one that formed and dissolved like a picture flash in the dark, only it was day.

I looked Arlo's way, just as his Bazooka Joe rolled from his lip and hit the dirt.

"So…you all see it too, huh?" I had to ask. Don't know why, but it seemed important that we all saw it, or nobody did.

I looked around, checking the street, the yards in view, the cars driving by on Elm, just to see the town's reaction. There was none. Not a bit. Nobody stopped their cars to jump out and point, nobody stopped in mid-stride to gaze at the brilliant flashes. Nobody except us. The gang of four. A few more blazed into sight and abruptly disappeared as they crossed the sky. I suddenly felt like we were part of an exclusive, chosen few. Mr. Holley's…ah, Buddy's words rang in my head…

You got a problem here in Harper's Mill, Pete. A big problem.

Yes, that was a sure thing.

Find it, Pete. You and the boys find it and you'll know you're in the right place. The Prayer cloth!

I looked at the gang, all wearing a look of total bewilderment on their faces. It was time to come clean with them. Time for us to answer our calling. I cleared my throat.

" Guys…?" They all turned in unison at the sound of my voice. "We need to talk." They stared at me, I stared back. "At the culvert." Those words brought the focus back into their eyes. "Last one there does the spider-check!" I yelled, and the race was on.

Nobody liked to do spider duty. I was the first one to my bike and I wasted no time. A running start and a bank robber's leap onto my seat put me out front. I had to trust they would all show up.

CHAPTER FIFTEEN

2011

MARGIE HAD ENTERED THE cafeteria with a feeling of overwhelming panic. Too much had happened too fast and she was reeling as it all crashed down on her. Clarice was the first to see it in her face, see the raw emotion spill from Margie as she approached. She was the first up and grabbed Margie with all the strength her 74-year-old body could muster.

"There, there, honey," Clarice said, patting Margie on her back with a frail hand. "We'll get through this. Peter will pull out of it, you know? He's a fighter, and I should know. He came out charging the day he was born." Her own words brought a cautious smile to her face.

Margie felt other arms, too. When she lifted her head, Millie, Peter Jr., Bill and Percy were around them, hands and arms trying to assure her that she was not alone. She pulled herself from Clarice's embrace and stood back, wiping her eyes, trying to shake off her despair.

"I know," she said, looking around at their faces. She knew then that this moment had to change, the scenery had to change. "I need to go home for a little bit. You're all more than welcome to come over. I can pull together something, not much, but something for us to eat. Make some coffee." She let that hang there as she looked around.

"That would be just fine," Bill said, glancing at Clarice for affirmation.

"I can help you rustle something up, Mom," said Millie. Peter Jr. nodded at Millie, silently offering the same.

"I think I can swing that." Percy spoke up. "Wanda's at a conference in Ashville this week and our house gets pretty quiet in the evenings. Too quiet, in fact." He was rubbing his head, brow furrowed, a distasteful look on his face.

"Good," Margie said, relieved. She would have their company for a while longer.

Martin strode in from the hallway, a dazed look on his face, and didn't say anything as he pulled up a seat and sat down.

Margie could see something was bothering him and thought he needed some company, too. That notion made her realize she was not alone. Not at all. They all needed company, needed each other, in the wake of this disaster.

"Martin, we're all going over to my house for a bit to…." She couldn't think of the right words.

"To make some sense of it all," Bill said, as if there couldn't possibly be any other reason.

A cafeteria attendant was mopping the floors around their table now, the clank of his bucket and mop ringer bringing Martin back to the present.

He looked up at Margie and smiled. "Sure Marg, that would be great."

The lights were being shut down systematically as they filed out of the cafeteria and made their way to the parking lot.

Millie, Peter Jr. and Martin rode with Margie in the minivan. Percy, Bill and Clarice took a separate car. It was fifteen minutes to Peter and Margie's house in Forest Acres, a gated, upscale community in North Raleigh. The ride in Margie's van had been relatively quiet until Martin reached over and turned on the radio. It was a casual gesture, automatic to Martin when he traveled anywhere in a car. A commercial was wrapping up, the DJ queuing the next song in a smooth transition.

Margie concentrated on the road, her mind lost on deeper thoughts, glancing in the rearview for the others, when the first notes of *White Lightning* spilled through the car's speakers. It took her a moment to process the sound. Her foot almost slammed on the brakes. Instead, the van slowed as if it had suddenly run out of gas. She pulled over in the breakdown lane and sat perfectly still.

I'm coming back, riding White Lightning, I'm coming back, to do it again.

I'm coming back, riding White Lightning, I'm coming back, to all of my friends....

I'm coming back, Margie, I'm coming back!

Buddy Holly broke into his aggressive guitar riff, the speakers buzzing like an angry hornet with his finger work.

"Mom, what's wrong?" Millie asked over the music, scooting forward to get a better look at her mother. Peter Jr. did the same.

Margie just sat there. She hadn't heard that song in over twenty years. It was an obscure song released after Holly's death and it rarely got airplay. *Odd that I would hear it now. Did he say Margie? Was that how the song went?* She could feel Martin staring at her. She looked over at him. Neither spoke. Their eye contact said it all.

"Nothing, honey." Margie shook her head. "Nothing at all."

She turned on her blinker and slipped back onto the road, watching in her mirror as the other car followed suit, and headed for the place she and Peter called home…only, without her Peter.

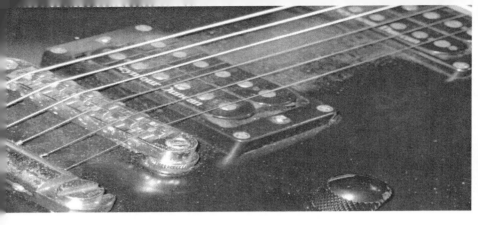

CHAPTER SIXTEEN

Peter

THE LIGHTS ENTICE ME as I study them against the black canvas that surrounds the thing that I have become. There are four now, four from the many that twinkled in the beginning. But they scare me when two become one. They scare me because for that moment, that second when they collide, the one from two becomes a black orb reflecting the remaining lights. In that black orb, for just an instant, I see the evil I saw that day of reckoning over Edwards Pond, and I shiver.

Whatever it is, it's playing with my emotions on a level that conscious man has no awareness of. Like magic. A magic that confuses, scares and awes me all at once. I wish only to return to what I was. To who I was.

I was confused that day at the culvert, but I wasn't scared. What I confused as magic, as I would later understand, was nothing more than a gift. A gift, like the eye of God. I've dealt with many from the world of Rock and Roll since I started in the music business. But the being that used the gift that day, the persona that all others in the Rock and Roll world would follow for years to come, was unlike anything I'd ever seen. My grandmother used to say that God worked in mysterious ways, and I've since grown to understand her meaning. There was nothing more mysterious to me than what we faced in that culvert, and nothing more horrifying than the evil it exposed.

Nothing.

'Culvert' was a fancy, adult name for it. It was really a mosquito-infested, overgrown run-off dead in the middle of town. But run-off was not exactly accurate either, as only a trickle of water seeped through the pipe every now and then, dripping to the dry creek bed below. In the summertime, it was fairly cool under the canopy of trees that surrounded it and hid it from the everyday world, which was just what we needed now.

I got there first, of course, and stashed my bike behind the bramble of wild raspberries that grew around the edge of the oasis. The entrance was indistinguishable from the road, but if you knew which tree branch to duck under, the path was well worn from there on. As I made my way through the undergrowth, I did what any decent kid would do.

"Anyone here?" I shouted toward the culvert. Hey, you never knew who else might find this place.

There was no response. I walked further in and rounded an old oak that must have been mentioned in the Bible. It *looked* that old, anyway. The leaf-strewn ground sloped gently down toward the culvert pipe and I could see the edge of it as I started down, trying to keep my balance in the moldy leaves. I stopped, grabbing a branch above my head for support before I reached it. Two black leather-clad legs, skinny things with grey snakeskin boots attached to the ends, dangled from the pipe.

"Who's there?" I said loudly, hoping he would look out from the shadows.

"Who wants to know?" The voice was slow and dreamy. Hip. I'd heard that voice before. For some reason, a song from the radio came to mind, but its name and melody eluded me at the moment. Both legs swung lazily back and forth and there was no attempt by this person to reveal himself. I moved closer, stopping only a few feet away.

" I'm Pete...Pete Travers. Who are you?"

The next few seconds were silent. I looked around to see if the gang was near, but they were nowhere in sight. When I turned back, the legs were gone, but a mop of hair surrounding a smiling, handsome face hung from the pipe.

"Pete! I've been expecting you. Where is the rest of your gang at?" One leg moved into view, presumably for balance.

"They're...they're coming." I took a step back. *Who the heck was this? Expecting me?*

"Good." He extended his hand out around the culvert pipe. "Some people call me Lizard. My friends call me Mojo Risin'...or just Mojo. Whatever works better on your lips, man." He grinned.

I stepped forward and shook his hand. *There was that tingling again!* Suddenly it hit home. "Then you know Hardin. Hardin Holley?"

He grinned again. I took that for a yes.

"Come on up, Pete. I have something to show you. Your friends will find out in due time...." He disappeared into the pipe.

I hesitated a minute, then moved to the rim of the concrete monster. The dirt beneath it had eroded away, exposing a large protruding tree root like a bent arm. Lizard...Mojo...was standing hunched over in the pipe. His form was ghost-like against the darkness. I placed my foot on the root and grabbed the edge, pulling my thin frame into the space in one swift motion.

"Good reflexes, man. You'll need them."

I stood up, almost bashing my skull against the pipe. Mojo squatted and I followed suit. We were facing each other, feet splayed apart over the stained center of the pipe. I took a good look at him in the limited light. Black leather pants, a big, chunky belt with large symbols all around it, and a dark velvet sheen shirt that shimmered when his body shifted. And the boots, of course.

"You know this thing is full of spiders, right?" My eyes were scanning the walls rapidly.

"Yeah, I know about them, Pete. But I've sent them on their way so you can relax."

He pointed between his legs and I followed the end of his finger. A column of hairy appendages moved slowly down the pipe toward the opening. The whole thing looked like a living snake, and the hairs on my neck stood out like needles.

"Holy crap!" I screamed, leaping to one side just as the mass started to crawl between my legs. I was trying to get a grip on the smooth concrete wall, but that wasn't working. I held my feet in place and drew in big gulps of air as I tried to calm myself.

"If that scares you, Pete, we are in serious trouble." Mojo smiled and shook the hair from his eyes. It was an impressive mane of dark, shoulder length hair and I wondered if I would ever have one like it. I glanced outside but still no Arlo, or anyone else for that matter. I squatted again with my back against the pipe wall.

"Pay attention, Pete. We don't have much time." He swung partially around and waved his arm toward the shadows. *Clearing spider webs?*

The dark area behind him lit up like a picture window. I felt like the Wicked Witch of the West gazing into her crystal ball. My jaw fell open.

The view was straight down Main Street, looking east. Cars drove into view and slowed as they approached the stoplight. People were strolling down the sidewalks in both directions, enjoying the sunshine, chatting and waving to their neighbors. "This is your town, man. Notice anything different?" His expression was quizzical. I just stared at him. "They're happy, man!"

I nodded my head. *Yes, they are happy, but this is Harper's Mill, and I know that people aren't happy now.*

"That's hypnotic, man!" He smiled a beatific smile at me. *Was he reading my mind?* "You're smart. This isn't how your town is now, but it's how you want to see it, Pete. You're not seeing what I'm showing you, you're seeing what you want to see!" Another grin like the sun. "But there's some things you can't see and things you weren't even around to see. That's why I'm here, dig?"

I dug...*I think.*

He waved that arm again and the scene changed. Old Mr. Rogers, who runs the Texaco filling station, was groping Miss Mabel Harrington, town librarian, somewhere around section **Ra - St** of the fiction aisle in the Harper's Mill Library. I guess he was either forcefully returning a book or offering to check under her hood for her. *Good thing he made it to church last Sunday.*

Mojo was still grinning, all his attention turned on me, when I said, "Ah, mister Mojo? I don't think I should be seeing *that*...." I pointed. He glanced back.

Muttering something under his breath, he waved his arm frantically. The scene flicked through several brief images, like bad TV reception, before it stopped. What filled the opening now made me cringe, my fingers clawing tighter against the concrete.

There were four of them in the dusky light, standing in the bed of an old pickup. Men in white robes with their backs turned to us, and they were busy. Two held what looked like a struggling young

Negro man, another held him by his thick hair, while the fourth struggled to put the rope around his head. There was shouting coming from all five, the Negro man's of terror, and the rest of anger and hatred. The scene before me flickered for an instant, faded, then resumed as the truck moved out of view. The young man swung slowly, kicking his feet wildly, hands tightly bound behind his back.

I turned away from the horror. Bile rose in my throat, and I knew I was going to be sick.

"Pete." Mojo spoke to me, but I ignored him. "Pete, you need to watch this." There was graveness to his tone. I slowly cut my eyes back to the scene.

The body was still now, but the rope slowly spun him around until I could see his face. The skin was ashen above the neck, his face muscles slack. I'd never seen death firsthand before and I lurched to the culvert edge and spewed bile until my eyes threatened to fall out and roll away.

"Pete, that's just the beginning. You need to know this stuff. I know it's hard man, but you've been chosen."

I wiped my mouth with my sleeve and made my way back. The culvert space was black again. Mojo flicked his hand in the darkness and the portal came to life. I flinched, but the body was gone. The scene was a pile of dirt. From somewhere off to the right came another spray of dirt and I caught a glimpse of a shovelhead before it moved out of sight. Another load was tossed on and the shovel began tamping the dirt down. Up and down. There was a shuffling sound and somewhere, faintly, I heard the splash of water. The scene faded to black.

"Hey! What tha'…?"

The sound startled me and my heart caught in my throat. Arlo, Percy and Martin were peering over the edge of the pipe. Sixteen white and nine black knuckles underlined their sweaty faces.

"Who's that?" Arlo nodded toward Mojo.

"He, eh…" I started. *Wait. They could see him?*

Mojo flipped them a peace sign and grinned. "Come on up, gang!" He summoned them with both index fingers, arms resting on his knees. His coolness seemed natural. "Nice sextuplet, Percy." He winked at Percy. I guess the nine black knuckles gave him away. "We don't have much time, so hurry! Pete can catch you up later."

The three of them scrambled over the edge of the pipe and lined the walls. I stared at them, wondering if they would be here very long. My intention to share what I knew with them had been eclipsed by Mojo's appearance. It would be interesting to see what happened next.

"Okay boys, pay attention." Mojo flicked his hand again and the blackness glowed to life. Six white eyes doubled in size as Arlo, Percy and Martin all shifted back several inches, mouths hanging open in surprise. Not a sound was uttered.

A long blacktop road lay before us, running in a straight line until it crested a hill some distance away. It appeared to be about dusk and we all drew a breath in when an old brown wood-paneled station wagon shot into view on the right, heading away from us. Without warning a loud *pop* made us all jump, and the station wagon slowed down, pulling over onto the grassy bank. A tall, aging Negro man stepped out of the driver's side and walked back to the rear of the wagon where he squatted next to the left tire. We couldn't see if it was flat from our vantage point, but that seemed to be the case.

"He's got a flat." Martin spoke to no one in particular. We all looked at each other and rolled our eyes. *At least they all seemed to have accepted their predicament.*

"Pay attention, gents." Mojo pointed back at the scene.

The man opened the trunk and dug around with one hand, swatting at yellow flies with the other. Within minutes, he had the car jacked up and had pulled out a spare. We watched, time crawling along in a pregnant silence. I opened my mouth to ask Mojo why we were watching this when he jerked his hand out, palm up, to silence me. From the top of the rise in the distance two headlights appeared. The man didn't look up, but seemed to be struggling with a lug nut, his back to the approaching car. I could tell the car was moving fast because the headlights grew bigger by the second. My heart started racing. It seemed as if it was going to run *us* down. I could see now that it was a dark blue Cadillac. Suddenly it swerved across the line and made a beeline for the crippled car.

"Look out!" Percy and Arlo screamed at the same time.

The car jerked violently back toward the center line, but not before it clipped the station wagon and connected with the man holding the tire iron. A sickening *thump* left no doubt in our minds. His body flew across the ditch where his head met a stately pine head-on, crumpling him in a heap on the bank.

The Cadillac locked brakes hard and did a one eighty on the blacktop, stopping with its taillights directly in front of us, rubber smoke rising and drifting across our vision. Arlo had grabbed my arm somewhere in the action, squeezing his fingers into my skin with enough force to leave fingernail marks. Martin looked away toward the culvert opening. Percy sat there, a single tear falling from the corner of one eye.

The scene started to fade a bit but Mojo quickly flicked his hand and made it vivid again.

"Let go of my arm!" I said as I jerked it from Arlo's grip. Mojo made a *quiet* gesture again, finger to lips. "Why?" I spit at him. Not only was I horrified, but I was angry. He ignored me.

Both driver and front passenger doors opened simultaneously, a man emerging from each. They each wore sunglasses in the fading light, but the similarities ended there. The driver was tall and broad shouldered with close-cropped blond hair. He swaggered as he moved around to the front of the car. The other man had very wavy hair fashioned into a ducktail and greased up to a high sheen. His walk betrayed his nervousness.

"What the heck!" Ducktail yelled at Crew Cut. He seemed very agitated.

"Shut up," said Crew Cut. "Ain't nobody 'round and the coon was asking for it."

"Asking for it?" Ducktail's voice rose to a shrill. "You gotta stop doing this crap!" He had jumped the ditch and stood over the body, shaking his head. "He's dead! Now what are we going to do with him? What if someone comes along here right now?"

Crew Cut looked up and down the road mockingly. "Nobody as far as I can see." He spit on the pavement and wiped his mouth on his sleeve. "Throw him in the trunk." He gestured with his thumb over his shoulder.

"He's a big one…maybe you can give me a hand instead of just standing there? It was your idea, you know!" Ducktail stood with his hands on his hip, lip stuck out.

Crew Cut sauntered over, clearing the ditch in one long stride, and slapped Ducktail sharply. "You just remember who I am…who *we* are." He stared at the other man for a long second and grabbed the dead man's feet. "Well? Get your butt in gear!"

Ducktail, still smarting from the slap, grabbed the man's shoulders and they carried the body over to the waiting car. After opening the trunk, they spent a few minutes of rearranging the contents, including spreading a sheet out, then they hoisted the body in and slammed the lid. No more words were spoken as they climbed in and drove away.

"Hey!" shouted Martin. "I know that car!" We all looked at him like he was daffy. "It's over in Mr. Rogers' junk yard behind the Texaco station! I remember the plates…RJO-745…yeah, that's it. I seen it one day when I was looking for a side mirror for my uncle's car. It was all rusted out and under a pile of junkers." We all looked at each other. I hadn't memorized the plates, but RJO stood out in my mind as I stared at the long stretch of road.

"Anyone else see something or someone they recognized?" Mojo said. He was staring right at me, a smirk on his face. I swallowed hard.

"I did." I let the words hang there a minute.

"Well?" Mojo swiveled on me, as cool as a rain-soaked lizard.

"That was Russell Beecham and Fred Sessom…a long time ago." A smile grew across Mojo's face. "And I'll tell you something else…" I looked around at each of them as I calculated my next words. "…what we just saw seems mighty similar to what we saw at Edwards Pond. In fact—"

"Hold on," said Mojo, waving his open palm at me. It was the first time I noticed the huge ring on his finger. Light played off of it like a kaleidoscope. "Pay attention one last time." He waved his arm toward the blackness and the portal glowed to life like the tail of a lightning bug. "We have one more little matter to attend to…."

The scene was full of trees and thick undergrowth. Sunlight filtered through the leaves, casting an eerie shimmer across everything. Without warning, an orange blur burst from the bushes and the orangutan beast appeared dragging a very large bag with a zipper that ran its full length. He stopped and released the bag, threw his head back and let go a screech like the hounds of hell. Everyone around me jumped, but their attention was drawn back quickly as three white robes pushed through the bushes and stopped a few steps away from the bag. They were hoodless.

"You gonna control that thing, Lath?" Fred Sessom spoke, whirling on Lath Edwards with his fist clinched. I sucked my breath in as I watched. Lath Edwards *without a wheelchair!* It wasn't a big surprise 'cause I always felt there was something not right about him. The other boys looked at me with puzzled faces. I shrugged.

"Just calm down, Fred." Lath held up his hands. "We got it under control. Unless you'd like to haul Kim around on your shoulders...." He smiled at the big man.

Kim? Mr. Kim?

"Just keep him under control..." Fred growled, showing Lath his fist.

The orangutan's fiery neck fur rose up as he stood, and his long arms flew up in attack mode. Sharp, numerous fangs completed the threat. Fred backed up a few steps.

"Whoa, you two...eh, three...." Russell Beecham chimed in. "Let's just get him in there and get out of here. That body bag ain't gonna move itself. Lath, call off that doggone monkey so we can get this done."

Lath gave Fred a look of contempt and stuck his fingers in his mouth, letting go a shrill whistle that hurt even my ears. The orangutan deflated and took off through the bushes.

Fred walked over to the bag and kicked it hard, eliciting a grunt from somewhere inside.

"I still say we make quick work of him an' be done with it."

Russell and Lath looked at each other. "What we gonna do with the other one, Fred?" Lath asked cautiously. Fred smiled at them both...

The portal went black.

"So!" Mojo almost yelled, clapping his hands together loudly as he half stood. We all jumped a little. I think I might have soiled my briefs…just a bit. "The floor is yours, Pete! As for me, I've got to get back to my gig, man!"

He brushed past us and leapt toward the opening like gossamer catching a wind current, dissolving into a zillion specks of sparkling dust…and he was gone, just like that. I turned to find the others moving their hands around in the darkness where the portal had been. It was time, I decided, to complete the charge. To bond together against something as tangible as the shoes on my feet. Something as heartless as a stone. Something full of hate. I clenched my fist and cleared my throat.

"Guys, sit down."

They turned and looked at me. For just a second I saw Arlo hesitating, trying to find a quick way out of this situation, then he relaxed and slumped down against the concrete. Percy and Martin reluctantly did the same.

"Okay. I didn't ask for this and neither did you." I scanned their faces, all of which held the same expression Fang used when I corrected him for peeing on the floor. I continued, anyway. "There's been a lot of weird stuff going on here. Weirder than you know. We all saw the lights at the school." Mojo's dazzling exit flitted across my thoughts. "And that stuff out at Edwards Pond." Three heads nodded in unison. "Well, it gets better... or worse in this case. Mr. Kim went missing, just vanished as we all know. But he's not the only one." Arlo raised his eyebrows, then furrowed them in bewilderment. "Mr. Freeman Davis is missing now."

Arlo waved his arm to interrupt. "How do you know that?"

"I'll get to that in a minute…let me finish." Arlo sulked at that. "Edwards Pond is a strange place and it don't sit right with me. Lath Edwards and that overgrown ape give me the creeps. My dad's been acting weird and my mom's been locked up for something she didn't do. Shanty Town's been torched and—"

"And that Mojo guy vanished into thin air!" Arlo blurted out.

"Yes, that Mojo guy...well, he's not the only one. There's another fellow you haven't met. Hardin Holley. At least that's what he calls himself." I paused and took a deep breath. "You guys believe in ghosts?" There, I said it. They remained stony faced, so I took that as a yes. After all, they *had* experienced Mojo just moments ago. "Mojo...the Lizard King." *Here it goes.* "I'm pretty sure that's Jim Morrison, ex-singer for the Doors. I think he died in a bathtub in Paris. And Hardin? He's the late Buddy Holly. I think Hardin... ah, Buddy and I share some kind of bond, but I won't go into that. That one was a plane crash a long time ago. Point is, both are dead and both are here now...somewhere."

"Wait," Percy said. "You're saying we have two dead guys haunting this town?"

"Not haunting us. I think they're here for a reason. And I think we're the only ones who can see them. They're trying to warn us about something. Something important. We just have to figure it out. I think what Mojo showed us is the key. Now, here's one thing that we all know now, especially since Mojo let us see into the past like that. The Klan is alive here just like it was twenty years ago. I knew Big Fred was in it, but Russell and Lath were a surprise. In fact, it looks like they've been at it a while." Percy's eyes grew a little wider at this, although I knew it was no surprise to him.

"Yeah," Martin interrupted. "I saw 'em out there when I was running milk with my pa." I nodded my affirmation in his direction.

"All right," I continued. "I think ...well, I think all this Klan business is behind all these disappearances. And I can't figure out where my mom's arrest fits into it all. Or why my dad's been acting strange. And the orangutan, and that fish thing...what has it got to do with all this?" I stopped, hoping for all the answers to come bumbling out of their mouths. They remained silent for a minute, then Arlo cleared his throat.

"But why Mr. Kim and Mr. Davis?" He scratched at his red mop of hair. "And who were the others Mojo showed us?"

Arlo's naivety was understandable. I doubted his dad had ever discussed the workings of the KKK with him. The only thing Arlo had cared about throughout his bully years was being a bully. Everything else, the important stuff, took a backseat. He just knew they existed.

"That's what they do." Percy spoke up, kinda quiet-like. "They harass and harm folks that don't have skin as white as theirs. My mom and grandma told me all about them and their bad doings." He stared at his feet and pushed his black frame glasses up on his skinny nose. Suddenly I felt pretty bad for him. "And they kill folks, too."

Arlo looked shocked and embarrassed at the same time. He retreated into his thoughts.

"Okay, here's the deal," I said, trying to keep this on track. "We know they're a mean bunch, and we saw what comes of those they don't like. Problem we got here is we don't know where Mr. Kim and Mr. Davis are. Another problem is a bit more complicated. Fred and Russell are respected adults in this community and both sit on the Town Council. We can't just run off and tell the police what we know. They'd laugh us out of the station."

Martin cleared his throat. "I got a hunch, if anyone wants to hear it." He stared at us and we stared back. I was getting impatient. "Well?"

"I don't know for sure, but that place where they had that body bag seemed a lot like Edwards Pond. Just saying…." He shrugged his tank top clad shoulders to make his point.

We all suspected that body bag held either Mr. Kim or Mr.

Davis. And Martin was right. Those trees and brush did look a lot like what we tangled our way through out there at Edwards Pond. *That was it. I had no other option. I had to talk to Dad about this and the sooner the better.*

"I got to go, guys." I stood up halfway and made my way toward the opening. Everyone followed but Percy, who hung back a moment and felt around in the air where the portal had been. I grabbed Arlo's sleeve before we jumped down. "We'll meet again tomorrow. I'll call you." He nodded, a solemn look plastered on his boyish face. I think the gravity of it all was weighing heavily on him and I was not surprised. The whole thing felt like King Kong was trying to piggyback ride on *my* shoulders, too.

CHAPTER SEVENTEEN

2011

MARGIE UNLOCKED THE FRONT door and led them all inside, turning on lights as she went. Bill Travers dashed for the bathroom, familiar with the layout of the house. The rest made themselves at home, seated or wandering about in the living room while Margie and Millie dug around in the kitchen and threw together what they could find as fresh coffee brewed.

"I remember this," Percy said, picking up an old 5x7 photograph from the mantle. Clarice wandered over to see which picture he'd picked up.

"Yes. Peter loved that getup, even though he'd outgrown it quite a bit." Clarice smiled over Percy's shoulder.

In the photograph, Peter, Martin, Percy and Arlo stood in the Travers' backyard, arms around necks as they posed. Peter had on a large, gawdy pirate hat, a homemade painted sword in his hand. Percy squinted, bandana wrapped tight on his head, six-fingered hand over his brow to block out the sun. Martin and Arlo had on eye patches, both their faces shadowed with shoe polish to look mannish, compliments of Kiwi.

Percy chuckled, looked over his shoulder at Clarice.

"Peter always did like to imagine himself a fearless pirate of the high seas. He took that sword to the freshman Halloween Ball that night and accidently poked Principal Taylor in the butt with it, if I recall."

They both laughed as he placed the picture back on the mantle.

Martin pulled out his cell phone and walked out to the deck from the kitchen, speaking to someone as the storm door closed behind him. Bill Travers came out of the bathroom and shuffled around as if lost. Peter Jr. sat with his head in his hands, looking at his shoes.

Margie came from the kitchen, wiping her hands with a dishtowel. "What we have is on the table. Coffee's ready. It's decaf, Bill," she said, looking at Peter's dad.

They all filed by her just as the phone rang. She walked over and picked up the handset on the end table.

"Hello?"

"Margie! You little peach! It's Arlo!"

"Arlo? My Lord! How have you been?"

"Aw, well, you know…busy with the professional wrestling business. Always a few young bucks trying to take on the world, you know."

"Where are you?" They hadn't heard from him for years and the sound of his voice brought another bit of comfort to her.

"Well, I'm at the airport here in Raleigh. Thought I'd give you and Pete a ring to see if I could drop by for old times' sake… maybe knock back a beer or two with my bud."

Margie hesitated, gripping the phone tighter. "Yes, Arlo… that…that would be great, but haven't you heard?"

She was met with silence. Finally, he spoke. "Heard what, Margie? Is something wrong?" His voice had gone deeper, rougher. Arlo had been like a big brother to her and Peter since Edwards

Pond. Her tone had apparently raised his flags.

"Arlo, Peter was in a bad accident this morning." She swallowed hard.

"Is he all right?"

"He's alive, Arlo…but he's in a coma." Tears welled up, blurring her vision.

Arlo was silent for a few seconds, then, almost as to himself, "I knew it. I knew something was up."

"What?" Margie wasn't sure she heard him correctly.

"You guys still over in that Forest Acres place? 4857?"

"Yes."

"I'll be there in thirty, Margie." He hung up.

"Who was that, Mom?" Peter Jr. asked, walking back into the room.

Margie wiped her eyes, sat down on the couch. "It was Mr. Hankshaw, honey."

Peter Jr.'s. face lit up, and Margie realized, bittersweet, that he was only a few years beyond the innocence of boyhood. "*The Hankshaw Hacksaw? The* wrestling legend?"

"Yes," she said. "But we call him Arlo." Margie managed a smile at her son's reaction.

He gained his composure, seeing the look on her face, and nodded. "That's cool." He turned and joined the others in the kitchen.

Margie sat on the sofa, emotions building inside her like a storm on the horizon. Her hand settled on her stomach. On her secret. No one knew but her, and she couldn't tell them. Not until she told Peter, who was perhaps as close to death as one could get without actually dying.

Forcing back the urge to cry again, she stared toward the kitchen door. Plates clanking, voices low, she was suddenly glad they were here with her. Not just for support, but as old friends. But there was something strange in all this, something she couldn't put her finger on. The last piece of this gathering was on his way now; the cement, as Peter said, that held him together as they started down that dark path so many years ago.

Arlo Hankshaw.

Margie was standing on the porch with Martin and Percy when Arlo drove up. It lightened her heart to see both of them bound down the steps to greet him. The door swung open and Arlo emerged, stopping them in their tracks before they reached the car.

Arlo Hankshaw was a massive man. His biceps looked like tree trunks. His legs reminded Margie of bridge spans. She and Peter had spoken with him years ago, but they never got together in person. And she didn't care for professional wrestling, so she never saw him on the television. His radical transformation from a chunky fifteen-year-old to an aged professional wrestler made the corners of her mouth turn up slightly. *Good old Arlo.*

Martin whistled and slapped his knees. "Man, look at you!"

Percy just stood there with his mouth hanging open as Arlo closed the car door. He was in a business suit made with enough fabric to cover three people. His trademark red hair, although thinning in places, was spiked with green tips. He wore rings on every finger, *big* rings, and a silver St. Christopher the size of an egg around his neck.

"Arlo?" Percy said, eyes squinted, brow furrowed.

Margie walked up and opened her arms. "Come here, you big lug!"

Arlo embraced her like a grizzly bear.

"Margie, you look like a million dollars, baby!" He swung her around gently and stood her back on her feet.

"Percy...um, Pastor Smith!" Arlo held out his hand. Percy broke into a broad smile, shook it.

"Good to see you, Arlo. What's with..." he pointed at his head, indicating Arlo's hair.

"Aw, it's just part of the business, Percy. Sports entertainment! I'm not wrestling anymore, bones can't take it. But I have to be the face of the industry, right?"

Percy smiled and shook his head.

Martin reached out and grabbed Arlo's arm. "Dang, Arlo. What are they feeding you these days?"

Both of them broke into a laugh.

Margie stood back and watched. It was like they were all fifteen again. But she could still see the worry on their faces, feel it hanging there like dead weight. *There's one still missing.*

"All right, boys, let's get inside. I know Arlo must be hungry."

She herded them up the steps and through the door, grabbing Arlo's arm as the others continued down the hall. "Arlo." She looked him in the eyes, searching for something she didn't quite understand yet. "Are you sure you didn't know something was wrong when you called here?"

He turned, watched the others disappear into the kitchen, then faced her. A nervous tick worked at the corner of his mouth.

"I never said that, Margie. I never said that at all." He swallowed hard, glancing over her shoulder at the yard outside. "We need to talk." He locked his gaze with hers. "Just the four of us."

He turned and walked away, leaving Margie in the doorway, somewhere between inside and out, much like Peter.

CHAPTER EIGHTEEN

Peter

I WONDER IF THE me that I am, the me between this and that, between something and nothing, is dead? But when I feel the approaching lights, their coldness, I know I'm alive in some way, and they make me wish I were dead.

Can life and death coexist in one soul?

I'm so tired, and there's no sleep here, no state of wakefulness from which to fall asleep. I'm cold, too, in a way I've never been before. *Why am I so cold?*

I think of flying. The lights make their journey, moving this way and that in my direction, like God exhaled and set a constellation adrift, the stars whirling and spinning toward a vast, endless void. Toward me.

I think of flying. The way boys fly off rooftops or tree branches, with beach towel capes and adventurous dreams.

I think of flying. The way I flew from a rough-hewn plank, the wind in my hair, light dancing off chrome and reflectors, with dreams of rising above the things I didn't understand in my youth.

I think of Margie. I can't feel her life force. I want her next to me. I need her next to me, just like I needed her then, long ago. I feared for her, wanted to protect her. But I still needed her.

And I need her now. I need to tell her something, desperately. *Margie?*

Dusk was approaching rapidly as I rounded the corner on my bike and started down the hill to our house. As I got closer, I spotted the plank I'd seen the little Anderson kid next door prop at an angle on the curb between our houses yesterday. The urge to jump it came on me strong.

I haven't done that in years.

Grabbing the handlebars tightly, planting my feet on the pedals, I gained momentum as I zeroed in on the makeshift ramp. Wind buffeted my face, bugs bounced off my forehead. I veered to the right, lining my wheel up for launch. With a *woo-hoo!* I made contact with the wood and soared over the curb, cool in my coolness, confident in my form...until my bottom half sped past my upper half and I turned upside down, approaching a hard looking spot in the yard.

I knew it would hurt like heck and I wasn't disappointed. My butt hit the ground at an angle, knocking the wind from my lungs. The seat smashed my doodads so hard I saw stars. I'd held the handles with a death grip, realizing only seconds later that I should have kicked the metal hellion away from me in mid-air. The bike halted...no, *hovered*, over my bruised body and I hastily covered my face. Satisfied with its work, it tumbled over to the side and came to rest next to me. I lifted my head to examine the damage just as Fang rounded the corner of the house with a carefree gait, tooth leading the way. He cautiously approached me, sniffing the air for any sign of Death. Once this was done, he licked my face and his tail got all happy.

"Nice one, Pete!" someone shouted.

Startled, I sat up and looked around. Mrs. Elwood was pruning her roses up the street. Fang sat on his haunches, staring at the house. Those were the only two living things around me. Mrs. Elwood was eighty years old if she was a day and I doubted she could have shouted at me from two houses away. I looked at Fang with wonderment until I realized he was looking *over* the house.

"You might try to stay in one piece until this business is done, Evel Knievel."

I looked up at the roofline and there sat Hardin, or Buddy, as I really thought of him. He was perched with his butt on the peak, white socks glaring from beneath his pant legs. The opposite ends of an electric Gibson guitar stuck out on either side of his lanky frame, held on by the leather strap across his chest that said *Buddy Holly* in bold white.

I glanced up the street at Mrs. Elwood, but she was oblivious to Holly's presence.

"What do you want?" I asked. "And why are you on top of my house?" I rubbed my head and squinted harder to make him out. Fang looked at me, then back to Holly, wagging his tail. Not one bark. I sensed he was enjoying this.

"Just making sure you're all right, Pete. I trust Mojo gave you the big picture?" He spread his arms and hands over his head in a wide gesture.

I nodded yes, lost for words.

"Good. You'll have some more help as this gets deeper." He grinned. "Take care, Pete."

He faded away into a gazillion black dots until the breeze scattered them to unknown points across Harper's Mill. Fang's tail became jubilant. He stood, barked sharply three times in what I took to be a dog's goodbye.

Pulling myself up, I brushed the grass off the seat of my pants and discovered a hole there. Funny thing about holes...we tend to stick our fingers in them. I absentmindedly wiggled mine in there for a few seconds, wondering where Dad was. Our car was nowhere in sight.

"Pete!"

I turned sharply, finger caught in the fabric, and there stood Margie in all her glory.

I told you we were an item that summer. That was an understatement. I fell hard for Margie. I bought that friendship bracelet I'd worked so hard for and had it engraved with words from my heart. *With all my Love, Pete.* But wait, that was just one side. The other side, with a little heart etched next to the words, read *Margie and Pete Forever.* I'd never made a girl cry before, but at least she was smiling, too, when I gave it to her one day over sodas.

To me, she was the best thing since homemade peach ice cream. We were the same height...well, maybe she was an inch taller, and she had shoulder length, auburn hair. She wore skirts to school and little sweaters with tatted lace on the sleeves and collar. But she was not all sugar and spice. I'd seen her down at her father's hardware store helping him unload lawnmowers and heavy yard equipment, dressed in overalls and work shirt, her sleeves rolled up, hair pulled back. Mom said it was a sign of good character and strong work ethic. I guess I was attracted to that in some way.

But it was her eyes that made my heart skip a beat and tango in my chest. There was something dreamy about them, and I was sure, at least as sure as my heart could be, that they were true windows to a gentle soul. Okay, I read that in a mushy book one time, but it seemed to fit. Anyway, we'd been going steady for a few weeks now and things seemed fine. I pulled my finger from the hole in my pants.

"Margie...what are you doing here?" I wasn't expecting to see her because she always went with her family over to Leesville on Sundays to visit her Grandma McMillan in the old folks' home. Plus, I was not exactly presentable at the moment. Fang had wandered off around the house with more important matters to attend to, I guess.

"Grandma has a bad cold and Dad said we...." She stopped and tilted her neck, looking at me like I had a knife sticking out of my forehead. "What in the heck happened to you, Pete?"

She eyed me from head to toe. I probably looked like I'd been run over and left for dead.

"I just had an accident with my bike." It occurred to me she might have been there longer than I realized. "You just get here? I didn't hear you...." I waited, sure she'd seen Buddy on the roof.

"Yeah." She pointed to her bike out by the curb. "I was on my way to Miss Taylor's to get Mom some flour for a cake she's baking for her Women's Club meeting tomorrow night. Thought I'd swing by here and see if you were home." She kept her gaze glued to mine. "You sure you're all right, Pete?"

I fidgeted, roughing the grass with my right foot. *She's gonna help you, Pete. Trust her...*Mojo's voice moved through my head smoothly, like thin grease on hot tin. It suddenly occurred to me that this was not so much an awkward moment as it was an opportunity. Why wouldn't I want my girl at my side while I battled the forces of evil? I mean, that's what this was, right?

Because she might get hurt?

That was my conscience, not Mojo. I faltered in my logic for a moment, looking into her eyes for a clue. *No, Pete...this is the way it has to be...without her you won't succeed,* Mojo warned, swimming through my skull again.

She crossed her arms, a sure sign she was getting impatient with me. "Well, if you don't want me here...." She turned to make for her bicycle. I had to do it now!

"Margie! Don't go...." I stepped forward and pleaded with my open hands. It was enough to stop her. She turned to face me, a hurt look on her face. "Just wait a second. We need to talk. I mean...I need to tell you something."

Her face scrunched up a bit and anger replaced the hurt. "You breaking up with me, Pete?"

I saw the bracelet dangling from her wrist, her fist clenched with white knuckles. This caught me off guard, and I tried to think of a quick way to make this right.

"I need your help...we...need your help." The words came out sounding more desperate and wacko than I intended.

That got her attention. "What?" She placed her hands on her hips, cocked her head to the side.

"I said we need your help. Me and the guys...and the town." I kicked at the grass again.

"Pete, what are you talking about? What kind of help? The guys?" Confusion replaced the anger on her beautiful face.

Now I just had to lay it out for her, and standing here in my yard didn't seem like the right place to do it.

"Come on," I said, grabbing her hand. "Let's go down to Jim's and I'll tell you about it."

We hopped our bikes and took off for town. Mine rattled quite a bit, but it was still in one piece. Margie kept the lead, at all costs it seemed, and I wondered if she was still angry at our misunderstanding or just being standoffish like girls are sometimes. I watched her hair blowing in the breeze, like a goddess mounted on a white stallion, and decided she could take the lead whenever she wanted and it was all right with me. Jim's loomed ahead and I collected my thoughts, hoping this would go well.

Jim's was open on Sundays between four and nine in the evening for a dinner crowd, mostly church folks, but while the menu was limited, french fries were always available. I still had a few bucks in my pocket from mowing the grass, so we ordered a plate full and two cokes. I emptied half a shaker of salt on those hot spuds and Margie squeezed a ton of ketchup in crisscrossing lines, just the way we liked them. We devoured a dozen or so of the too-hot fries before I finally got to the problem at hand.

"Notice anything strange about Harper's Mill lately?" I looked her straight in the eyes as I wiped at some ketchup on my chin.

"Like what?" Her brows knitted up. Margie could get real serious, real quick. There was a piece of french fry on the corner of her mouth, but I suppressed the urge to tell her.

"I don't know…like the way people are acting, maybe?"

She shrugged her shoulders and bit into another fry. I could tell this wasn't going to be easy. There were only a few tables occupied and it was fairly quiet in the place. I took a more direct approach.

"Do you believe in ghosts, Margie?"

I waited for a second, sure she would laugh at me. She wiped her mouth with a napkin and looked around before bending forward a bit to reply.

"Yes!" She said in a low whisper, grinning like she'd just been asked out on a date with David Cassidy, eyes lit up with excitement. "I saw one today! I was riding over to see you and saw a man standing at the crosswalk over on Second Street. Weird guy dressed all in black, long hair, looked like a hippie…a cool hippie. I stopped my bike across the street and pretended to mess with the chain, like it was messed up or something. I kept sneaking a look at him. There was something familiar about him, but I couldn't figure it out. Anyway, he just seemed creepy, like he wasn't all there… like he was shimmering." She looked over both shoulders again and turned back to me. "Then I saw Mr. Beecham approach that exact same crosswalk…and he walked right through him! Never stopped, just walked through him like he wasn't there!" She giggled at that, keeping it low.

"What's so funny?" I frowned, not seeing the humor in it.

"As soon as Mr. Beecham started across the street, this hippie guy held out both middle fingers in his direction. Just stood there grinning…it was so cool!" She covered her mouth to suppress any more laughter. Her eyes twinkled.

A smile worked at the corners of my mouth. I wasn't sure if the double finger was cool, but I *was* sure it was Mojo. Margie's casual acceptance of the dead walking our streets was a shock to me. She could've been talking about the latest Funny Face drink mix flavor. I laid a ketchup-sticky hand across hers. I knew she wouldn't mind.

"Okay, this is good. That hippie you saw? That was Mojo. But not really Mojo…." I wasn't sure how far I wanted to go with this, but what the heck. "I'm positive that's the lead singer…*was* the lead singer for the Doors."

Her face went slack, eyes big. I told her about Hardin, formerly known as Buddy, and our cosmic connection. I told her about everything. The more I talked, the more mesmerized she seemed. She leaned forward, chin propped on the knuckles of her hands, hanging onto my every word. I was so emboldened by her rapt attention, I rambled on until Jim's was about to call it closing time. When I was done, she sat silent for a minute before she spoke.

"That's the coolest thing I've ever heard, Pete," she said. "The craziest, but definitely the coolest." A smile spread across her face.

I sat back, waiting for the questions to start, but they never came. Still, I could see her thinking about it all behind those beautiful eyes. The place had emptied, except for us, so we paid our bill and walked outside. She kissed me on the cheek and climbed on her bike to leave.

"Wait!" I walked over to her. "You didn't say if you'd help us or not."

"I wouldn't miss it for the world." She smiled like sunshine, turned her bike around, and rode off into the evening.

I wasn't sure what just happened, but I felt like a million bucks. Girls could be so weird. I took her cue and headed for my own house, wondering if Dad would be there.

CHAPTER NINETEEN

2011

THEY ALL GATHERED IN the kitchen, Margie finding a few extra chairs to make them comfortable. Arlo had removed his suit jacket and was wearing a canary yellow shirt, his tie loosened at the collar, sleeves rolled up on his big, hairy arms. Millie sat back, keeping a cautious eye on him, while Peter Jr. just glowed from where he sat across the table. Margie knew he wouldn't be able to hold it in much longer, and he didn't.

"Mr. Hacksaw, can I ask you a question?"

"Sure. What's on your mind?"

Margie watched their exchange from across the table, a smile playing on her lips. Peter Jr. looked like a twelve-year-old again, next to Arlo. *Who wouldn't? His presence at the table was like having tea with an elephant.*

"What was it like, winning the world wrestling championship fourteen times?"

"Well, the last thirteen were like the first." He grinned. "It's not so much about winning the match as it is about winning the confidence of the company that pays you. When I got that first championship match with The Crusher in Tokyo, I thought I'd finally made the big time. But when he pulled out that board of nails four minutes into the match, I knew they wanted to see if I had it in me."

"Oh, come on," Percy said, throwing up his hands. "Not real nails? They wouldn't let someone—"

Arlo stood up and pulled his shirt from his pants, turned around and hiked it up. All of them drew in a sharp breath.

"Oh my Lord," Clarice said, her hand to her mouth.

Arlo's back was a canvas of scars, small puckered indentions of ugly red tissue. He lowered his shirt and sat back down.

"As I was saying," he continued, winking at Margie, "I knew I had to prove my worth to them to get that belt. When he slipped in my blood, I went for the kill...well, not a real kill."

"Ewww," Millie said, twisting her face up.

"Aw, it wasn't that bad, Millie. But it was the first time any wrestler ever begged me to go for the finishing move." He smiled

"So, what do you do now?" Martin asked.

"Mostly scouting new talent. I head a training facility in Tallahassee, Florida and work between there and New York." Arlo rubbed his eyes with his knuckles and yawned.

"Sounds like a great job." Bill unfolded his arms, laid his hand on Clarice's.

Clarice glanced around the table and smiled. "If you young folks will excuse me, I think it's time I retired for the night." She turned to Margie. "Guest room, dear?"

Margie nodded and helped Clarice up from her chair. "You know where everything's at, Mom." She kissed Clarice on the forehead and watched her carefully mount the stairs. While Bill and Clarice were like family to her, at this moment she felt a renewed loss for her own parents.

Peter Jr. pushed back from the table. "I'm going to crash. See everyone in the morning."

"Me, too," Millie said. "It's been a long day." She hugged Margie and fell in behind her brother.

"Goodnight, you two!" Margie yelled as they disappeared up the stairs.

"Still keep their old rooms just the way they left them?" Percy grinned.

"Yes," Margie said, smiling at the thought. The pride at being a doting mom felt good at that moment, with everything else going on.

Arlo brought both palms down on the tabletop, making Martin jump.

"All right, boys and girls…." He looked at Bill and nodded. "Mr. Travers." Everyone turned their attention to Arlo. "I don't know about you all, but I need—"

"Wait!" Margie interrupted. "I know what *I* need." She walked over to the pantry and pulled out a bottle of bourbon and several shot glasses.

"Margie, I didn't know…." Martin feigned shock, bringing a hand to his mouth.

"I don't," she said, setting the liquor and glasses on the table and punching him playfully on the arm. "But if anyone has a reason to take a shot today, it's me." She poured herself a small amount and slammed it back, her eyes watering as she gasped. "Besides, I'm hoping it will help me sleep tonight."

Arlo and Martin each poured one and followed her lead. Percy and Bill abstained, Bill with amusement on his face.

"That hits the spot," Arlo said. "I'm a one shot guy, though. Never been able to stomach the stuff much."

Everyone acknowledged Arlo's sentiment, nodding.

Arlo laid his hands flat on the table. "Now that we're all here…

all but Pete," he looked down at his hands, "I have something to tell you." He took a deep breath. "I was scouting at a show in Baltimore three days ago. Medium venue, three-quarter filled. The final match of the night had just started and I was hanging out close to the ramp." He looked at each of them, one at a time, measuring his next words carefully. "I would've never seen him if the Quartermaster hadn't of tossed the Tango Kid over the top rope."

"Seen who?" Bill asked.

Arlo leaned in, his face growing serious. "Mojo." He leaned back, watching his friends. They all looked at each other, eyebrows raised.

Martin was the first to speak. "Arlo, are you sure?"

Arlo nodded. "Never been more sure of anything in my life. You don't meet many Mojos. Especially dead ones. I was already on my way here to see you and Pete, Margie. I just felt that something was up, you know? Like the world slipped a foot off kilter and nobody noticed but me."

Martin shook his head and looked around the table until his gaze settled on Arlo again. "I noticed, Arlo." They all turned at Martin's words. "I was coming out of the airport, heading for the taxi queue when I spotted her." Nobody said a word. "Pearl was sitting there in her taxi, smoke rolling out, sun reflecting off of those pink tinted glasses. I just knew she was looking at me, watching." He looked around nervously. "It was the same old yellow taxi. It looked so out of place, but it was as real as anything else. There's no way anyone could have seen that but me. It would have caused a stir."

Mouths were hanging open now. Margie felt the little whiskey shot go to her head like an ocean wave breaks over rocks. She was watching Martin, waiting for him to say it, but she couldn't wait any longer.

"And there was the song on the radio, too." They looked at her, Martin acknowledging that fact on his face. "When we were coming home from the hospital. It was that Buddy Holly song, *White Lightning*, only…I think…I think he was singing it to me."

"What makes you say that, Margie?" Bill spoke up.

"At the end he said he was coming back…it's part of the lyrics *'I'm coming back, I'm coming back'*, except he said *'I'm coming back, Margie, I'm coming back'.*"

Bill nodded thoughtfully. He looked over at Percy.

"Percy?"

Percy hung his head low. Margie could see the gray starting to creep in over his ears here and there, and it reminded her of how quickly their own youth had slipped away.

"I've seen no dead rock stars," he said, still looking at his hands. "But I've been having dreams, or should I say a *certain* dream, for the last month. Always the same one." He squeezed his palms to his temples and shook his head. "I'm standing in front of Butterbean's Fixit and the sun is shining so bright the ground shimmers." He rubbed his eyes hard. "And Mr. Davis, God rest his soul, is sitting there, just sitting there smiling at me. He waves at me and I wave back. He's drinking a Nehi grape soda, and I'm thinking how bad I want that soda. My mouth is so dry…so dry." Percy clasped his hands together and raised his face toward the ceiling, closing his eyes. "And then he just fades away, just blinks out, right there on that bench. It's the same every night. Every blasted night."

The only sound in the quiet that followed was the tick-tick-tick of the wall clock. Nobody knew what to say. Looks were passed, hands wrung with trepidation. It was Arlo that plunged back in with both feet.

"I'm not sure how that plays in here, Percy. Though, I am sorry you're losing sleep with that dream. Freeman Davis was a fine man." He rubbed his chin, studying the forgotten liquor bottle on the table, then switched gears. "As for our heavenly rockers, that leaves only one unaccounted for," he pointed out.

"Jimi Hendrix," Margie said in a flat voice, staring glassy-eyed at some point on the wall beyond Arlo.

Percy slid his chair back abruptly, stood up, and started pacing in front of the sink. "But why? After thirty-seven years, why?"

"That's a good question, Percy," Bill said, standing up. "That's something you kids will have to figure out. In the meantime, it don't feel right, me in the middle of this..." he indicated the four of them with a finger, "special group." He shook his head, looking down at his hands, tired-like. "You know I'm here if you need me...just like before." He waved goodnight and climbed the stairs to join Clarice.

Nobody said a word. Margie wandered over to the counter and leaned against it, hugging herself. Her body ached for Peter's embrace right now. For Peter, period. She was studying the shapes in the floor tile, a small part of her brain connecting the repeating patterns, when it clicked somewhere in her skull. Suddenly, she knew. Much like a mother lion knows when her cubs are in danger.

"It's Peter," she said.

Everyone turned to look at her, Percy stopping in his tracks.

"This is about Peter." A tear ran off her cheek. "They're back because of him...his accident...if it was an accident." She scanned their faces, lower lip trembling.

"Or he's half dead because of them?" Arlo said, more as a statement than a question.

A stalemate hung over the room. Even with Margie's intuition, no one seemed able to piece together the chain of events. Martin stood up and put an arm around Margie's shoulders.

"We all need some sleep. Why don't we turn in?" he said. "We'll all see Peter first thing in the morning."

They all agreed that would be best. Margie pulled out linens from the hall closet and led them to the furnished basement.

"Two of you can sleep in the spare bedroom and one out here on the futon." She divvied out the sheets and blankets.

"I'll take the futon," said Arlo. "I've slept on so many airplanes, buses and backstage cots, it'll be like home to me."

They all managed strained smiles, then Margie climbed the steps to her own bed, Percy's question still rattling around in her head like a nickel in a dryer. *After thirty-seven years, why?* Although she knew in her heart Peter was at the center of it, the question was still relevant…and haunting.

Why?

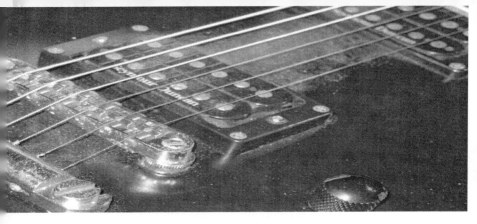

CHAPTER TWENTY

Peter

THERE ARE OTHER LIGHTS now, different lights. I think of them as sentinels because they do not approach, do not retreat, do not converge as the others do. They are strange. Close, but so far. Full of electrical charges that grasp at their orbs in bluish light. I sense a strength, a peace within them. They simply watch. Or wait. Wait for the dancing lights to reach me, perhaps?

I've thought about Margie for so long, I somehow found my way to her. She's lying in our bed as I move closer. Her warmth radiates toward me as I bend over her, trying to smell her, wanting to embrace her.

I've become something in my mind, something tangible.

She's lying on her back. Her face, the face I've kissed a thousand times, looks so peaceful. I recall the earlier dreams, the dreams I had when our journey began. Is she searching for me in *her* dreams now?

I just want to kiss her, maybe for the last time. I bend slowly, gently...but stop. I feel another warmth from her, separate, but within. I lay my hand on her stomach and quickly draw it back. *A baby?* The elation I suddenly feel threatens to send this thing, this tangible dream, exploding into the void in which I exist.

Why didn't she tell me?

How long has she known?

I watch her, absorb her as much as I can until I'm filled with a sadness I can't describe. I remember those dreams before and I realize this will be nothing more than that. A dream.

I bend over again, this time with my hand on her stomach, and kiss her with the lightness of an angel's breath.

Then I'm gone from her side.

Gone into the void.

The car was parked along the side of the house when I pulled my bike into the driveway and walked it around to the tiny garage in back. I parked it and hurried back around to the screen porch and into the house. Dad was in bed with the light on, book on his belly, chin on his chest, fast asleep. I didn't want to wake him so I turned off his bedside lamp and shut the door quietly behind me.

I went to the kitchen to pour a glass of milk and spotted the note on the fridge.

Pete, there's some spaghetti in the fridge if you're hungry. I have to be over in Leesville early tomorrow on business. Might sell a few life policies if I'm lucky! Anyway, I should be back after lunch. Maybe we can go see your mom. She sees the judge on Tuesday. Stay out of trouble and I'll see you tomorrow afternoon.   Dad

I folded the note and stuck it in my shirt pocket, trying to gather my thoughts as I poured a glass of milk. I started for my room when I noticed Dad's jacket on the back of a kitchen chair. Something scratched at my brain. I had the strangest feeling that all wasn't right with this scene. There was something pulling his coat almost to the floor. I knew he'd be upset if it were on the floor by morning, so I walked over and shifted it back on the chair like it should be. It was heavy, and the weight clanged against the chair leg. I reached down and felt in the pocket just to… *a gun*! I pulled my hand away quickly. *Why did he have a gun?* I stood there a moment, afraid that any second a loudspeaker would start yelling *Pete's messing with your gun! Pete found your gun! He touched it! He touched it!* I took a few steps back. It wasn't as if he'd never had a gun. I'd seen it on his duty belt many times when he was a policeman. *But that was in another life*, my brain told me, *what does an insurance salesman need with a gun?*

Suddenly, I felt exhausted. I took a final glance at the jacket and headed for my room. After drinking my milk and a half-hearted attempt at brushing my teeth, I made my way to bed and crawled under the sheet. I wasn't sure what Dad was up to, but it was just another layer of problems I seemed to be buried under.

Sleep came quickly, with nightmares dead on its heels, as usual.

I woke with a start, sitting straight up in bed. My heart was slamming around in my chest and it took a minute to get my breath. The doorbell was chiming. I jumped up and threw on my pajama pants, almost falling on my face as my feet got tangled up.

"I'm coming!" I yelled, as I passed by the kitchen and noticed Dad's jacket was gone.

I looked out the peep hole. At first I didn't see anything, then someone stepped into view. It was like looking at a fish bowl. The man's nose looked huge and he had a big, bushy mustache, black hair combed back nicely with a dab of Brill cream, I guessed. His blue service coat had some kind of tag on it but I couldn't read what it said. A white tow truck sat out by the curb. I could make out the words *Ca n's Towing Service* on the side. *Ca n's Towing Service? There was no Ca n's Towing Service in Harper's Mill…was there? Cain's, maybe?* I unlocked the door handle and pulled it open. Dan, as his nametag implied, was standing there with a clipboard in his hand.

"Hi, Son. Is your father home?" he asked through the screen door. He smiled at me from behind a pair of dark shade glasses.

"No, sir. He's over in Leesville, working today." I rubbed my eyes to clear away the last of my sleep.

"Leesville, huh? Well, you expecting him back soon?" He scratched at his mustache with his finger.

"Sometime this afternoon, I guess."

He looked up and down the street, and as he did a flash of metal from inside his coat caught my eye. I was sure it was a gun. *Seems to be a lot of those around here lately.* I eased partially behind the door, gripping the handle.

"Okay. Maybe I'll drop by later to see if he's home yet. Kinda late to still be in your jammies, ain't it?" He grinned, then turned and headed for his truck.

I closed the door and glanced at the living room clock. He was right. It was after ten on a Monday morning and way too late to be in my pajamas, summer break or not.

But for now I had something else to worry about. Why was a man carrying a gun looking for Dad? He didn't seem like a tow driver to me. What would Dad need with a wrecker anyway?

I let all that jumble around in my head as I got dressed and filled one of Mom's cake mixing bowls full of Cap'n Crunch. Skipping dinner last night had near about put my stomach against my backbone. Thinking of Dad's note while I ate, I decided I couldn't wait until he got home to go see Mom this afternoon. I needed to see her now.

I rinsed my bowl and headed outside to my bike. Fang was sitting next to it. He cocked his head as I approached, trying to read my intentions. He was a smart dog and was already two houses up the street ahead of me as I took off for town.

When I pulled into the City Hall parking lot I did a double take. The tow truck that had been at my house moments before was wedged between a utilities van and a sanitation truck on the back row of the lot. I leaned my bike against the building and walked over to it, looking around to make sure nobody was watching. Fang stayed close at my heels, his eyes and ears alert. The "i" was missing from the word *Cain's* on the side panel and the hood was still warm. *Why was this truck here?* I knew the town didn't run a towing business. I returned to the side entrance and Fang stayed next to my bike as I made my way inside and entered the Police Department.

Chief Lewis looked up at me and smiled. "Pete! How are you doing, Son?"

I've always liked Jerry Lee. I'd never felt a bad vibe in his presence. But today his smile faltered after a second. "Your mom's in there with Toby Bryson right now." He pointed toward a room off to the left. "He'll be representing her tomorrow, you know."

"How long do ya' think they'll be?"

"Don't know." He looked at the file folder lying open on his desk. "Bryson scheduled an hour, and they just went in fifteen minutes ago." Closing it, he looked back up at me. His extremely wavy hair gleamed with a tonic or something, reflecting the ceiling lights. "Why don't you come back later with your dad…and bring Fang in next time. I'm sure Clarice would love to see him." He stared at me like a man who needed to get back to work real soon.

"Okay. I'll be back later."

I reached the door just as the tow driver opened it and walked past me like he owned the place. He said "Hi" to Chief Lewis and disappeared into the back room. I was about to ask Chief Lewis about him, but he glanced at me with a look of caution and that was all I needed. I stepped out and started to pull the door closed when I had an idea. I eased forward, knob in hand, until only an inch remained open. I placed my ear to the crack and held my breath.

I was not disappointed. I heard the towing man re-enter the room.

"I'm all done in Shantytown." I could hear him pouring coffee as he spoke to the Chief. "No witnesses, but someone said they saw a strange car drivin' slow through there just before the fire. Course, they didn't get the plates down. We'll have to wait for Arson to file their report."

The Chief grumbled and mumbled something, but it wasn't clear.

"We might have a lead on that Kim fellow."

"What?" I heard the Chief's chair slide back.

"Calm down, now. It may be a cold one when we start chasin' it down. Nothing on that Freeman Davis fella, though."

"Dang! This mess is driving me crazy!" I heard someone let out a long sigh, and I suspected it was the Chief. "All right. We can only do what we can do, I guess." Papers shuffled on the desk.

"I'm heading down to Jim's for some dogs and fries. Want me to bring you anything?" asked the towing man.

"Naw. This dern heartburn is branding my gut this morning. I'll just—"

That's all I heard before a hand clamped over my mouth and pain shot down the side of my head from my ear being twisted upside down. Miss Harrington, the town librarian, shuffled me back away from the door to the other side of the hallway, keeping a tight grip as we went. When we were out of earshot of the door, she ear-guided me into one of the wooden appointment seats along the wall and let go. My ear felt like it'd been pulled off and re-attached with thread and glue.

"Peter Travers!" she hissed in her low librarian tone. "What are you doing?" Her voluminous bust loomed over me, blocking out the dim light from the hallway. I envisioned Mr. Rogers trying to climb up it like Spiderman, so I focused on my shoes.

"Nothing, Ma'am. I just came to see my ma and they said to come back later."

I looked up at her with the same eyes Fang uses when he begs for food. Her face softened a bit and I realized how pretty she was behind those horn-rimmed glasses. She had nice hair and smelled good, too, like lilac powder.

"Well, I thought…okay, just get on along now and stay out of trouble…you hear?" She straightened up and smoothed out her old maid dress.

"Yes Ma'am."

I jumped up and bee-lined for the side door where I found Fang panting from the heat, but ever diligent. I mounted my bike and struck out for home. I had to get the grass mowed soon and this seemed like as good a time as any.

What I'd learned down at the station was enough to confirm what I'd heard so far. I was sure our local Klansmen were responsible for that Shantytown blaze. I think Chief Lewis knew it, too. And I figured out he was having a hard time figuring out exactly who was involved, and how much of this town—the old family bloodlines—he wanted to shake up.

When I got home, Buddy was not on my roof. That was a good thing…I think. I mowed the grass and fed Fang. Dad came back mid-afternoon like he said he would and we went back down to see Mom. No Towing man, no ghosts on roofs, nothing out of the ordinary. The day ended with a whisper instead of a bang. Too bad I couldn't say that for the rest of the week.

Mom saw the judge Tuesday morning and things didn't go too well. Dad posted bail by noon. We spent the afternoon as a family, lots of hugging, ice cream on the porch, and generally enjoying the moment. I wanted to spill the beans about all that had happened to me and the gang, and Harper's Mill, but it just didn't seem like the right time. Had I known then what I know now, I would have laid my soul bare. I would've been laughed out of the house, but I'd have done it anyway.

That Wednesday, the town was shocked once again when twenty prime cows were found dead on a farm outside of town. All had been shot, white paint tossed by the buckets full on each and every one. They all belonged to a black farmer named Amos McCauley. No one saw anything, as the crime had been committed in the dead of night. And strange as it was, no one heard gunfire.

Thursday brought anger to the town of Harper's Mill. Theo Smith, the high school's black star running back, was found around sundown beaten and bloodied in a rural ditch just south of the city limits. He was transported to the county hospital and was still unconscious as late as Friday evening. Again, no witnesses came forward.

Friday would prove to be even worse.

Mom spent the day cleaning house and crying. Watching her soaps and crying. Talking on the phone and crying. Dad called to say he would be working late, and when she hung up the phone she was…well, crying. I had planned to spend the day with her, but the crying was getting me down. Way down.

Fang and I had found retreat under the cherry tree in the back yard, me reading a dog-eared copy of Rolling Stone magazine and listening to Eric Clapton confess to shooting a sheriff through the miracle of my transistor radio. Fang lay like a corpse next to me. He got these lazy ways about him sometimes. Eric was bragging how he didn't shoot the deputy, when Mom raised the kitchen window and called out to me. "Pete! Telephone!" She didn't wait for my reply, just closed the window.

I crammed the transistor in my pocket and told Fang to guard my Rolling Stone, tossing it gently over his head. As if to affirm his laziness, he didn't move an inch. Running around the side of the porch, I jumped up and slapped the lowest branch of the red maple that grew by the door. I was getting more and more of that branch as summer wore on.

The phone was off the hook where Mom had left it. I picked it up and pressed it to my ear, unsure if I was going to hear Buddy, or Mojo, or Mr. Kim…maybe Elvis, at this point. I was in a weird mood.

"Hello?"

"Pete." It was Arlo. "Martin said his parents are giving him a ride to the Summer Carnival over at the high school ball field tonight. Wanna tag along? His folks said it was okay."

I looked over at Mom, stretched out on the couch with a box of bonbons, a box of tissues and a Life magazine occupying her mood. This was no place for me.

I covered the mouthpiece. "Mom, can I go to the Carnival with Martin and his parents tonight?"

She pulled a tissue from the box and waved it in my direction, like a queen dismissing her subjects. I took it for a *yes*.

"Yeah, I can go." Another thought crossed my mind out of the blue. "But I'm bringing Margie if she can go. You think his parents would mind?" I heard wet kissing noises on the other end. Arlo never missed a chance to be a clown at the expense of my romantic interest. "Cut it out, Arlo." He snickered.

"I'll ask, but I don't think they'll mind. They're picking me up at six-thirty, so we should be there just after that. Bye Romeo!" He made a big kissy sound on his end and hung up. I called Margie, and in a few minutes we were all set. My summer earnings would be well spent.

Summer Carnival was held at the Harper's Mill High School (home of the Asteroids) every year. The food vendors, games and what few rides they had were the highlights, all situated on the football field behind the school. We arrived at dusk and piled out of the car. Martin's dad gave him a few dollars and told us to be back at the car by ten o'clock.

We waded into the fairway giggling and horsing around, our nostrils filled with the smells of cotton candy, candy apples, popcorn, fried chicken, french fries, roasted peanuts and about a dozen more scents that made our mouths water. We played games, rode rides, and ate things that would rot our teeth and give us acne. Arlo got cotton candy stuck in his hair and Martin swore he chipped a tooth on a candy apple. Percy was tossing peanuts up and catching them in his mouth. Margie and I held on to each other, laughing at their antics. Music filled the air and the night seemed magical.

I spotted the first one behind the Ferris wheel, on the slight rise that surrounded the field. I froze, gripping Margie's hand a bit too tight. Arlo, Martin and Percy kept walking, unaware.

"Pete, what's wrong?"

"There." I pointed. "Behind the Ferris wheel, just to the left." She followed my finger and drew her breath in sharply.

A figure was standing there, light from the carnival illuminating the white robe with an eerie glow, pointy hood with two black holes surveying the crowd, the evening breeze rippling the fabric like it was floating.

"Pete! Look!" I turned to Margie and saw her pointing toward the goal post on the south end. Another robed figure stood defiantly on the rise, as still as a stone. I whirled around now, confirming my suspicion that there were more. The whole carnival was surrounded by sheeted figures every fifty feet along the rise. The gang, realizing we were not around anymore, came back to where we stood.

"Hey! What's the matter with you two?" Martin asked, poking at his chipped tooth with his forefinger.

"They're the matter," I said, pointing to the rise and doing a three-sixty to show them all.

"What the...." Arlo stopped picking at the sticky mess in his hair and spun slowly in a circle, mouth hanging open.

At that moment the lights went out, leaving us in total darkness. Boos and mutterings of indignation rose from the people around us. Margie clung tightly to my arm and I felt the other three crowd in instinctively. A loud hissing sound erupted from our left and I heard the clanking of metal as something hit the ground real close to where we stood. That was followed by a series of hissing, clanking noises across the carnival grounds that lasted about twenty seconds by my estimation. Arlo broke into a coughing fit, followed by Martin, then Percy. I covered my mouth. My eyes were burning as Margie buried her head in my shoulder, her frame shaking as she coughed. People were running by us, panicked, and the din from the crowd rose as small children screamed and parents rushed to corral them to safety, colliding in the smoky haze creeping through the fairway.

"That's tear gas! What the h—" I heard a large man yell as he ran by, dragging his wife and kids in tow. All were retching and crying, much like the five of us.

"Come on!" I yelled at the gang. "We have to get to the car!"

"My mom and dad...." Martin yelled back at me, his teary, swollen eyes trying to search the crowd for a sign of them.

I grabbed his sleeve, Margie still clinging to me for dear life.

"They'll be all right!" I had to trust that they'd be waiting for us back at the car. "Let's go...*now!*"

I pulled Martin along, Margie clinging, Arlo and Percy staying close on our heels. It was hard to see, and we all tripped several times, stopping to help each other up as we made our way in the dark.

We were working our way up the gravel roadway to the parking lot, as best I could tell, when suddenly the smoke around us illuminated and I could see ghost-like shapes of people, big and small, moving off to my left. The smoke was thicker than I'd imagined. Arlo let out a low, guttural moan and I turned to see what was wrong.

"Arlo, what's the matter...?" The words froze on my lips as my watery eyes locked on the source of light. The other three turned to follow our gaze.

What lay before us looked like a battlefield illuminated. The tops of tents and vendor booths peeked through a sea of roiling grey smoke, wispy fingers rising toward the night sky. But what made the fuzz on my arms tingle were the crosses. Four of them, one behind each goal post and one on each side of the field, ablaze on the surrounding rise. It looked like Hades unleashed, as Pastor Stevens would preach. Glowing embers, spat from the pop and sizzle of wood resin, twirled skyward as the flames grew hotter. Margie leaned in hard against me and I could feel her trembling. Somewhere in the distance I could hear the town's emergency warning sirens wailing away. We were stunned. This whole situation had just taken a wicked turn for the worse.

"Scare you a bit, sweetheart?"

I almost jumped out of my skin. The voice rode on a low, whispery, hot breath across my ear. I turned to look Pearl dead in the eyes. She had that loopy grin on her face. Her wardrobe was as colorful as I remembered it the last time, but the smoke curling from her cigarette was lost in the haze that surrounded us. The light from the flames played off her red hair. I could see myself reflected in the lens of her rosy glasses. This time she seemed *very* real to me. Margie squeezed my arm and I looked down to find her gazing at Pearl with teary eyes and a half-smile of wonderment on her face. Arlo, Martin and Percy walked up behind us and leaned in a little, squinting their eyes against the smoke.

"Don't let them get to ya, kids. That's a groovy fire show, ya know? But remember this..." She leaned into our group, her jewelry jangling as she did so. "...love is stronger than hate." She turned her fiery head, looking directly at me. "And music is love. They're just men who hate. Don't let them jive you with this spooky stuff, ya hear darlings?"

Everyone, including myself, nodded a yes. Her words went to my heart, and at that moment I knew the five of us held a special bond. A bond that would be tested without mercy.

Pearl turned and strode away, purple feather boas in her hair swirling in the smoke, until she disappeared.

Pete, baby,... Mojo, Buddy...the whole gang will be there when y'all need us, darlin'— just stand your ground. It's almost show time! Pearl's parting words filled my head and I smiled.

"Who was that?" Margie shook my arm a little, pointing off where Pearl had vanished.

"Just a friend of Buddy's…and Mojo's…and probably some other really cool people."

"You mean she's…?" The words hung on Margie's lips, her eyes huge and watery.

The others stared at me in unison, waiting for the word.

"Dead? Yes." I paused for a moment. "But maybe not. Maybe not as much as we think." I smiled at the thought.

"Marty!" Martin's dad broke the spell as he walked toward us through the haze. "You kids all right?" He put his hand on Martin's shoulder, scanning our faces with a nervous smile.

"Yeah, Dad. We're okay…let's just go home," Martin said. We all nodded in agreement.

When we reached the car, Martin's mom was waiting for us in the front seat. "Oh kids, that was just awful!" She went into a coughing fit, straightened up. "Everyone in the car." Arlo grabbed me by the sleeve and drew me aside.

"Okay, Pete. We got the KKK running wild, dead people popping up everywhere, people missing, people being arrested, and you have the goo-goo eyes for Margie something awful…." He paused to gather his thoughts. "You want us to fix all this? The five of us?"

I stood there, meeting Arlo eye for eye, no expression, no words. His face softened.

"All right…you don't have to say anything, Pete. I know you, and that look says it all. You're my bud, man. If you think we can do this…well, I guess we can." He let go of my sleeve and started for the car door, turning around at the last minute. "Oh, but one thing…." He hesitated for a second, then sighed. "Just don't let that goo-goo eyed thing get in the way of what we have to do."

I saw a bit of scared in him at that moment. He needed reassuring.

"Okay." I'm not sure I said the right thing, but there it was.

And that was that.

They dropped us off, each at our own houses, Margie's being the last. When we pulled up to mine, I opened the door to step out and Margie held my arm. "Pete..." she started, a sparkle in her eyes, "don't worry. We can do this." She choked up a bit on that, then whispered, "I love you, Pete Travers." She bent forward and planted a wet kiss on my cheek. I was thrown off balance, heady with sudden emotion. Working my mouth, I tried to tell her the same, but Martin's dad piped up.

"Let's go, kids, it's not getting any earlier!"

I stepped out and shut the door. I was still off balance as their car drove away. I made my way inside and found Mom on the sofa, still crying. This was reaching critical stage. I sat down next to her, gingerly.

"You okay, Mom?" It was a stupid thing to ask, but I felt awkward.

She turned to look at me and I knew the answer. I just wasn't expecting what came next.

"Your dad's not come home yet, Pete! He hasn't called...oh-h-h...where is he?" With that, she broke into a fresh sob.

I got up and went to my room. I felt shell-shocked, a bit overwhelmed. *Where was he?* I didn't want to think of the possibilities. I took off my clothes and crawled in bed smelling like a spent firecracker. It took a long time to fall asleep, and when I did I found little comfort.

It was dark where I stood. I could smell the summer undergrowth beneath my feet, pungent with life. My legs shuffled forward, tangling in vines and roots as I lumbered toward something. The culvert pipe was suddenly in front of me, light shooting out like an atomic kaleidoscope. Laughter rolled out of the opening, high and joyous. I stepped to the pipe's edge and peered in, momentarily blinded. Images began to materialize before me and I was filled with awe. Buddy, Mojo, Pearl, and someone I couldn't quite see, sat around a tiny table. Tiny wings, like a baby chick's, protruded from the back of the three I could see. They all turned and waved at me. I tried to say something but realized, to my horror, I had no voice.

Without warning, the ground trembled and shook, like a mighty hammer had struck the earth. The culvert dissolved before me and I was left in darkness. The hammer slammed, slammed, again and again, getting stronger and louder with each fall. Trees snapped, and a foul wind blew my hair back as my eyes tried to focus in the dark. Like a boulder breaking from a cliff, I could sense something heavy descending toward me from above and I held up my arms to protect myself.

Then quiet fell, and when I dared look, hell was upon me.

Large, white, needle-like teeth, ten foot across, in two perfect rows, hung above me as putrid, steamy air whirled about my head. They seemed to float on air, and I felt something warm run down my leg. From far off I heard someone scream…and I knew it was Margie. I could hear legs and feet running, fast and crazy in my direction. "Pete! Run! Run now!" came Margie's cries from the darkness. My legs were frozen as the teeth above parted and I stared into a black maw, a depthless vortex of death.

Like a leaf on a breeze a small white cloth floated from the blackness and landed at my feet. It had red squiggly lines and something round in the center. Something grabbed at my shirt. When I turned around, Lucifer let out a roar inches from my face that made my legs go weak. The monkey shrieked and grabbed me with both hands, shaking me like a rag doll. I tried to push away, to get my footing, but those powerful arms were like iron bands. As he shook me harder, Margie's screams began to fade and I knew he was going to kill me. Spots floated across my vision…

I sat upright in bed with a start. Eyes wide, my fingers gripped the bed covers until the knuckles were white. My breath came in ragged gasps, sweat pouring down my face, hair sodden and plastered to my scalp. The night had abated beyond my curtains. I turned on my lamp and looked at the clock. *07:03.*

Crawling out of bed, I walked to the den, where I found Mom asleep on the sofa. Dad was still not home.

And I knew…I knew why.

CHAPTER TWENTY-ONE

2011

MARGIE WOKE WITH A start, eyes wide, head plastered to the pillow. With fingertips, she brushed her lips lightly where they tingled. Her hand move toward her stomach, where it brushed another hand, a rougher hand—and she sat bolt upright.

Was I dreaming?

She felt different, like some part of her had been restored, renewed.

Lying back down, she watched the blades of the ceiling fan rotate in slow motion. There was no nervousness inside of her, no fear. Only a sense of wholeness. A sense that Peter had been here, lying beside her.

That thought suddenly filled her with dread. *Didn't dead people, spirits, sometimes try to visit their loved ones after they passed away?*

Light streamed through the curtains as she crawled out of bed in a panic and headed for the bathroom. Thirty minutes later she had everyone rousted out of bed and set out for the kitchen to start coffee and round up enough food to at least get them started. She was focused on one thing and one thing only and that was getting to the hospital by nine o'clock for visiting hours. Toast, hard-boiled eggs, jams, microwave bacon, cereals, juice and milk were on the table as people straggled in from the upper and lower floors.

"Good morning, Mom," Millie said, kissing Margie on the cheek as she poured herself coffee.

Arlo stomped up from the basement and entered the kitchen. "Morning, all!" He pulled up a chair and eyed Margie. "You wouldn't be in a hurry to get somewhere this morning, would you Margie?"

She sat down across from him. "Of course I'm in a hurry, Arlo." She squeezed her coffee cup, nervous. "Why would you ask such a thing?"

"Oh, no reason. I just saw your sweatshirt is on inside out and backwards." He grinned at her.

Margie looked down, her face flushed. "Okay, so I was in a hurry." She turned to Millie. "Thanks for telling me I look like a three-year-old that dressed herself."

Millie shrugged, took a glass of orange juice and an egg into the living room and turned on the television.

Martin and Percy entered from the basement and exchanged good mornings with Margie and Arlo as they poured their coffees and sat down. Martin glanced at Margie.

"I know, I know," she said. "I'll change before we leave if you think you can hold your laughter in that long."

"Now Margie, there's nothing wrong with feeling upside down when the world turns you upside down," Percy said, trying to hold his own composure as he stirred his coffee.

Arlo abruptly changed the subject. "I was thinking," he said, stopping to smear strawberry jam on two pieces of toast. "We need to be alone with Pete for a few minutes this morning."

He didn't elaborate. Everyone watched as he put four strips of bacon in the toast and made a sandwich.

Martin was absently peeling an egg as he watched. "And why is that?"

Arlo took two bites and the sandwich was lodged in his mouth. Gone, just like that. He looked at Percy with his eyebrows raised while he chewed, deferring the answer to him.

Percy was eating a bowl of cereal when he looked up and realized Arlo was waiting. A drop of milk hung on his lip as he contemplated the question. Then he looked at Martin. "Because…if what Margie said last night is right, if this is starting all over again," he glanced at Arlo and Margie, "then we have to be together. Like before."

Arlo nodded. "Maybe the only way our dead friends can communicate with us now is if we are together." He looked everyone in the eye, gauging their reaction. "It's just a hunch."

They were each contemplating this revelation when Bill and Clarice came downstairs with Peter Jr. on their heels.

"Good morning," Bill said to a round of greetings as he pulled a chair out for his wife.

Margie glanced at the clock on the wall. "Excuse me, everyone. I have to go dress myself properly. Bill, you can have my chair."

She went to her bedroom and chose a nice blouse and light over-jacket, but decided to keep her jeans on. Percy's words kept playing around in her head. "I hope you're right, my friend," she replied to the empty room.

Just as she started to leave, a picture of Peter on the dresser caught her eye. It was one shot from a series of photos *Spin* magazine had taken back in the nineties. A side shot caught against a black background, Peter gazing upward. She'd liked it so much she'd insisted they have it framed. She walked over and picked it up.

Minutes passed.

Without a word, she dropped down beside the bed, letting his picture fall on the bedspread, and clasped her hands together. She prayed.

It was all she could think of to do.

CHAPTER TWENTY-TWO

Peter

I'M GETTING WEAKER. NOT in body, for that's a thing I don't feel familiar with anymore, but in my mind, my soul. The contents of my life beyond youth, those years that were rich with love and music and the laughter of my children, flee desperately through my thoughts now. I find I have but two regrets. Two things that I would've done different once the situation was clear to me in the years that followed. I would have prayed. Prayed for a different end, a different purpose than the one I now must fulfill. Prayed for God to reconsider.

And I would've shared it with Margie.

I feel a change in the darkness around me. The sentinels have moved to a place opposite from the dancing lights.

And they have begun their approach.

What's left of me, what may be nothing more than a single thought, will be taken like a prize when these lights, these things, reach me as One. I know that now. I know what the dancing lights are, the things that bring such coldness to me. They are the keepers of a destiny. A destiny that marked me from my first breath. Keepers that must collect me for a purpose.

The only thing I don't know is what these sentinels are, who they are.

I can only wait, now. Helpless and cold.

But there was a time when I could not wait. A time when things drove me forward into the unknown, and I went fearlessly in the eyes of those that were drawn to me. A time when God had another purpose for me. For us.

I slipped on my clothes and started for the door when my guitar caught my eye. I don't know why, but the thought came out of nowhere. I had a powerful urge to move those strings, maybe for the last time. I picked it up and sat on the bed, getting my fingers into position. *Forgive me, George*, I thought, as I started strumming *My Sweet Lord*, keeping it low as to not wake Mom. I was slow at first, but I played it straight through, the melody bringing a quietness to me that felt right. When I was done, I sat it in the corner and silently left the house by the side door.

The moon was pale and low in the sky, the air warm and moist. Crickets serenaded the shadows in the dewy grass as I pushed my bike to the curb and mounted. A low rumble of thunder sounded off to the east, announcing that a less than perfect summer day lay ahead. Fang swaggered up beside me and sat down, an indication that he was ready to rock and roll with whatever I had in mind. His ears were perked like antennas.

I pulled my Wolfpack ball cap down tight on my head and gripped my handlebars. Everything felt off-center, my body tingled like I was peeing on an electric fence. So much had happened that my head felt like it would explode. One thing burned crystal clear in my mind, though. The town was under attack, and like Pearl said, it was almost show time.

It was my turn to pebble some windows.

As I peddled toward town, my head began to clear. Making a mental inventory of the situation, I felt a little better about what lay ahead. After all, Buddy had been sent back to help us and that was a good thing, right? We had a connection, Buddy and I, and that meant a higher power was at work here, right? *Right.*

I neared the intersection of Frazier and Elm, lost in thought, when flashing lights bounding off the surrounding buildings brought me back to the moment. As I slowed down, I realized the parking lot by the Police Department was full of cars, emergency lights lit up on every one of them. I moved onto the curb and walked my bike over to the lot fence, keeping just out of sight. There were three plain cars, three sheriff's cars, the two town patrol cars and a large black van with the words Special Crimes Unit across the side. I could make out what looked like about twenty men standing in a loose circle, five of them dressed all in black. I listened intently, trying to pick up what conversation I could…

"…we got reports that they are somewhere north of town… Edwar… Pond vicinity and…found that Kim fellow's car…arrest warrant…" a tall one with an FBI jacket on said.

Then…

"…my boys know the wa…and it's a tight road, but…" I recognized Chief Lewis' voice.

"…channel 4, if backup is needed…" Someone pulled away in a police car.

And…

"…a new development with Bill Trav…and we have a lead that's reliable for…" that sounded a lot like the tow driver that came to the house, "…but we have to be care…" the rest trailed off.

Wait, did he say Bill Travers?

So, there it was. Not that I needed it confirmed, but hearing it made my stomach sink. Dad was now one of the missing. If I had any doubt about what lay ahead of us, this erased it for me. "Mojo...Buddy...Pearl...." I said under my breath. "Don't let me down...us down." Fang whimpered somewhere in the shadows at my feet. "Shhh, now" I whispered, "It's okay, boy." I reached down and patted his head. I wasn't too sure about my words, but I had to believe. "Come on, boy. Let's get out of here."

We slipped away from the fence quietly and backtracked to Moore Street, where we hung a left and pushed on toward Arlo's house. The horizon to the east grew a lighter grey as the day arrived, the rumble still promising a skin-soaker by noon. Martin would be on a delivery with his dad, so Percy would be our first stop, then Margie. That is, if I could get Arlo's butt out of bed without his dad finding out.

I peddled like a demon, my mind working overtime. It was obvious where we had to go...Mojo had shown us that. But what we would find was anyone's guess. I turned on Maple, scraping my peddle on the asphalt, and was about to cut through the Taylor's property when the police cruiser came out of nowhere and blocked my path. I jammed my peddles in reverse and slid six feet before I came to a stop just inches from the bumper. Feet on the road, I stood there, legs trembling from the near miss. *Fang!* I looked around frantically and spotted him, standing on the Taylor's lawn, eyes wide, tail pointed upward. He was as surprised as I was.

"Pete? Is that you?" It was the thief, yelling from his window. He emerged from his car and made his way over to me on visibly shaky legs. "What in the Sam Hill are you doing whippin' around out here at this hour of the morning, Son? Why ain't you at home?" He pushed his hat back an inch and rubbed his forehead. "Holy smokes, boy. I almost ran over you. Are you okay?"

I was glad he asked that second question before I had to answer the first.

"I'm all right, sir." I barely got that out. I was strung as tight as a guitar string.

The lines on the Chief's face softened a bit. "Well, while we're both out here at this God-forsaken hour, you might as well climb in and let's chat a bit." He motioned toward the car and turned before I could say anything.

I walked my bike over to the curb and popped the kickstand out, dreading the conversation that I knew was coming. I wasn't sure what the police were going to do, but I knew what we had to do and I really needed to get to Arlo's soon. I walked over, opened the cruiser door and crawled inside where he was waiting. The cloudy morning cast a dreary light inside the car, which matched my mood.

"Pete..." he began, then paused. "Pete, I have to tell you something and I don't want you to get upset...well, that's a dumb thing to say, I guess." He hesitated, rubbed his forehead. "I just want to..." He turned to me and looked me straight in the eyes. "Pete, your dad's been abducted...kidnapped, we think." His eyes searched mine, waiting for a response. I held my tongue, not wanting to reveal that I'd overheard them in the parking lot. I had to think— quick!

"What?" I put on my surprised face. "Where is he? Who...who took him? Why?" I feigned hurt, fear and hysteria, which I felt on the verge of anyway, but like I said, I didn't want him to know I already knew.

He turned, stared out the window and took a deep breath. "I probably shouldn't be telling you this. Your dad should be doing it, but he's...he's..." He massaged his temples real hard. "Well, he should be telling you, that's all. But I guess it's time you knew." He got real quiet again.

Then, "Pete, your dad ain't no insurance salesman anymore. He's working for the State Bureau of Investigations now. The SBI. Has been for the last year, in fact. We think that's the reason he's missing. We *know* that's the reason. He's been working on a case, this case..." He jabbed his finger hard toward the windshield. "... along with the FBI and my police department." He kept his eyes dead ahead.

It was my turn to take a deep breath and stare out into the dawn. *Dad was still doing police work? But...*

"Your dad wanted back in police work real bad. Told me that himself. I guess I'm the reason he's in this mess and, well, I feel I owe you an explanation. The whole insurance job was a good front, to start with. Once he quit the real one, we set up a phony company and the state paid him under the company's name, like a contract. It was kept way under the radar, as they say. But he ain't sold enough insurance to fill a gnat's head."

He licked his lips.

"Here's the deal, Pete. We've been running an undercover operation on the KKK for months now, and your dad, he's been in the thick of it. They've been real dormant in these parts for many years, but lately...lately they've grown a pair, a big pair, and...." He glanced at me, then back at the road, looking a little embarrassed by his words. "Mr. Kim's disappearance was the trigger for us. Then old man Davis, and their big meetings outside of town, and their parades, and that whole intimidation thing last night with the crosses. We've had a lot of folks to come forward and tell us things that always lead back to them."

I was facing him now, eyes wide, because he was telling me part of what I already knew, and part of what I didn't, but suspected. A knot grew in my stomach.

Clap. Clap. Clap. I cut my eyes toward the back seat and there sat Mojo.

"Bravo! Pete. Bravo! You're playing it beautiful, man. Just beautiful." He grinned. "Don't be late to you-know-where!" Then he was gone. Just like that.

I glanced at the Chief, but he apparently hadn't heard, or seen, a thing. Relief washed over me.

"And that thing with your mom? They set her up, Pete. I know Sessom, and I know who and what he is," he continued. "They knew Mr. Kim's wife wouldn't be able to run that store properly once he was out of the picture. They also discovered that their paperwork for citizenship was falsified. That brother-in-law of Russell Beecham's, Thelonious Nichols, dug that up for them. That's all supposed to go to court next week, then that property will go up for auction. And guess who plans to bid on it?" He eyed me for a moment, contempt glaring in his eyes. "And guess who's gonna strong-arm anyone who bids against them?"

I shrugged.

"I don't know what riled that organization up, Pete, but it's just been crazy these last few years. Bobby Kennedy shot. Martin Luther King shot. That Manson gang killing them folks. Our boys dying over there in Vietnam…just a nightmare. I guess they just want to make a name for themselves again." He shook his head in disgust.

I was getting antsy. Thunder boomed off in the distance. I had to get away from here, and soon.

"I want to ask you to keep this to yourself, Pete. I could lose my job if it ever got out that I told you all this." He smiled a sad smile at me as he reached over and patted my shoulder. "How 'bout I run you home so you can take care of your mom? We'll get your dad back…." He choked up a bit on that. "We'll get him back today, in fact." That familiar steely look returned to his face as he gained his composure. He reached down and picked up his aviator shades and slipped them on against the daylight.

I was processing a lot and knew I had to skedaddle soon, but at that moment, watching Chief Lewis was like watching the posse saddle up. I felt encouraged.

"If you don't mind, sir, I'd like to go home alone…at my own pace." I replaced my 'worried' face with a sad one, hoping the Chief would understand.

"Okay, Pete. I understand. But don't be too long. I'm headed there now anyway to tell your mom the bad news…and maybe more. She'll need a man around the house after that." He cranked his car up and smiled at me from behind his shades.

I opened the door and climbed out, trying not to seem too anxious as I picked up my bike and straddled the seat. Chief Lewis pulled away from the curb and drove on down to Robinson Street, took a right and disappeared from sight. I knew I should go home and be with Mom, but this couldn't wait. With Dad's disappearance, the game just became uglier…and closer to home.

I took off with a new sense of urgency, peddling standing up, as was the standard for boys trying to save the world. Three blocks from Arlo's house, I spotted Charlie Russ sitting on the curb. Flies swarmed Charlie's head as he belched and swatted at them with soiled hands. I pulled to the curb and stopped with both feet. He paused his swatting and looked up at me with a smile on his hairy face.

"Hey, Charlie." I really didn't have time to shoot the breeze with Charlie, and we weren't the best of friends, but something tugged at my brain, telling me that this was the right thing to do. Fang wandered up to Charlie, sniffed at his leg, and immediately backtracked, his tail between his legs, head shaking to get the smell from his nostrils.

"Hey." He was not a man of many words. "You seen a cab come by here?" His eyes looked full of hope…and dazed. A fly landed on his lip and distracted me for a second.

"No, I just got here. You waiting on a cab?" I didn't think he could afford one, much less have the sense to call one. He shook his head yes at me and looked down the road in the opposite direction.

I followed his gaze, not expecting to see anything. At least not the things he was seeing. Just as I started to say bye and get on with my business, a bright yellow cab turned the corner and barreled down the road toward us like there was no tomorrow. I grabbed my bike and jumped the curb just as it came to a screeching halt a foot from the curb and about a quarter inch from Charlie's toes. I exhaled.

Pearl leaned over the passenger seat and hollered in his direction through the open window. "You call a cab, Charlie?" She was dolled up in pastels of sheer fabric, wild jewelry dangled from her arms and ears, and a cigarette from her lips. Her rose colored glasses hid her eyes from us.

Charlie's eyes lit up as he staggered to his feet and grasped the cab door. "Where ya headed?"

"On an adventure, baby!" She grinned, laughed her throaty laugh, and turned her head in my direction. "You got a handle on it, sweetheart?"

I opened my mouth to speak but a voice in my head interrupted me. *You need to put a fire under it, baby…some heavy stuff goin' down and we're all counting on you and the gang.* I nodded my head and she smiled at me. Charlie was climbing into the backseat, which baffled me, but that was of no consequence in my current situation.

I grabbed my bike and made to strike out for Arlo's house, but paused and turned to look at Pearl's cab as it pulled away. I wasn't sure if I should laugh or cry, standing there in the road. What I saw might have made another person go loony on the spot. Both of them floated away from me on thin air, their legs out of sight, Pearl slightly ahead and to the left of Charlie. The breeze blew her hair through the now invisible window, but nothing else moved on them as they glided down the road. Just two people…ah, one ghost and one lost soul, I guess, floating away from me in an imaginary cab.

I filed it away in a far corner of my brain and hoped that when this was all over, if I lived through it, I wouldn't be left to die in a padded room in a straight jacket. I turned my sights on Arlo's and took off on my bike.

The clouds were building up fast, churning across the sky like an oily black tide. Thunder rumbled louder as the storm grew closer. I approached Arlo's house and jumped the curb Evel Kneivel-style and came to a stop under his carport. Their car was gone. I panicked. Dropping my bike, I made my way around to Arlo's bedroom window and looked around to be sure no one was watching.

"Arlo!" My whisper was almost a yell…almost. I tapped on the window with my knuckle. Nothing. I peeked over the ledge, through the curtains. Arlo lay tangled in his sheets, his underwear halfway down his butt, lost in a dream. "Arlo! Get up! Arlo!" I rapped the window with all four knuckles now, praying that Bobby Hankshaw was nowhere around. He rustled around in the sheets and sat up on the edge of the bed, eyes puffy and dazed. I rapped the glass again.

"Pete?" he mouthed at me through the window. He rubbed his eyes and looked at my bobbing head again. "What…?" He stood up and shuffled over to the window, undid the latch and shoved it up. I stepped back.

"Pete, what's the matter? It's…" He looked around his room, for a clock I guess, and turned back to me. "…really early, Pete. Why'd you wake me so early?" He tugged his briefs up, thankfully, and bent down, sticking his head through the window.

"It's time, Arlo." I let that hang between us for a moment as we stared at each other, unspoken words passing between us. When my words finally made their way through the circuit of Arlo's brain, his eyes lit up and his mouth dropped open.

"Now?" He blinked and looked down at his underwear. When he looked up he had that old crooked Arlo grin on his face. "Just a minute!"

He turned, scurried back into his room, hunting for pants and whatever else he could throw on. I looked around, still wary of Bobby Hankshaw, but too anxious to let it ruin the moment. The wind was picking up and I felt a splatter of rain on my cheek. Lightning flashed off in the distance. Arlo had his clothes on and ran to the window, that wild look in his eyes.

"Come on!"

I grabbed his elbow to give him balance as he climbed through the window, but his big bulk caught us both off guard and he fell out, bringing us crashing to the ground. Arlo looked at me as I looked back and we both started laughing. A nervous laugh at first, then we guffawed there in the grass until our sides felt like they would bust. After a few seconds that brought tears to our eyes, we pulled ourselves up and stood facing each other. The look between us said it all— the heck with the neighbors and Bobby Hankshaw. We both knew we may never come back from where we were headed.

"I think my mom's still asleep. Hold on!" Arlo ran to the shed and grabbed his bike. I was standing with mine in the carport when he came back. We both took a deep breath.

"We gotta' get Percy and Margie. Martin's probably out deliverin' with his dad. Then we have to get to Edwards Pond. I think—"

"Why Edwards Pond?" Arlo interrupted me, a quizzical look plastered on his face. Arlo had a short memory.

"It's where we think they're all at, Arlo...remember?" I paused, taking another deep breath. "All of them that went missing... including my dad."

Arlo's jaw dropped. "They got your dad?"

"And Mr. Kim...and Mr. Davis..." I shook my head. "Let's go...." I started to mount my bike and stopped. "Arlo." I turned to him. "I suspect Martin was right about those...those visions Mojo showed us. I hope not, but I suspect he was. It's gonna be crazy out there." I paused, trying to fill in the pieces. "You know about Mojo, no surprise there. And I told you, Martin, and Percy about Buddy." Arlo nodded his head in agreement. "Well, I think I know who Pearl is."

"The cab driver?"

"Yes." The image of Pearl and Charlie still burned on my brain.

"Who?"

"I think she's another dead rock star, Arlo. She's Janis. Janis Joplin." I waited for him to speak again, but he didn't. "What I'm trying to say is, this ain't just about kidnapping's and killin' and the KKK. It's gonna get real weird, Arlo. Chief Lewis, the SBI and the FBI...and even my dad, they've..."

"Your dad?"

"Yes. Chief Lewis told me he's been working for the law on this case. I guess that's why they took him. I had no idea...but what I'm saying is..." I tried to warn him, I really tried, but the words weren't there. So I did the next best thing. "Arlo, I just want you to know that you're my best friend in the whole world. And I...well, I just wanted to say that." He stood there and smiled.

Smiled like a goony bird with a silver tooth. I felt my face flushing and decided we should get moving before I burst into flames from embarrassment. "Come on, let's go."

We took off to gather the rest of our gang, the rain pelting our faces with small drops as the storm moved in. The air smelled electric as lightning moved in closer all around us. I could hear Mojo singing *Riders on the Storm* in my head and it sent a chill up my dampening back. The roads were fairly empty for a Saturday morning, even at this hour. Apparently the news about the carnival incident had spread through town like a wildfire, leaving an already wary town a bit more terrified. Martin and Percy must have sensed it too because they were both waiting for us at Percy's house, wide-eyed and on edge. "We couldn't sleep." they both said in unison when Arlo and I rode up.

"Okay," I said as we gathered around Martin's porch. "We have to...wait...." I looked at Martin. "Why aren't you out with your dad on deliveries?" I'd plumb forgot about that little detail.

"He told me to stay home this morning. Said it wasn't too safe to be out today."

I nodded thoughtfully, mulling it over for a moment. Considering what we were going to do, I was sure his dad would've thought otherwise had he known the truth.

"We need to get Margie before—"

Arlo cut me off. "Do we have to?"

I shot him a look that said *Yes, Arlo, we do!* and he sulked for a few seconds while I ignored him.

"Like I was saying, we need to go get Margie and—"

"What about the others?" Percy broke in.

"Others?"

"Yeah, you know. Buddy and Mojo and—"

"Oh, yeah. I don't know, Percy. We'll just have to see." That's about all I could say. I just hoped they were there when we needed them. The rain had eased up to a sprinkle, teasing us. I felt the pull again. "Let's go."

I climbed on my bike as the others mounted theirs, and in minutes we were all pulling up in front of Margie's. Percy started cleaning his glasses with his shirt, and I imagined that even a few sprinkles could render him sightless. I pulled my cap down tighter, happy to have it.

"You guys wait here." I laid my bike down. "I'll go see if she's up yet."

It was close to 9:15 by my watch and I chose to take the front door approach, crossing under an old oak that took up most of the front yard. I pushed the doorbell and knocked three times for good measure. After a few seconds, the door opened and Mrs. McMillan stood there in a yellow sundress, her apron covered in flour. She was unusually bright-eyed for a Saturday morning as she pushed the screen door open and leaned out, the smell of fresh lavender preceding her.

"Pete! What brings you out so early?" She smiled, her hair and make-up perfect for such an hour. I wondered if she slept that way, or if she slept at all.

"Hi, Mrs. McMillan." I suddenly felt awkward standing here so early in the morning. "I know it's early, but is Margie up yet?"

She brushed her hands on her apron as she held the screen open with her leg.

"She was up early, too! Said something about cheerleading tryouts?" Her face scrunched up, but the smile remained. "Woke me up before she left, but I'll tell her you were here, okay? I just hope she gets out of this mess." She squinted toward the sky. I could smell fresh baked biscuits and country ham through the screen door. Suddenly I was starving.

"Okay. Thanks." I turned and headed back to the others, a little disappointed. *Cheerleading tryouts?* That was the first I'd heard about that.

The boys were waiting by the curb, anxious.

"Well?" Arlo asked, arms crossed.

"She's at—"

"Hey! Pete!"

The sound startled us. I looked toward the front door, but it was closed.

"Up here! Is my mom gone?" The leaves on the lowest oak branch shook.

"Margie?" It took me a moment to get the picture. "Yeah, she's gone. What you doing up there?" I tried to keep my voice low, and I suddenly remembered Grandpa telling me once that a tree was like a lightning rod. Not a good thing, this.

She made her way down, swinging precariously from the branches, and dropped to the ground. Her backpack looked stuffed to the point of overflowing. I ran up and steadied her with my hand.

"I got us some sandwiches and Kool-Aid for later…and apples, Mary Janes and Pixie Stix for dessert." She smiled, and I could see nothing but mischief in her eyes. Her hair was back in a ponytail, bangs hanging wildly across her forehead, freckled cheeks radiant. "Oh! And some Honey Buns."

I was seriously in love with this girl!

"How did you know we were coming?" Martin asked. All of them had joined us under the oak.

"I couldn't sleep last night. I felt something…" She looked up, and I could see the roiling clouds reflecting off her irises. "…coming. I don't know why, but something told me y'all would be here soon. I guess it's time, huh?"

We shook our heads in unison. Margie grabbed my hand. It was a simple gesture, but Martin reached out and took my other one. Arlo grabbed Martin's and Percy closed the circle between Arlo and Margie. We stood there, all looking at each other, no words spoken. I could feel it, and by their looks, they could, too. Like an electric wave, something moved between us, sending our loose hair standing on end. Fang barked and backed away from our ring with his tail between his legs, eyes locked on us. Air swirled upward, filling our nostrils and suddenly we were all holding on tight to keep our balance. I glanced over at the oak and not a single leaf was moving.

"Look!" It was Percy. He gazed downward and all eyes followed. Between us the grass appeared to blur in a swirling motion, spinning out to the edges of our toes. "What's that?"

Arlo started to step back, but Martin and Percy held tight. "No!" they both shouted at once.

The green beneath us spun until it grew hazy white. It took a second, but then I realized we were looking at clouds. Before I could say as much, the clouds drifted apart and a tiny body of water surrounded by trees came into view. My head swam from the height.

"It's Edwards Pond." Margie said.

"How do you know that?" Percy looked at her suspiciously.

"Mr. Barber had some local topography maps in our science class last year. I recognize the shape." She bent forward a little, squinting against the air flow for a better look. The air was moist from the rain clouds and I gripped her hand tighter "What are those lights?" I braced my legs better as she leaned a little more.

"What lights?" Arlo leaned forward, too, for a better look, but he was trembling and white as a sheet. I knew it was his fear of heights. The only consolation I felt was that if we all fell forward at once, our heads butted together might stop us.

"There, there…and there. Around the pond." Margie pointed, releasing Percy's hand. He grabbed her shoulder, and I nodded a thanks in his direction.

She was right. Three small, pulsing lights hovered in a semicircle around the pond's outline. It seemed impossible to tell how high they hovered over the pond and how high we hovered above them.

"Pete." Martin looked at me and I looked back at him. "Do those look familiar?"

It took a second to put his words together in my head, and then it hit me.

"The fireballs. At the school."

Arlo and Percy nodded their heads in agreement. Margie turned to me.

"What fireballs?"

Before we could answer her….

"*You kids enjoying the view?*"

The voice was all around us and nowhere at once. We all looked at each other, except Arlo. His gaze remained on the hole, no doubt contemplating throwing up. The voice sounded very familiar. *Mojo! I should have known.*

"Look at the light by the road!" Arlo pointed and we all looked.

"*It's time to rock and roll, little ones.*" The voice started to fade. "*Don't forget your transistor radio, Pete!*"

"Did you see that?" Arlo looked spooked. We all did, I'm sure. The light he pointed out had pulsed with the sound of Mojo's voice. Syllable for syllable. For some reason the movie *It's a Wonderful Life* flashed in my head. "Does that mean…?"

Before he could finish, the hole, or whatever you would call it, closed with a loud *swish!* Just a patch of grass remained. Everyone looked around, pale and a bit shook up. Discouraged, as my dad would say. Percy's glasses were fogged up with moisture, but he made no move to clean them. We all dropped our hands. I took advantage of the moment.

"Margie, you know this but the rest of you don't. Buddy died and I was born just about the same time." They stood there, bewildered. "Don't you see? This has always been my destiny. And all of you, my friends, are my friends for a reason! You were meant to be here... now... to do this thing." I smiled, hoping my words would work, and waited for someone to respond, but they all stood there with their mouths ajar. Margie looked cool and collected. Percy was the first to open his mouth.

"So you're saying...?"

"What I'm saying is, Buddy, Mojo, Pearl...they're all here for one reason. To help us." Arlo looked up like something clicked in his head. I nodded at him and continued. "From what I can tell, there's the FBI, the SBI and Chief Lewis, all headed out there to fix this."

Percy and Martin raised their heads, small tugs came to the corners of their mouths. Arlo opened his mouth and threw in the wrench, as usual.

"But what do *we* do? Why do they need us? There'll be guns and stuff...them KKK are mean."

I shrugged my shoulders, at a loss for words. I knew why, but saying it was hard. I looked at Margie. She seemed to be in a trance or something.

"Because this isn't business as usual, boys." Her lips barely moved, voice low and gravelly. "There's something, a force at work here, that needs our attention. Something only we can stop. But you have to be there...that's the way...the only way." She stared straight ahead and we stared at her. I had to get her attention. She was creeping us out.

"Margie?"

She turned to look at me, sweat beading on her forehead and upper lip.

"What?"

She sounded normal again, eyes clear and focused. I was relieved. I decided to let it go, even though the whole thing made my doodads feel tighter than a balloon hat. I was sure it was Pearl I heard when Margie spoke, but we would figure that out later.

"We got to go. Come on, you can ride with me." I reached for her hand.

"Wait!" It was Arlo again. "What's wrong with Percy?"

We all looked over at Percy. His face was scrunched up and tears rolling down his cheeks.

"Percy?" I walked over to him and laid my hand on his shoulder. His glasses had cleared a bit and I could see his eyes were red. "What's wrong?"

He held up his trembling left hand and I heard Margie gasp. His sixth finger, a double pinkie, was as white and translucent as a quartz stone.

"Holy moly!" Arlo mumbled as they all moved closer to us.

"It hurts!" It was all Percy could say between sobs.

"What...what's happening to it?"

We all stared at his sixth digit as it began to pulse with a faint glow, like a heartbeat.

"Wow!" Arlo said, light reflecting off his tooth.

Martin and I stood speechless. Margie stood back a few steps, starting to sob quietly. Her cheeks looked all blotchy, and I wondered if she was going to make it.

"It's..."

Martin started to speak, but before he could finish, Percy's finger darkened and solidified to its natural brown color. He was still trembling when I felt that tug in my mind again.

"Okay." I gathered myself and turned to the others. "We have to go now...no matter what. Come on." Something told me we were running out of time, fast.

Percy wiped his eyes and grabbed his bike. The others grabbed theirs as Margie climbed onto the back of mine. I turned to her.

"You all right?"

She looked at me, blotchy and wet-eyed, and nodded her head as she smiled. I pushed off and away we went. The rain started again and pelted us as we headed toward town on our way to Edwards Pond.

When we arrived at Main Street, I stopped my bike and the others pulled up behind me. Looking down Main was like looking at a graveyard. Nothing moved except the flow of rainwater along the curbs as it worked its way to the city drainage system. Margie squeezed me tight from behind. I looked at the others and they shrugged, but concern was written all over their faces. They knew what I was thinking. The clock on the Bank sign blinked 10:00 and Harper's Mill was usually bustling with Saturday morning shoppers and gossipers by now.

"This is so-o-o weird," Martin uttered. We all nodded in agreement, but that was the end of it. We started up Main again, each of us scared, determined, and unsure of what lay ahead.

CHAPTER TWENTY-THREE

2011

THEY WERE ALL IN the kitchen finishing their breakfast when Margie came down. Millie and Peter Jr. were rinsing the dishes and putting things away.

"Everybody ready?" she asked with a smile, trying to keep their spirits up, not to mention her own. Nods and gestures were given as a yes. "Good. We'll take the van, ride together, if nobody minds. Millie, Peter...just leave those."

Everyone grabbed their personal effects and followed Margie out to the van. Black clouds were building off to the east as they all stepped to the edge of the drive.

"Looks like we're in for a pretty bad one," Bill said, gazing off in that direction. Clarice put her arm in his and pulled herself closer against him.

Arlo was grabbing a jacket from his car when Bill spoke. Now he stood there, jacket in hand, looking at Margie with her hand on the van's door handle. Martin and Percy shared a glance. The kids were buried in their smartphones.

"What?" Bill asked, confused by the reaction to his words.

Arlo closed his car door and walked over to Margie. "Do you

think it…?"

"I don't know." She shook her head, released the door handle. "After all this time, who knows?"

Martin and Percy walked up, both glancing back at the clouds that were moving too fast now in their direction.

"I say we give it a try." Martin locked eyes with Margie, nodded, then looked at the others.

"I'm in," Percy said, raising his eyes upward. "God, please forgive me if this is against your word." He grabbed Martin's hand.

Martin grabbed Margie's and she grabbed Arlo's. Arlo and Percy hesitated a moment, looking down at their hands.

"It's the right thing to do, Percy," Arlo said. He reached for Percy's hand and took it gently into his own.

Four stood in a circle, and four stood back. The wind howled ahead of the storm front, trees began to sway as droplets of water struck their skin and clothes. Arlo was the first to look down, and then the others followed his lead. The grass swayed and bent, one way, then the other, until it formed a concentric circle and turned fluid, blurring as it rotated between their feet.

The bottom dropped out.

PART III

Deadly Convergence

CHAPTER TWENTY-FOUR

Peter

THERE ARE ONLY TWO dancing lights now. Two that will merge as one…and they're almost upon me. The sentinels are almost here, too. Friend or foe, I feel their essence, their being, emanating from those orbs, cautiously probing the thing that is me. I feel like injured prey, stricken and left for dead on the roadside, a black, hot sun bearing down. Scavengers circling above, more crouched in the bushes, inching ever closer.

I don't have the fight I had when I was younger. The years of a good life have softened me and I find myself on a strange, dark battlefield, unarmed and disoriented. I can only turn my thoughts to God now, and pray he'll change my fate.

And if he won't do that, I can only hope he'll give me my dignity, give me the same courage I had then, when the world was still a place of heroes and hope. Give me the strength and determination I had that day….

We rode single file up Open Bridge Road. Nobody spoke, but

nobody had to because we all knew what the other was thinking. Fang had disappeared from my periphery, going off to be a dog. I'd hoped he would be there with me, but maybe he sensed just how bad things would probably get. I hoped not. Dark clouds moved low now with a fury, wind pushing at our backs. The rain continued to pelt us like metal tacks and we were soaked to the bone, Percy bringing up the rear because his glasses were smeared with moisture. Lightning was all around us. I thought of how crazy it must look to anyone who saw us out here running around in it.

I was guessing we had about a half mile to the pond when I heard sirens approaching behind us. I stopped my bike and looked back, bringing the others to a halt. Two state troopers barreled down on us and we shuffled into the grass and weeds off the side of the road to get out of their way. They blew by us in a roar, sending another gust of air and a fine mist across us that nearly toppled me and Margie into the ditch.

"Look!" yelled Martin. He pointed off in the distance and we all turned at once. Two helicopters were coming in low from the west. My heartbeat quickened. Suddenly it seemed it was all coming a little too fast for me. I took a deep breath, remembering Dad was out there and he was in big trouble, maybe *deadly trouble*. I removed my cap and wiped the moisture from my face.

"Come on, guys!"

I pushed off with Margie holding on, and soon we were moving as a pack again. My legs were getting tired and Margie was getting heavier. Then I remembered her backpack, and stopped complaining to myself about it. Martin surprised me when he passed us. The look on his face was intense, almost painful, but I didn't say anything.

"What's wrong with him?" Margie had moved up a bit and spoke close to my ear.

"Just nervous…and anxious, I guess," I yelled back at her.

"No! His back…what's wrong with it?"

I looked at Martin's back as he peddled ahead of us. His tee shirt was plastered to his skin, much like the rest of us, but something didn't look right. I shrugged. Just then I heard the tires of approaching cars and started to swerve over, but they blew by our left so fast that they were gone before I could react. Dirty water splattered us again. I heard everyone let out an *aaawww* at the suddenness of it. There were three of them, but the only thing I saw was the 'GOV' of the license plate of the last one.

We finally reached the bridge and I stopped everyone except Martin with my hand. I yelled at him to stop. He backtracked and joined us.

"Why're we stopping?" Arlo asked as he banged the side of his head to get the water out of his ears I presumed.

"So I can clean my glasses, moron." Percy shot him a look and proceeded to dismount and squat down. He pulled his pant leg up and stretched his sock top out to dry his glasses. *That's a smart one*, I thought. I eyed his extra finger and it seemed normal…for now, anyway. Arlo kept banging his hand against his head and shaking it like a dog.

"Do you think we're too late, Pete?" Martin looked at me as he scrunched his shoulders back and pulled at his soggy tee shirt, obviously uncomfortable.

Lightning struck so close that we all jumped, and I think I heard Arlo fart but I wasn't sure. It wouldn't be too pleasant to have him around if he left more than just tracks in his drawers.

I looked in the direction of Edwards Pond, but all I could see were the tops of the trees from this distance. The helicopters had disappeared and I assumed they were on the ground by now.

"I don't think we're late at all."

Glancing around at their faces, I saw four miserable souls looking back at me. Suddenly, I felt bad about dragging them all into this. I started to tell them they could all go back home when several loud *whoomppps!* drew my attention back toward the direction of the pond. Smoke climbed up through the tree tops in the distance.

"What was that?" Margie was squinting toward the smoke and I counted six dark blotches on her face now. Was it the rain? Or nerves?

Martin turned to us with a deadpan expression. "That's probably tear gas. They're shooting tear gas at something. My uncle told me about how police do that sometimes to flush people out. Criminals and such." He twisted his face up again and scratched over his shoulder.

I looked back at the rising smoke. Whatever Buddy and his friends expected us to do, we weren't going to do it just standing here in the road. "Let's go." I said.

We started up again with a renewed urgency. If it was going down, it was going down now. The wind whipped at our backs with fine sheets of rain, but I think we were so waterlogged no one noticed. Water steadily dripped off the brim of my cap. As we grew closer, I could see Lath's driveway up ahead, and several cars down at his trailer. All along Open Bridge Road sat more police cars and emergency vehicles, as well as the Special Crimes Unit van that I'd spotted back in town. My eye caught something I'd never seen before; a few hundred yards beyond Lath's trailer sat an old, weathered barn with a massive two-panel door. It was butted right up against the woods and I made a mental note. I was about to call everyone together to assess the situation when the sounds of *Run Through the Jungle* came blaring out of my pants.

Darn!

I skidded to a halt with my feet on the pavement and fumbled for the bread bag I'd wrapped my transistor in and tucked in my waistband. With trembling fingers I turned the dial down and shut it off. Everyone had pulled up and stopped next to me with amazement on their faces. Up ahead, one of the men dressed in a yellow rain slicker was looking down the road in our direction.

"You brought your transistor?" Arlo was gaping at me as he jerked his head in that funny way.

"Shut up!" I was still shaking. The words kept banging around in my head. "Mojo told me not to forget the radio."

The man up ahead was waving now, gesturing for us to go back. Only we couldn't be turned back now. Not when we were so close. The gang was looking down the road when Percy turned to me.

"What do we do now?"

"We go on anyway. Just follow me."

When we reached the cars and the men standing there, the one that had waved us back walked up and held out his hand. "You kids need to turn around and go back the way you came. This ain't no place for youngun's to be right now." Water dripped off the brim of his fedora. I caught a glimpse of his .38 holster as the wind whipped at his slicker. Margie squeezed me and I knew it was to urge me on.

"But sir, we're just passing through. My mom sent me...us, out here to check on my grandma. To make sure she was all right...with the storm and all."

"In this weather?" He took his fedora off and shook it, sending rain droplets in all directions.

"Yes sir. Mom's sick in bed. And my dad's out of town on business." I played for his sympathy.

"All right. Just keep going down this road and don't stop until you get where you're going." He turned and walked back, shaking his head.

I waved everyone in closer, taking advantage of the moment since we weren't likely to get another chance.

"Listen up! We got to get to that other path down there and get in without being seen."

"But what about that road we saw last time we were here?" Arlo asked.

"Yeah, I remember that, too. But I don't know where it is. Do you?"

Arlo shook his head and looked at his soggy shoes.

"We're gonna go on like they expect us to, and when we reach that path, I'll give the signal. Y'all need to get down it like greased weasels. Okay?" I looked at each of them, twice at Arlo, to make sure they understood.

All heads nodded and we got underway, riding past the cars with flashing emergency lights and the men next to them. I kept my eyes straight ahead until we were out of hearing range. The weed-choked path was about twenty yards ahead when I glanced back over my shoulder to see if anyone was paying attention to us. The men who stopped us were now walking back toward Lath's driveway and I knew this was it. As I came almost even with the cut-off, I signaled with my arm and turned my bike on a dime toward the ditch. "Hold on!" I shouted to Margie as we bucked and bounced down the muddy bank, almost losing my grip on the handlebars. I could hear the others rattling down behind us, and then a big *umfff!* as Arlo was thrown over into the mud and reeds. We pulled up just short of the woods and I motioned for everyone to stay down as our heads would easily be seen if anyone took to looking hard enough. Arlo walked up grinning, mud on the left side of his face. We gathered around tightly.

"We need to hide our bikes around in this tall stuff...." I motioned to the thick growth around us. "Make sure it's hidden good." They all nodded. "Then, we all go in together. Got it?" More nodding. "Good."

A few minutes later we were all back together. Margie passed out an apple to each of us. Arlo frowned.

"You can have the Mary Janes and Pixie Stix after you've had your sandwich…later." She admonished him like a mother would.

We all grinned and savored the juicy, red fruit for a few minutes. That is, everyone but Arlo. He took a bite and crammed the rest in his pants pocket, where it protruded at a ridiculous length from his leg.

"We'll go in through here. Stay low…and stay together." I pulled my cap down tight and crab walked through the first few yards of wet undergrowth, pushing at the low branches that tried to slap me. A squad car flew by on the road and I looked back, glad to see Arlo safely inside the foliage. *Where were the police going?*

"Pete!" Percy was trying to get my attention.

"What?"

"Your hat!"

My hat? It suddenly dawned on me. My bright red Wolfpack hat was like a beacon. I pulled it off and stuffed it in my rear pocket.

We finally cleared the thick stuff and stood up in the path. It was gloomy, large drops of rain falling on us as we stood there getting our bearings. Martin was tugging at his shirt again and Arlo still whacked and shook his head at every chance. Margie moved close to me.

"What do we do now, Pete?"

I could just make out her face and what I saw stopped the words on my lips. She had three large, red boils on her face and some that were not quite there yet. Boils as big as my thumb. I stepped back on reflex.

"What's wrong with you?" She was looking at me hurt-like. I

decided to play stupid.

"Nothing. You feeling okay?"

"I guess. Why?" She scratched at her face, and I wondered why she didn't feel them.

It could have been a trick of the eyes, since mine were watering a little, but those things seemed to move, like they were alive. My stomach did a flip-flop. I glanced around and the averting of eyes told me the others saw them, too. They said nothing.

"Just asking," I muttered.

"Anyone feel that?" Percy asked. He had his glasses off, rubbing his eyes. In fact, we were all rubbing at our eyes.

"Must be the tear gas." Martin spoke, continuing to scratch at his shoulders.

We were wasting time standing here. I motioned for everyone to follow me and turned in the direction of the pond. We kept as quiet as we could until we were near the water, and crouched down behind a growth of weeds and vines. I signaled everyone to be quiet with a finger to my lips. I pulled the wet leaves apart, just enough to get a view. Percy and Arlo crowded in on me as we peered toward the bank. What we saw surprised and confused us at once.

A tall man stood on the bank with his back to us, dressed in a silky green robe. His hood was down on his shoulders. I could tell it was Fred Sessom by his spiky blond crew cut. He stood stiff, head bowed toward the water, swaying slightly like a tree in the breeze. Rain pelted the surface of the pond, and I wondered what he could be doing.

"Look!" Margie whispered in my ear. "Down in front of him…."

We craned our necks to get a good look at the water. It was covered in tiny ripples as the rain came down, but something dark lurked just below the surface. A ring of black, about the size of a shoe polish can, opened and disappeared, over and over where the shadow was. It took me a second to realize where I'd seen such a thing before. *That's a fish's mouth. But what's it doing?* I looked back up at Fred Sessom, and it hit me. I turned to the others.

"You're not going to believe this…there's a fish talking to him."

I watched their expressions turn from confusion to disbelief. I could see those boils on Margie's face real close now. They *were* moving. My stomach knotted, sending bile up my throat. I almost gagged, but held it in. *Oh crap!*

The air was broken by a shrill *squawk!* We all jumped.

"*This is the police! This area is surrounded. Under the jurisdiction of the State of North Carolina, the County of Johnston, and with the cooperation of the Harper's Mill Police Department, you are hereby being served with arrest warrants for the following persons….*"

Fred seemed to come out of his trance at the sound of the bullhorn. He looked around, luckily not spotting us as we crouched down further, and made for the bushes some twenty yards away. I waited until he disappeared before I stepped out.

"*…Fredric Sessom…*"

"Pete! Where are you going?" Arlo was halfway up, strung like a piano wire ready to snap.

"*…Lath Edwards…*"

"Just wait there a minute!" I shooshed him back with my hand and walked to the edge of the pond. The shadow was still there. *What was I doing?* I waited a few seconds but the fish mouth didn't appear. *This is crazy….* The images of my nightmare washing over me, I shivered uncontrollably, stepping back from the algae-ooze that marked the water line.

"*…Thelonious Nichols…*"

A loud *boom!* rocked the ground to the north, just as two more *whoomppps!* were heard, followed by shattering glass. *Must be firing at the old cabin.* I bent over and scurried back to the bushes, hands eagerly pulling me in to safety.

"*...and Russell Beecham. Anyone in the company of these men will be held for questioning. The time is 11:15 a.m.. You have fifteen minutes to surrender yourselves into our custody.*"

"Well?" Percy blinked at me through his misty glasses.

"The fish isn't talking no more." I shrugged.

"Oh, yes he is."

I looked at Arlo. A single tear ran down his left cheek. He wasn't slapping at his head anymore, and that made me feel uneasy for some reason. The mosquitoes were getting bad. I slapped my arm, smearing one in the hairs.

"What do you mean?"

He took a slow, deep breath. "I mean he's in my head, Pete. Has been since we left Margie's. At first I didn't know what was happening, but when we saw Mr. Sessom standing there, the words made sense. It wasn't talking to me anymore. I heard what it said to Sessom...." Arlo choked up a bit.

"You mean that thing was talking in your head? How? Is it still talking?" I blurted everything out at once, my tongue almost tripping over itself.

"Yes." Arlo's face sagged.

"I know what we can do." Percy spoke as he moved between me and Arlo. "Give me that radio, Pete." I hesitated as he dug around in his pocket, finally pulling out a small twist of wire. He looked at me impatiently. "Pete, it's for our own good. Now give me the radio...please."

I dug it from my pants, removing the bread bag, and handed it to him. He opened the back and worked the little speaker free from the case, leaving all the wires intact. I stared at it, my jaw hanging open. He handed the loose wire to Arlo.

"Unwind that wire and wrap one end around your silver tooth,

Arlo. Keep your finger on it and hand me the other end when you're done," Percy instructed.

Arlo carefully wound the wire around his tooth and handed Percy the other end, keeping his finger on his work. Percy checked the power dial, then hooked the wire end and slid it around some exposed wire at the base of the speaker coil. He studied his work for a second, pushed his glasses back up his nose and looked around at us. A mosquito landed on his neck and he slapped it flat, leaving a little dark smear. He never lost his composure.

"Ready?"

We all nodded and he rolled his thumb across the switch. The radio made a small popping sound, then settled on a barely audible hiss. It reminded me of a conch shell I'd held up to my ear at the beach one summer. Percy moved the dial up slowly. *Wild World* was mesmerizing the airwaves in tight acoustic style.

The hiss grew louder and overtook Cat Stevens. We could hear something faintly in the background noise, just above a whisper…

"…*arlo is a useless boy… a bully…a ugly, ugly boy…you will die with your friends arlo…die die die.…*"

We all looked at each other, then back at Arlo, then back to the radio. The noise faded out and Cat came growling back, reminding the world that it's wild out there. But the hissing returned.

"…*die a horrible death…the angels cannot save you now arlo… everyone will die die die.…*"

I reached over and turned it off. I'd heard enough. I made eye contact with Arlo.

"What else did it say, Arlo?"

"That's pretty much it. Not much else…except.…" Tears rolled from Arlo's eyes freely now. "It seemed…" he shuddered. "It seemed old, Pete. Real old. I don't like it." He brought his crying under control, seemingly noticing for the first time that there was a girl present. "And…and what it told Mr. Sessom…told him to kill them all…kill them all."

I thought about this a moment and noticed Martin out of the corner of my eye. He had smeared mud across his face and neck, and was in the process of covering his arms.

"Not a bad idea, Martin."

The others took notice and we all started to do the same, except Margie. She studied us for a moment, then looked out at the pond. I guess it was too much for a girl, even a tomboy like her, to cover herself with mud. I looked at Percy and grinned. Apparently, he had dug his hands into a pocket of clay at his feet.

"Whaaat?" He stopped in mid-smear.

"Nothing…except you're whiter now than before." I grinned. The others looked at him.

"Yeah, you are." Martin was grinning now, although I noticed he was trying to smear mud across his shoulder blades.

"Dangit!" Percy took off his shirt and started wiping off the clay.

"We need to find that road. It was that way, if I remember right." I pointed at the woods off to our left.

Someone said, "Lead the way, Daniel Boone." And I did.

The rain was now reduced to drips from the trees as we all moved through the underbrush, staying low, me in the lead and Martin bringing up the rear. When we reached the road, there wasn't a lot of cover to be had, but the old outhouses were still there, backed up to the wild honeysuckle bushes. I ran up behind the first one and motioned for Margie to follow. Martin, Arlo and Percy did the same behind the other one. From my side I could see down the road to the bend. Margie positioned herself on the other side with a view between the old crappers.

"There's some cars over there, Pete!" Arlo said, peering around from his vantage point.

I looked over Margie's shoulder and sure enough, there sat three vehicles I'd seen before. A black Bonneville, an El Camino and an old VW van, all parked in front of the cabin.

"Look!" Margie had shifted and was pointing in the opposite direction down the road.

I moved back over to see what she was talking about. The police van was creeping slowly around the bend in the road.

Kaboom!

The ground around it lit up in a fiery flash, sending the van five or six feet off the ground. The top peeled open like a sardine can, and men and pieces of men flew in all directions, some smoldering like green oak on a bonfire, some completely aflame. We'd all ducked to the ground instinctively, partially covering our heads.

"We have to get out of here, fast!" I yelled.

We spilled out into the road, heading in the opposite direction. KKK or not, we couldn't just sit here. The last piece of van hadn't hit the ground yet when Margie screamed behind me, a loud scream full of terror and pain. I whirled on her and grabbed her arms to calm her down, suspecting the bloody carnage was more than she could stand.

"Oh my God...."

I dropped her arms and took a step back. She stood there, hands inches from her tear streaked, contorted face, crying in great sobs. The boils on her face weren't really boils anymore. They were people. People's faces. Writhing faces with the same contorted, horrified expression as Margie had at the moment. Small screams erupted from their mouths. I looked closer and saw several colored men and an oriental man...*and my dad.*

"Pete…Pete…help me…it hurts so bad Pete…it hurts so-o-o ba-a-a-d…." Dad pleaded.

The other faces were speaking and screaming in unison, but it was my dad's image that brought tears to my eyes and shut out everything around me. *Was he already dead?* I started to reach for Margie…for my dad, when Percy stepped up and placed his six-fingered hand across Margie's face. *His* face was calm as his finger began to grow brighter, illuminating the humid air around us, lighting up Margie until we couldn't see her head, or the end of Percy's arm anymore. He looked at me, light dancing off his glasses.

"It's just trying to scare us." That was all he said. Calm, just like that.

I heard a thump behind me and turned to see Martin on the ground, tearing at his shirt until the fabric gave way with a *rip!* "Oh God, oh God, I'm on fire!" he screamed, rolling around on the muddy road. Arlo ran over to him and grabbed his arm.

"Pete! Look… look at his back!" Arlo shouted, trying to hold Martin still. He finally managed to put his knee on Martin's shoulder and grab his other arm.

I left Percy with Margie, shielding my eyes as I ran to the struggling pair. I stopped just inches from Martin's leg and immediately took a step back. *So this is what he was scratching and pulling at.* His back looked blistering red, but I could make out the writing there, like someone had scrawled across his flesh with a nail.

YOU WILL ALL DIE

DEAD

DEAD

Martin wriggled around, clawing at the dirt, screaming.

"Augghhh…awww…it burns, Pete, it burns…stop it, pleeeaassss…."

I felt a hand on my shoulder and looked up at Percy, still calm.

Margie's beautiful face appeared next to him and my heart swelled. Not a boil or screaming face to be seen.

"Let me, Pete." Percy bent down and placed his hand on Martin's back. The light returned, brilliant and blinding to his finger, but we didn't turn away this time. The color grew and swirled around us, sucking up sound and time, filled with whispers of color I couldn't quite place. I could've sworn I heard music in there somewhere, like old flutes and drums, and maybe a harp. But then my mind just went blank. The light began to dim. We all stood gape-mouthed at Martin's baby smooth back.

I was helping him up when a screen door slammed behind us and we all turned to see Fred Sessom and Lath standing on the cabin porch. And they looked mad. Not just mad, but enraged.

CHAPTER TWENTY-FIVE

2011

"CRAP!" ARLO TOOK A step back, almost breaking the chain, but Percy and Margie held him in place.

"Don't!" Margie yanked his arm. "We have to stay together."

The hole between them was not what they expected, what they remembered. It was black, a void that seemed infinite and pulled at their minds like a vacuum. Only seven things were visible to them, and it seemed they were a million miles away and within arm's reach all at once.

"What are they?" Martin was leaning a bit too far forward. Margie tightened her grip,

"Lights," Percy said under his breath. No one disputed him.

The largest floated at the center, faintly illuminated, weakening as it pulsed. Two brighter lights danced, inching closer to it. Four more lights approached from the opposite direction, blue to the eye and full of energy.

"What are they doing?" Arlo seemed mesmerized.

Margie felt a small tingle in her stomach, an excitement that she knew was not from her own soul. It was the baby. At that moment the curtains of her mind dropped and she knew what she was seeing. The baby, however small and underdeveloped, knew too.

"It's Peter," she said, her voice flat. "It's Peter, and they're coming for him. For some reason, they're coming for him."

The other three looked up at her. Only Arlo had a look of horror on his face.

"I remember Margie," he said. Tears started running down his leathery cheeks as he spoke. "I remember something I'd forgot. I never told everything that day at the pond. I never—"

"Told what, Arlo?" Margie's voice was high, full of fear.

"I never told y'all everything I heard…all that the voice…*those* voices, said to me." He looked around at them, pleading with his eyes for understanding. "It wasn't just that old thing's voice, there was another one speaking in my head that day."

"Who?" Percy asked.

They all glanced down at the hole and back up at Arlo, waiting for his answer. Margie could see the younger Arlo in his face now. A younger and scared Arlo.

"Some old black man's voice…I don't know. He said something about Peter. That he would come for Peter one day. Something about seeing what's in the pot? Said not to worry about Peter, that he would be safe." His face contorted with grief.

"That's who they are." Margie scanned their faces. "They're coming back for him. This was no accident, don't you all see?"

A loud sound, like a zipper in heaven, reached their ears and they looked down just in time to see the hole close up and the grass resume its struggle with the wind. They stood like that for a few minutes, afraid to let go of each other.

"Mom, are you all right?" It was Peter Jr., gripping her by the arm.

She looked up, pieces of her past falling away like dandelion spores in a breeze.

"Yes, Son. I'm okay."

They all dropped their hands and stood back.

Bill and Clarice approached with Millie at their side. Clarice was crying. Bill turned to her when they reached the group.

"It's all right, Clarice." He kissed her head and turned to the others. "Lord, lord," he said. "Almost forty years and I got to explain it all to her now." He shook his head, gazed up at the sky. "But what in blue thunder *was* that?"

"It was blue thunder, Mr. Travers," Martin said. There was no humor in his voice.

Margie started for the van. "We have to go…now! Percy, you drive." She threw him the keys as she passed. It was an order, and nobody argued, especially Percy.

Three minutes later they were speeding toward the hospital in Margie's minivan.

Percy fought to keep traction in the deluge of water standing on the road. The windows were fogged despite the defroster being on high. Day had turned to night as they made their way down the interstate. Everyone was deep in thought as the sound of over-worked wipers filled the van. Margie sat silent, staring out at the cold, wet world.

Light in the rearview mirror nearly blinded Percy and he let up a little on the gas. A roar like a jet closed in on them and all heads turned as a motorcycle blew past, a jet of water splashing across the van's side. The driver, dressed in leather, wore goggles that strapped around his huge afro. His guitar case was all they could see as he moved further up and pulled back in front of them. Percy swerved to the right momentarily before gaining control again.

"Did you guys see that?" Arlo asked.

"Yes." Martin didn't look at him. He kept his eyes on the back of the motorcycle.

"I guess the fourth one is now accounted for," Bill said.

Nobody said a word.

Percy took the exit ramp, and ten minutes later they pulled into the hospital parking lot.

CHAPTER TWENTY-SIX

Peter

I CAN FEEL MYSELF descending, now. Descending through time and space, but the scene before me remains. The two lights have merged and the one they have become is upon me. I can't stop it, so I wait.

Images from my youth flash before me quickly, then fade away only to be replaced by others. My dog Fang, Arlo taking a beating, white hoods and burning crosses, a mystical portal. On and on they emerge, like so many scenes from a forgotten home movie. And there is the music, weaving through it all like a ghostly soundtrack. It was always the warp thread in my cloth, in my life. These things pull at me now with a longing I can't describe.

I feel weightless and weak of spirit, but I have not given up. I have not surrendered my dignity. I can still feel those that love me. They are close by, and I hear their voices sometimes. I hear them calling out to God. Asking for a better deal, for a second chance.

Oh yes, I hear godliness in them, a small but enduring belief in the good, just like I once heard the evil and hatred in those we confronted so long ago.

"You children shouldn't of come down here!" Fred shouted. "Especially that lil' nigger boy there." He pointed at Percy. Lath hovered at his side, standing straight as a board, those thick glasses magnifying his eyes.

I could see hate in Fred's eyes...all over his face, in fact. And there was something else, something I couldn't place. The hairs prickled on my neck like porcupine quills on alert. I shouted for everyone to follow as I took off in the direction we had been headed before all the weirdness started.

"Dangit!" I heard Fred shout, and then they were behind us.

It was a foot race. I looked back and everyone was close but Percy and Margie. Percy's glasses had bounced off his face in the ensuing chase and he was trying to retrieve them when Lath snatched his arm, nearly dislocating it. The contrast of Percy struggling against his pale, hairy bulk was shocking. A boning knife materialized in Lath's hand and just that quick he had it against Percy's throat. Fred Sessom's long legs pulled in behind Margie fast, and then he had her by the hair. She let out a scream as he jammed a gun under her chin. He was grinning like a madman.

I stopped at that sound and turned around to face them, feet planted. We were all in the center of the road now, Arlo hanging close at my side, Martin a few feet back. I'm not sure what happened at that point, except to say I'd had enough. Enough of the Freds and Laths and the *hate* of this world. Of the bullies and ugliness. A calm washed over me. If the three of us were going to die here, so be it. I just hoped Arlo and Martin had enough sense to run.

"What you looking at boy? You come out here to save the darkie and the china man? Or maybe your snitchin' weasel of a daddy?"

Fred was taunting me. Lath cackled loudly, amused by Fred's

words as Percy's small frame struggled in his clutches. He pressed the knife closer to Percy's throat.

A sound started behind us like a train in the distance. Arlo pulled at my arm.

"Pete?"

I glanced over at him, followed his gaze. Martin did the same.

In the distance, above the tree line, appeared a light, faint at first, but growing brighter and larger as the sound grew near. Martin took a step closer to us. The sky there suddenly exploded into a brilliant spectrum of white, then dimmed slightly as it came through the treetops, breaking and shredding limbs along the way. Then it dipped close to the road, heading directly for us. And it was moving fast!

"Run!" Arlo screamed, and we scrambled to the sides of the road like crabs in a flashlight beam.

Martin was the first to spot it. He jumped up and down, laughing and clapping his hands like a loon. The light came to a halt and the front of Pearl's cab rolled out of the glare like it was on a Sunday drive. The car pulled up next to us, covered in some clear goop, and stopped. The radio was wide open, *Mercedes Benz* blaring from the speakers, as Pearl's cigarette smoke rolled out the window. She tilted a bottle back and took a long pull of bourbon, bent over and smiled at us through the passenger window.

"Don't worry, sweethearts. This stuff don't do a thang for me anymore." She winked.

Both rear doors opened. Buddy stepped out, holding his Gibson by the neck, rattlesnake boots shining, fire in his eyes. Mojo glided from the other door, dressed in a long black cloak with purple suede boots. He gave us a peace sign as he strolled by.

I looked back at Fred and Lath, still holding their hostages, both men taking a few steps back, eyes like saucers. Lath was the first to bolt, pushing Percy to the ground and hightailing it through the bushes. Percy scrambled to his feet and scurried over to us, taking a step behind Arlo.

"You get back, ya hear?" Fred motioned toward Buddy and Mojo, cinching Margie tighter under the neck.

He was still moving backwards when Buddy made a beeline for him. Fred pulled the hammer back on his gun and stopped, a grin widening across his face.

"I don't know who or what you freaks are, but she's as good as dead!"

My gut clenched in a knot. There was no bluff in Fred Sessom's voice. *Margie could die!* I saw Arlo from the corner of my eye, working his way off to Fred's left, and figured he was making a run for it.

Buddy stopped fifteen yards from them and brought the Gibson up by the neck like a gunslinger. *What was he doing?* I rushed toward Buddy in a panic, knowing something bad was about to happen.

"No! Don't do it, Buddy!"

Arlo stepped forward and pitched his half-eaten apple like Don Drysdale, hard and fast, at Fred's head. It struck his temple with a wet thud, exploding like applesauce. He loosened his grip on Margie, who was struggling to break loose, and stumbled back a few steps, still clinging to a handful of her hair.

Mojo circled to Fred's right, smooth like a lizard, cloak loose and flowing like silk. Squatting, he nodded at Buddy. In an instant, from our left came a brown blur across the road that launched into the air and brought two sharp rows of teeth down on Fred's gun arm. Margie scrambled free and ran to us in a flash, tears streaming down her face. Fang hung on, flopping around like a wet dishrag as Fred screamed and tried to shake him off.

Then, as quick as greased lightning, that gun was in his free hand, jammed against Fang's head. The sound of it firing made me flinch, and I watched in horror as Fang went limp and fell from Fred's arm to the mud below. Tears formed in my eyes. I wiped at my face, but no one noticed. Buddy brought the Gibson up again, aiming the neck at Fred.

"Goodbye, Mr. Fred." Buddy's big teeth dazzled in that lop-sided grin.

He broke into *Peggy Sue*, holding the neck high on the fret board. Sparks shot from strings as the sound became shrill and high pitched, Buddy's fingers moving at a blur. An eerie white glow surrounded him, emanating in all directions, a burst of white energy tearing from the head on his Gibson. It struck Fred like a freight train. I could see the hair blown off him, the skin pushed back against bone until it started to tear. Then he exploded, sending particles so fine through the air that they appeared to be glittery dust motes. Everyone seemed frozen in place as the last of Fred Sessom shimmered in the air and winked out.

In the distance, I could hear sirens blaring as backup police and emergency vehicles arrived. *This wouldn't be their business yet. Not until it was over.*

The door to the cabin slammed open and out ran Thelonious Nichols and Russell Beecham, both armed with pistols. Mojo strolled toward them, hands out in a friendly greeting, cloak billowing out behind him. They opened fire. Bullets ricocheted off the vehicles, blowing out some windows in the process, and we all dropped down for cover. All except Buddy, Mojo and Pearl. Pearl was now sitting on the hood of the cab, cool as an ice-box Coke. Nothing seemed to touch Mojo and he stopped twenty feet from the steps. Buddy raised his guitar, but Mojo waved him off without looking in his direction. The guns simultaneously ran out, evidenced by the dry-fire clicking noise they were making.

"You fellas are being real ugly about this," Mojo said. He started to add something else, then paused, as if gathering his thoughts. "And for the record...I was just adjusting my zipper that night in Miami." He grinned and threw both hands out, sending two brilliant rainbow bursts toward the cabin. Russell threw himself off to the side and landed, smoldering, in the bushes. Thelonious simply exploded with the cabin. Boards, splinters and mortar chunks flew in all directions, some right through Mojo. In fact, it must have been two full minutes before the last piece hit the ground in front of the cab. And when it did, Pearl flicked her cigarette butt at it. We all just stayed on the ground and rolled over, some puking, some gagging. Thelonious Nichols' head rolled a few inches and finally came to rest propped against his nose.

I could see Pearl on the hood as she looked at it and shook her head sadly. "Don't pay to be a coward in a bully's business, Theo...." There was no hate, no joy, no evil in her face. Death truly made her sad.

I looked around for any sign of Lath, but he'd long since gone. Where *to* was another question altogether. Those helicopters appeared overhead again, flying low and fast. I guess they were assessing the situation. Pearl broke my concentration as if she'd read my thoughts.

"They can't get in here, Pete, honey. They contained these bad men for a reason, then we blocked *them* out to protect them. That police van was our mistake." She shook her head again. "We should've shut them out sooner than we did."

Well, that explained why the cavalry never showed up, or at least the real world cavalry.

The cabin was still on fire in some spots, but the flooring was still intact. I saw Mojo making his way through the debris without much worry. Buddy turned to face us.

"Pete, Arlo, Percy, Martin…and Margie." He said our names like roll call, then stood there clapping and grinning behind those things I once heard my dad call 'birth control' glasses while joking with Bud at the barber shop one day. "Follow me."

He started toward Mojo, climbing through the wreckage as he went. The rest of us followed, all a little shell-shocked. Martin stepped on something and bent down to pick it up.

"What's that, naked boy?" Arlo was kicking at an empty whisky bottle, glancing at Martin. It seemed he'd found part of his old self again.

"Probably why this place went up so fast?" He tossed the remains of a blasting cap at Arlo's feet, causing him to jump a little. Martin's dad had taught him well.

I spotted something partially under a pile of boards and pulled it out. The prayer cloth was soiled and ripped, but there was no mistaking what it was. I caught Buddy smiling at me. *Bingo* was all he mouthed at me silently. Mojo kicked the boards back and his foot struck something metal that jangled. He looked up at us.

"Well? You kids have some exploring to do." He stepped back and Arlo and I approached the spot.

"Be careful, Pete!" Margie said.

I looked at her and nodded.

Arlo and I grasped an over-sized metal ring and heaved the false floor up and back, letting it crash on the floor. A set of old wooden steps led down into darkness.

"Is that what they call a root cellar?" Percy peered over the edge and pushed his glasses up, then looked over at me.

"I don't know." I thought about it a second, about Buddy's words, *Mr. Kim's prayer cloth. Find it, Pete. You and the gang find it and you'll know you're in the right place.* I looked at the others. "They're down there…and we have to find them."

They all stared at me for a second, hesitant-like, then Margie said, "What about light, Pete? We don't have anything to see down there with."

"I know… but I'm going down anyway." The thought that Dad might be down there alive made me go against reason. I would go alone, if necessary.

I stepped on the first step and took a deep breath. Nobody moved, so down I went. The earth around me smelled old, damp. But there were underlying smells, things I couldn't quite identify. Ten steps, I kept my hands on the smooth dirt walls to balance myself…fifteen…then my foot struck dirt. I looked up at the opening where four heads were silhouetted against the daylight.

"You guys coming?" It was worth a try.

Four heads looked at each other then back into the hole. Arlo was the first to put his foot on the top step. I let out a sigh of relief and looked around as my eyes adjusted. I could hear water dripping somewhere, but the darkness still swallowed everything up. *Maybe they were right. How were we going to find anything in this place with no light?* Margie stepped off the bottom step and we were all down.

"Now what?" Percy asked.

"Now we go find those people…and Pete's daddy!" a voice said from the darkness.

We all jumped, Martin almost falling over the bottom step as he scrambled toward me. A light blinded us and Margie let out a shriek that made the hair stand up on my arms. Charlie stepped into the light coming from the stairway. He held an old nine-volt torch lamp in his hand.

"Charlie?" I said.

He took a bow. Now I knew what those underlying smells were, but I was relieved anyway. He had a light.

"What took y'all so long?" He grinned like a Cheshire cat.

"Well," I started, "we've been kind of busy, Charlie. You didn't hear—"

"Yeah, I heard it all. But I was getting a little spooked down here with all that noise and them men comin' and goin'. Mr. Mojo told me to wait it out." He pointed to his head and grinned again.

"How did you get—"

"I know'd a secret way in. I sleep here sometimes when it's cold."

"But how did you know—"

"Miss Pearl told me I need to help you find…them…" He aimed the light behind us. "…down there."

We all turned to look, following Charlie's light down the tunnel, which went about fifty feet and seemed to end where the light stopped.

"But it looks like a dead end." I glanced at him, then back down the tunnel again.

"No…no it ain't. That tunnel circles the pond. Been here over a hundred and forty years. Don't know why they dug it out, though." He scratched at his matted hair, the light bouncing crazily around the tunnel walls. "But they were smart cause that pond's dug into a bed of rock, so this cave is safe."

I hoped he knew what he was talking about. I looked at the others for support. No one protested. "Come on, then. Let's get this over with."

Charlie led the way, all of us falling in behind him. The tunnel ran down a ways and branched off to either side. That seemed about right, since the pond lay straight ahead. Charlie led us off to the left and we stayed as close as we could without walking all over each other. Being downwind from him was a battle in itself, but we had no choice. It was cool and dank, and I could just about taste dirt in my mouth.

"Where would you hide someone down here?" Arlo asked no

one in particular.

"You'll see," Charlie said as he continued down the tunnel. "I haven't been here since last winter, but when I heard about everyone disappearing and then Pearl told me about the KKK, well, I had a hunch."

We came to a halt. Charlie stepped to the side and threw the light beam on the opposite wall. Built into the dirt was a wooden support frame made of old railroad ties. But most surprising was the old wooden door it supported. Held together by rusted iron bands, the door looked old and warped. Charlie cleared his throat.

"I come down here sometimes in the winter. Don't know what they used these for but I stay pretty warm in here." He bent down and turned the old handle, giving the door a push with his foot. It popped open a foot or two and he bent down with the light.

At first all we saw was dirt and a few cobwebs around the doorframe. Charlie swept the light around the floor. A muffled sound came from the darkness beyond the beam. Charlie pushed the door open wider and raised the light to the far right corner... and there was Mr. Kim. He was tied hand and foot and stretched out on a dirty, moldy mattress with a rag stuffed in his mouth. He was trying to lift his head up to see us. Mr. Kim was never a big man, but my guess was that he weighed less than me now. His clothes were dirty and ragged, and he had sores on his skin anywhere you could see skin. I grabbed the light from Charlie and scrambled past him through the door to help the man. Arlo and Percy followed.

"Either of you got a knife or something?"

Arlo dug around in his pocket and pulled out a small pocketknife his dad had given him last Christmas. He handed it to me and I gave him the lantern to hold. I cut Mr. Kim free and removed the rag from his mouth. He tried to speak, but he was too raspy to understand so I told him to be quiet and we'd get him out of there. His glasses were in the dirt next to the mattress. I grabbed them, cleaned them a bit with my shirttail and handed them to him. He put them on and nodded at me with a smile. I helped him up, like lifting a feather, and walked him to the door, where Charlie and Martin grabbed him and pulled him out. I handed Arlo his knife.

"So that's what I tripped over...." It was Percy.

I looked around at Arlo, who was shining his light straight up. He and Percy were staring up at a piece of galvanized pipe that protruded through from above. I walked over and reached up beneath it. Cool air brushed my fingers.

"Yes..." I looked around the hole, "...to keep people alive until...." I suddenly thought about my dad. *We had to keep moving.*

The ground trembled a little and dirt rained down on our heads. Then it shook violently for about three seconds and stopped. I grabbed Arlo's arm and yanked him toward the door. *What's going on? We don't have earthquakes!*

"You guys, hurry!" Margie yelled from the tunnel.

The three of us fell out through the door, glad not to be buried alive in a dirt tomb. Arlo handed the light to Charlie, then he and Percy brushed the dirt out of their hair while I spoke to Mr. Kim. Charlie and Martin were still holding him up.

"Mr. Kim, are you okay?" It was a stupid question.

"I okay, Pete." It came out in a hoarse whisper as he smiled and nodded his head.

A thought occurred to me at that moment. Why was he still alive? They'd had him here for over two months. I couldn't go on without asking.

"Mr. Kim...why..." I paused a second, looking for the right words, "...why did they keep you down here so long? We thought they...we thought they would...." I couldn't say it.

"Kill me?" Mr. Kim asked, his voice like gravel under a boot. "They want money. I tell them I have no money, but they don't believe me. They think I have big bunch of money. They choke me and put cigarettes to my skin…say they make me tell them." His eyes grew watery. I could see the tremors in his face and lips as emotion welled up in him. "They not feed me for week at a time… but I tell truth!"

His voice was almost gone now, but the raw emotion was slowly being replaced with anger. It was an awkward moment for everyone. I turned my attention back to the gang.

"Come on, let's find my dad and Mr. Davis."

Arlo grabbed my arm and walked me a few feet away. "Pete… why don't we send Margie and Charlie back to the entrance with Mr. Kim? Someone needs to stay with him and we don't want to drag him around in these tunnels, do we?"

Arlo was right. We didn't know what lay ahead and this tunnel was getting very unstable. It was probably for the best, and I didn't want Margie getting hurt. I just hoped she'd take it well. We walked back to the group.

"Charlie? Margie? Would you two mind staying with Mr. Kim? He's in no shape to be running around in here. Y'all can take him back to the stairs and wait for us."

Charlie smiled and handed the light back to Arlo. Margie looked at me with hurt on her face, but I saw relief in her eyes, too. After a few awkward moments, she softened a bit and nodded.

Arlo, Martin, Percy and I took off down the tunnel in a hurry, looking for another door. The earth shook around us again as we ran, throwing dirt and dust into our eyes, but it didn't slow us down. After a few minutes, Arlo came to a stop and leveled the light at another door. It was almost identical to the first one except for one thing—it was locked. Arlo twisted the handle and pushed against it a few times, but it held fast.

"Wait," Percy said.

He moved next to Arlo and knelt down. I couldn't see what he was doing, but Arlo fell back on his butt and sat there with his mouth hanging open. I moved in closer. Percy's special finger, or his finger tip you might say, was jammed inside the keyhole and glowing like a hot poker. We watched as the metal softened and started to run in rivulets down the door front. After a few seconds, the lock mechanism fell into the dirt at his feet. He wiped his finger quickly on his pants as Arlo kicked the door in.

Mr. Davis was leaning against the back wall when Arlo's light fell across him. He shielded his eyes for a moment, then grinned as we all piled inside.

"'bout time you boys showed up. I was starting to lose my color down here."

Percy laughed. We all laughed as we helped him up. He was weak, but not too weak, and he walked out on his own. Not much else was said, but I felt he needed to know what was happening.

"We're going to get my dad. You can go back and leave, or come with us."

He looked off into the darkness, rubbing his chin, then studied our faces for a moment before his eyes settled back on me.

"Your daddy, huh?"

I nodded.

A grin broke loose on his weathered face. "Well, what are we waiting for?"

We all started down the tunnel again, a little slower this time. I could feel my heart picking up a pace, knowing we were getting closer. Arlo looked back and started to say something when a noise up ahead grabbed our attention. We stopped. He steadied the light along the tunnel. Something reflected it back for just a second, then was gone.

"What was that?" Percy whispered to Arlo.

Arlo remained silent. We started moving forward again at a snail's pace. After a few more feet, a dirty orange color moved into the edge of the light beam. We all stopped again. The orange took on shape, growing in stature as it moved cautiously into the light. I heard myself suck a sharp breath in as Lucifer stopped dead center in Arlo's beam.

"What the heck?" Arlo almost dropped the light.

Lucifer studied us for a few seconds, arms hanging low, teeth bared. It was so still I could hear the air coming and going from his nostrils. He was wearing no accessories now, just raw aggression.

"Don't move," I whispered. I could see a third door just past him. *He was guarding Dad.*

The ground shook again and Lucifer roared, beating his chest in a fury as dirt fell in his hairy coat and around his eyes. He took a step toward us. I felt Mr. Davis's hand on my shoulder, gently pushing me aside to get in front. I held up my hand slowly, stood my ground. He stopped next to me.

Like an elbow to the ribs, something nudged my brain: *the transistor radio!* I slowly reached down the front of my pants and pulled out the bread bag. I saw Lucifer hesitate, his brow furrow. I had to do this quick before he decided I was up to no-good. I removed the radio and carefully stuffed the bag in my pocket. Maintaining eye contact with him, I switched it on, keeping the volume low, and pointed the little speaker in his direction. Louis Armstrong was singing *What a Wonderful World.* I sighed with relief.

Lucifer stood there for a few seconds, teeth bared, body tense, and I wondered if this was just delaying the chaos he planned to unleash on us. Then, just like that, his teeth disappeared behind his lips, his brow relaxed and he slumped. Louis continued to soothe the savage beast as I took a step forward, slowly, and laid the radio at his feet, then stepped back in the same manner. We all watched him for a few minutes. Finally he leaned forward and picked up the radio, handling it gently. I prayed that The Who would not come on and launch into *My Generation.*

"Good thinking." Percy patted my back.

I didn't say a word, but watched as Lucifer turned and ambled further down the tunnel, radio against his ear. A loud explosion shook the ground and we couldn't tell where, or from what direction it came as more dirt covered us. Lucifer was not waiting around to find out. He disappeared into the darkness and away from us at a high speed, and I was glad. I took the light from Arlo, then reached down and turned the latch on the door. It wasn't locked.

"Dad?" I pushed the door in and thrust the lantern inside. Someone grabbed my arm and the light swung across a grizzled face.

"Pete?"

Dad stood there, a look of bewilderment and wonder on his face at once. The ground shook again, so violently that I had to grab him to keep us both upright. He let out a howl of pain as the tremor diminished.

"What's wrong?" I let the light fall down his side and discovered his arm hanging at a grotesque angle. He gently held it against his side.

"It's broke…and dislocated." He grimaced, sweat running down the sides of his face.

"We have to get out of here, Dad."

A small tremor shook below us and he nodded his head at me to lead the way. Mr. Davis helped me get him out, careful not to touch his bad arm, and stood supporting most of Dad's weight.

We started back down the tunnel, Arlo leading, Martin behind him, Mr. Davis and Dad, and Percy and I at the rear. We had just passed the second door when the shaking started again, and this time it was brutal. Trying to stay upright, we all grabbed at the walls, barely able to stand. Somewhere behind us I heard the distinct sound of water gushing.

"We have to run!" I shouted. "Back to the steps!"

We all took off, much faster this time, and reached the junction where we would turn in seconds. Arlo disappeared around the corner with Martin at his heels. I heard a yell as two bodies collided. When we rounded the corner I saw what the problem was. The exit was gone. *That must have been what the explosion was.* But where were Margie and Charlie…and Mr. Kim? The whole section where the stairs had been was now a wall of dirt. It grew thinner near the top, but covered the tunnel from wall to wall.

"Margie? Charlie?" I yelled, starting to worry now.

We all grew real still, waiting for a response. Just when I started to yell again, a few dirt clods and rocks rolled down from the top of the wall. Arlo trained his light up there and we all watched, a bit mesmerized, as more and more dirt and rocks rolled down. Finally, a small white arm thrust its way through the dirt.

"Margie?"

I clambered up the side of the mound and started digging away. Martin and Percy joined me, and in a few minutes we had Margie through. They went back to help Charlie and Mr. Kim out as I pulled Margie aside.

"What happened?"

"We were waiting for you guys when we heard someone at the top of those stairs. I started to call for help, but Charlie didn't think we should, so we hid over on that side in case someone…one of them came down here." She looked awful covered in all that dirt and grime…and beautiful, too. "I couldn't stand waiting so I ran up to just this side of the light….That's when I saw Mr. Lath's face at the top of the steps. He was looking away at something and I ducked and hurried back to Charlie and Mr. Kim. Then we heard the explosion. It was so loud, Pete. We couldn't hear anything for a while."

Her eyes got misty and I took her in my arms to comfort her. I heard a louder sound now, *lots* of water moving, if I wasn't mistaken. *Were we trapped down here?* We were all standing in the tunnel now. I looked at Charlie. He'd never really answered my question before.

"Charlie, how did you get in here? The door was in the cabin."

Charlie smiled at me. He was still beating dirt from his clothes when he answered.

"Probably the same way Lucifer got out." He kept brushing at his ratty pant knees.

"Wait," I said. "Are you telling me you knew Lucifer was down here?" We hadn't told them about our encounter yet. Suddenly, I was angry at Charlie.

"Well." He stopped brushing at his clothes and looked at me, looked around at all of us. He wasn't grinning any more. "I…I just guessed you might run into him. My mind don't work too good no more. When we…" he looked at Margie, "…got trapped, I thought I heard that screech, but I hear things in here all the time." He pointed to his head and lowered his eyes. "I saw him come in this place one day…from the other side. When he left, I came down here to see what it was." He grew silent.

I felt the steam go out of me. I couldn't be mad at someone like Charlie. His intentions were well meant.

I noticed the light Arlo held was growing dimmer.

A tremor hit at that moment that threw Charlie and Martin to the ground and showered us with dirt. A few old roots broke loose and dangled over our heads. We all held on to the walls, or each other, but it didn't stop. Mr. Davis kept Dad steady, but I could tell he was in a lot of pain with that arm. It sounded like an ocean was pouring in somewhere down the tunnel. I grabbed Martin and hauled him up as Charlie carefully pulled himself up against the wall.

"Give me your belts," I said to Arlo and Martin. They handed them to me, no questions asked. I buckled them together to form one long belt and went over to Dad and Mr. Davis. Dad raised his good arm, reading my mind it seemed, and I wrapped the belts around him, securing his bad arm to his side. He didn't make much sound. He winked at me and I winked back.

"We have to get out of here!" I yelled. "Charlie, lead us out!"

Arlo handed Charlie the lantern and he was off, moving like he'd been told there was a bag of old burgers in the dumpster behind Jim's Grill. We fell in behind him, chunks of the ceiling bombarding us. After a few seconds, it occurred to me that we were sloshing through mud and water, the water getting deeper with each step. A roar up ahead confirmed my suspicions.

Charlie swept the light further along the tunnel and we saw the source. Water shot out of several fissures along the wall with the pressure of a fire hose. Large chunks of dirt were washing away every second. He paused, causing a slight pile up.

"Keep moving!" I yelled at him.

"That's a lot of water." He looked terrified. I moved to the front and took the light away from him and grabbed his arm.

"If you think this is a lot of water, just keep standing here!" I shouted above the roar. "Now come on!" I gave him a good yank and he reluctantly followed.

We ran through the gushers, through the mud and ankle deep water, as fast as we could. I threw the light back a few times to make sure everyone was still with us. Mr. Davis and Dad were bringing up the rear as expected.

"It's up there…." Charlie said after a few minutes. He was panting, his body odor permeating the tunnel. We continued on as if a doorway would appear ahead like magic.

"Whoa, whoa!" Charlie was pulling at my arm. "We passed it!"

I stopped and swung the light around, still not seeing a way out.

"There." Charlie pointed at the top of the wall. My eyes followed until I saw it.

A square, rusty set of bars seemed to float on the wall above our heads. I studied it for a moment and realized there wouldn't be any concrete down here if the tunnel was as old as Charlie said. I reached out and touched the wall. The dirt had broken away in some places and I scratched at it a second until I exposed a wood beam about eight inches wide. I looked up…*lined up with the edge of the bars?* I moved over and discovered another one standing vertical under the dirt. *It was bolted to beams?* I turned to Charlie.

"Where does this lead?" Before he could answer, the ground rocked again and we all grabbed each other to stay upright. A rock fell and hit me on the crown of my head. I saw stars for a few seconds and felt something trickle down behind my ear. The tremor stopped.

"It leads down an old wooden chute…under the road and out into the woods." He stared up at it. "But it wasn't locked when I came down here."

Mr. Kim groaned in despair somewhere out of the light's range.

"So, how do we get that open?" Mr. Davis asked.

I swung the light up. Sure enough, there was a really old key lock holding it shut. *What else should we expect from Lucifer?* I looked at Percy. He shrugged and came over as I handed the light to Charlie and cupped my hands to boost him.

"Wait!" Arlo ambled over and dug out his pocketknife. "I can do this…." He poked his chest out a bit, and I knew we didn't have time for any competition at the moment.

"Arlo…I don't think…."

"It's okay," Percy said. He moved away.

Arlo stepped into my hands and I hoisted him up with all my strength. I could hear a grinding metal sound and a clicking noise, but couldn't see anything. "More light!" he shouted at Charlie. Charlie moved to the side for a better position. Arlo worked at it a few minutes, and I started to drop him back down and give Percy a try when I heard a metal snapping sound. The lock fell at my feet.

"I'm in!" Arlo shouted.

He swung the bars back on squeaky hinges and grappled with the opening, stepping up on my shoulder and finally pushing off from the top of my head when he got enough leverage. After a few seconds his head appeared where his feet had been. I felt relief, realizing the water was mid-way to my calf now.

"Give Margie the light and help her up…I'll grab her," Arlo said, arms and head dangling from the opening.

Mr. Davis motioned for Charlie to take hold of Dad. Charlie shouldered him and Mr. Davis came over to us. "Here, I'll do it, son. I'm taller than the rest of y'all." He stooped down, made a foothold for Margie and lifted her up. I handed her the lantern. Then Mr. Kim, Martin, Percy and myself. Charlie and Mr. Davis both hoisted Dad up, careful not to handle Dad's bad arm too much. I grabbed him and helped pull him into the chute. We all kept moving in a little ways to make room, and Charlie was next, but paused before he pulled himself up.

"What about you, Mr. Davis?"

"Don't worry about me none," he said, looking up at Charlie.

Charlie pulled himself up and crawled far enough in to make

room for Mr. Davis. We heard him leap up and grab the edge. After a few minutes, he'd clawed, drug and scrambled his way in.

Not bad for an old guy.

The chute was wet and moldy smelling, soft in a few places, as we made our way forward. I pulled Dad by his shirt collar on his bad side while he pulled with his good arm. It was slow going. After about thirty or forty feet, I heard Arlo up ahead say "Oh, great!" followed by a yelp and a thump. It grew a little brighter.

"Oh…" said Charlie, his voice bouncing off the walls. "I forgot to mention…there's a slight drop off…about five or six feet."

CHAPTER TWENTY-SEVEN

2011

MARGIE WAS THE FIRST one to Peter's room. When she opened the door, her heart skipped a beat. Two doctors and three nurses stood around Peter's bed, all of them looking back at her as she looked at them. Peter's doctor moved toward her.

"Mrs. Travers, can I speak with you in the hallway?" He didn't wait for her reply as he gently grabbed her elbow and led her back outside. The door shut behind them. "Mrs. Travers—"

"What's wrong with Peter?" she said. "Is there something wrong?" Tears welled up in her eyes.

"Mrs. Travers," he began again. "I'm afraid some of your husband's bodily functions are starting to fail. We're doing everything we can to stabilize him."

The others joined them, shaking rain off their clothes. Their expressions betrayed that something wasn't right.

"What's wrong?" Peter Jr. asked.

Margie didn't answer him. She pushed past the doctor and entered the room again, family and friends following. She stopped and looked at Peter on the bed, at the medical staff. "Would everyone please get out? I…we need a moment with my husband."

She kept her chin up, face calm.

They looked at each other, mumbling between themselves, pointing to a monitor or an IV line, then filed out of the room without saying another word. The door closed as the group moved to Peter's bedside.

"Margie?" Bill said, concern all over his face.

"Peter's body is shutting down." She said it evenly, keeping her eyes on Peter's face.

Clarice let out a sob. Bill led her over to a chair and helped her sit down. More sobs and cleared throats echoed in Margie's head. She thought about it for a moment, how cold it would sound. Everyone had a right to be here at Peter's side, but this wasn't just about Peter anymore. It was much bigger than that.

She cleared her throat and looked up, scanning their distraught faces. "Bill, Clarice," she turned toward them, then to Millie and Peter Jr., "Millie, Peter. I need you all to step out a minute, too. Please."

Clarice looked stunned. Millie started to protest, but caught the look in her mother's eyes. Bill and Peter Jr. gave her a look like they understood, in some way, what her motives were. Arlo, Percy and Martin stood there awkwardly, avoiding eye contact with them.

Bill helped Clarice up and led her toward the door. Peter Jr. opened it as Mille joined them and they all walked out, the door clicking softly behind them.

"Come here," Margie said, motioning for the others to gather closer around the bed. "Hold hands." They all held hands over Peter's still form. "Please pray for Peter." Her resolve almost broke. Closing her eyes, she took a deep breath and continued. "Pray for his strength, pray that God will give him the fight he needs to return." Her lips trembled. She bowed her head.

Monitors beeped, green lights went amber, then green again.

The respirator sounded labored, as if it were working against a great strain. The stillness of the room was suffocating, as if the void of one world had spilled over into the other. Five minutes passed. Something made a small clinking noise. Arlo lifted his head and looked around.

"Margie?" Arlo said.

She looked up. They all did.

Buddy, Mojo, Pearl and Jimi stood across the room. They looked exactly like they had thirty-seven years ago. The friends released their hands and moved to the foot of the bed. Four faced four, the air electrified.

"Margie," Buddy said, real concern in his ethereal eyes. "We're sorry about Peter." The other three nodded.

Margie's awe at their presence was quickly replaced with coldness. "Did you know?" she asked. "Did you know about the old black man? About some deal? Are you here to take Peter?" She moved to the front of the group now, her back like steel, fists clenched.

Mojo stepped up and held out his palms. Arlo flinched. "Now Margie, baby, we're not here to take Peter. We're here because we care."

"It's the Singing Man." Pearl said, moving next to Mojo. Sadness hung from her usually jovial face like dead weight. "His time as the Keeper is up, sweetheart. He's come to claim Peter."

"And you knew about this? You knew, even back then, that he would come for Peter one day?" Margie was visibly shaking.

"Yes," Jimi said. Phantom shadows danced across his dark features, disappeared. "Peter knew it, too."

His words took the fight out of Margie. *Peter knew this and never told me?* She stumbled back against the bed, grabbing for the railing.

A moment passed, then another.

"What can we do?" Margie pleaded, realizing suddenly that the game had changed.

Pearl shook her head, the purple boa tied there shimmering as she adjusted her pink sunglasses. Light from the ceiling reflected off her many rings. "Margie, darling, sometimes you gotta look to the past to figure out the future. Ouroboros, baby, it's all the same." A knowing smile tugged at the corners of her mouth.

Margie stared at her, at the lens of her rose-colored glasses, and then she knew. It all came down to the pond. Ground zero. They had to get to Edwards Pond. Peter was leaving, his body remaining behind, to meet his horrible destiny, and it would happen in a place from their past. A place between two worlds. She couldn't let him face that alone.

"But," Buddy stepped forward. "We can't interfere with the Singing Man, Margie. It's the Divine Law."

"I don't care!" she shouted. "We have to get to Edwards Pond!" She looked at Percy, Martin and Arlo. They needed no coaxing.

They were out the door and halfway to the elevators when Clarice called out to them. "Margie? Where are you going?"

Margie turned to her. "Just stay with Peter!"

They disappeared into the waiting elevator.

CHAPTER TWENTY-EIGHT

Peter

THE LIGHT ABSORBS ME, pulling me into a coldness that my mind can't fathom. There is chaos in this light, and I pray that I can keep my sanity. I cannot worry about the past now. Whatever has me propels me forward to the unknown with alarming speed.

The whiteness of the light is changing as I descend, red hues pulsing, deeper and deeper until I can sense nothing but crimson. A pulsing, blood red crimson.

And a noise. A high-pitched noise that threatens to rattle—to annihilate—the very core of my fragile, inner consciousness.

Is this what death feels like?

Arlo helped pull us out, headfirst. After I was free, Martin and Arlo helped me ease Dad out and set him down. Charlie wriggled to the opening and Arlo grabbed him, but let go just as Charlie leaned forward and clutched at his arm for support. Charlie fell out on his head. Arlo grinned and stepped around him to help Mr. Davis. Once we were all on the ground and accounted for, we plopped and sprawled out in the wet leaves that surrounded the chute opening.

We were not a pretty sight. Dad laid back and closed his eyes, probably fighting against the pain. I sprawled out like a snow angel, my whole body exhausted. Tiny tremors still shook the ground beneath us, like we were sitting atop an awakening beast, and that thought unsettled me. I started to sit up when my arm bumped against something hard under the leaves. I brushed them away... *My radio!* Lucifer must've dropped it, or hid it, when he came out. I picked it up and turned the switch on to be sure it still worked. The Three Dog Night were singing *Mama Told Me Not To Come.* Man, I loved that song. I started bobbing my head, lost in it, when a car skidded to a stop on the ridge above us, followed by the slam of a car door. I shut the radio off and crammed it in my pocket. Pearl came into view, her paisley print top fluttering in the breeze. She squatted and smiled.

"Ain't that the sweetest sight I've ever seen? Hope y'all are rested up cause you have one more thing that needs to be attended to." She stood up to leave and stopped. "And you better hurry."

I could hear a car engine revving in the distance and I knew instantly what she was talking about. *Lath!* I wasn't sure where exactly he could go, but he didn't deserve to go there, wherever it was.

"Come on, guys!" I pulled Dad up. Martin helped me get him up the slope. The rest followed until we were all on the road. The car was approaching as I hustled everyone into Pearl's cab, being careful with Dad's arm. Pearl sat still, smoking her cigarette with deliberation, checking the rearview mirror every few seconds. We were packed in there like sardines.

The car engine grew louder and Pearl sat up straight. "Let's rock and roll, honey!"

The battered El Camino blew by us. Pearl punched the gas. We took off, pressed against the seats by the force of acceleration, Margie's knuckles white as she squeezed my arm. Lath was moving fast toward...*the woods?* The road ahead seemed to end in shrubs and tall bushes and Lath was headed right for it...with Pearl on his tail.

"Pearl! Whoa! Pearl!" Arlo realized what was about to happen and grabbed the back of the seat in terror.

We all froze as Lath's El Camino hit the greenery and drove into...*what?* He crashed through the growth, leaving a flattened trail behind him, and entered the shadows of a barn through an open back wall, never slowing down. The front doors of the structure flew outward from the impact of the El Camino. Lath came barreling across a grass field.

Pearl drove through the bushes, into the barn, and rolled the cab to a stop. *This is what I saw from the road...there's no backside on this thing* I sat up for a better look.

"What's that?" Percy was pointing at a stand of trees where Lath was headed.

Mr. Davis sat up and let go of the arm rest. The tiny indentions his fingertips left were a testament to Pearl's driving. He looked through the windshield. "That's a field border. Used to have an irrigation ditch running through it. Looks like someone filled it up and drove on it over the years. Hummm...must be cool...and dark in them trees." He sat back and crossed his arms. "Wonder where it goes?"

Another boom rattled the cab and we all scrambled out as if on cue. All except Dad...he kept his seat. I didn't blame him. Even Pearl joined us, minus a cigarette for once.

"Holy—" The words stopped in Charlie's throat. We followed his awe-struck face to a point just above the trees. Three balls of blazing light converged at a point in the distance, directly in line with the trees in the field break, and grew brighter as they approached. Just as it seemed they were headed straight for us, they dropped toward the ground and disappeared.

Lath's El Camino hit the edge of the tree line and the tail lights lit up as he slammed on the brakes in the grass and brambles. After a few seconds, the El Camino slowly backed up a few feet and stopped.

"Guess he saw something he didn't like, huh?" Pearl looked around at us and smiled.

We heard them before we saw them. Three motorcycles rolled out slowly from the gloom of the trees and stopped in front of Lath's car. Feet planted, the riders revved their machines to ear-shattering levels and throttled them back before shutting them down completely. The two on either end were decked out from head to foot in leather, dark sunglasses and bandanas. Their bare, muscular arms looked flexed and sculpted as they gripped their machines and sat perfectly still. The one sitting between them was the centerpiece, and rightly so. A guitar bag strapped to a backrest towered over his head. Leather-clad, but a bit more colorful, sunglasses like mirrors, his long, lanky legs seemed way too long for his motorcycle. His afro was wind-swept, accented with a multi-colored bandana, and he exuded authority over his pack. Two snow-white arms were wrapped around his mid-section…*wait a minute…!*

I heard Charlie's breath intake sharply. He took a few steps forward before Pearl stopped him with her hand.

"I wouldn't go there, Charlie."

The Black Cats were back…and they had Jenny Lee with them.

Everyone stood still now, even Charlie. The air was so thick with tension you could cut out a slice. The lanky one dismounted his bike slowly, confidently, and strolled back to his guitar case. Jenny Lee sat there, calm and collected, her pink tassel-covered leather jacket accenting her beauty. She seemed to be nothing more than a spectator, and an indifferent one at that. I knew Charlie's heart was breaking all over again.

The biker unstrapped the case and withdrew a Stratocaster. He paused for a moment, caressing the neck and body with his long brown fingers. He didn't bother strapping it on, just turned and walked toward Lath's car.

The wind was picking up again and I felt the first few drops of what I was sure would be another torrential downpour.

Lath hadn't moved a muscle since his car stopped, and I wondered if he was terrified, or just too arrogant to see disaster coming. Taking several long strides, the man stepped onto the hood of Lath's El Camino and raised that Stratocaster above his head. The rain came down harder now, so hard, in fact, it was getting difficult to see the other two sitting on their bikes next to the trees.

With his bandana buffeted by the wind, and afro catching rain like glittering jewels, he ran his long fingers across the fret board like a man wrestling a python, quick sliding motions that sent a wall of shrieking guitar sounds in all directions. He took a deep breath and threw his head back, keeping the wailing instrument high above his head. Thunder boomed and cracked. A bolt of lightning snaked down and struck that Stratocaster, illuminating his body like a psychedelic rainbow. He held on, never losing his footing, never releasing the guitar, as the notes poured out of that heavenly amplifier from above.

It was still shrieking and reverberating when the colors faded, but flames now shot from the face of that Stratocaster. He lowered it, grabbing it by the neck like a baseball bat, and brought it down hard across Lath's windshield. Then again. And again, hammering with a fury at the man inside. The flames grew brighter, fueled by air, as glass flew in all directions. The guitar was coming apart, fiery pieces flying off with every swing to land inside the car. We could see Lath struggling to get out, fighting with the door, but he seemed to be trapped. Smoke started billowing from the shattered windshield as Lath screamed, loud and long... then went silent. His silhouette through the red glass disappeared in smoke and flames. The biker hopped backwards off the hood and stood there a second, lifting his glasses to assess the situation, then dropping them back in place.

I was stunned. Pearl was humming a tune behind me the whole time, and it sounded vaguely familiar. She smiled when I glanced back at her.

"An eye for an eye," Mr. Davis mumbled under his breath. I understood what he was saying and stayed silent.

The whole area behind us began to rumble and shake violently. I turned to see Buddy and Mojo strolling up the road toward us like gunslingers.

"Glad you could come, Jimi," Pearl said behind me.

Jimi?

When I looked back, they were embracing. But they weren't the only ones. Jenny Lee and Charlie met somewhere in the middle of the chaos, and Charlie had her in a bear hug, swinging her around, kissing her face and neck and...well, anywhere he could. I wondered how she could stand the smell. I walked over to the original gang, ground shaking beneath me, and hooked my thumb back over my shoulder.

"That's Jimi Hendrix," I said, poking my chest out like I knew everything. They all stared at Pearl and Jimi with bug eyes.

"Yes. That Jimi Hendrix," Mr. Kim said hoarsely, as Mr. Davis helped him walk over on shaky legs to join our group. We all smiled.

The trees around Edwards Pond were shaking and swaying from the tremors, steam rising like smoke from the center. Pearl and Jimi walked past us to join Buddy and Mojo. They all stood there in a circle for a few seconds. I couldn't hear what they were discussing, so I grabbed Margie's hand and squeezed it. She fell into my arms and we stood there a moment.

The roar from Edwards Pond was deafening. We all looked up, startled. I could feel goosebumps run up both my arms. Margie squeezed me tighter.

Mojo, Buddy, Pearl and Jimi turned to face us. "It's time!" Mojo shouted to all of us above the ungodly noise of pain and grief that echoed from the pond. "This is our battle now. Pete, Arlo, Martin, Percy, Margie…" he gave an exaggerated bow in our direction, "…thank you for all you've done. We love ya, man!" The four of them turned and walked side by side back toward the pond.

"What do you think they're doing?" Arlo asked. Martin and Percy had walked up with him.

"I don't know," I replied. "But whatever it is…we have to believe in them."

We watched as they disappeared into the gloom around Edwards Pond. Nobody spoke another word. Nobody had to.

As the car burned behind us, we all gathered together in the rain and faced the pond. Charlie held Jenny Lee, I held Margie. Mr. Kim and Mr. Davis were exchanging tales in the grass behind us. Arlo, Martin and Percy were huddled together, attention fixed on the trees ahead. Water ran into our eyes and dripped from our clothing, but it seemed insignificant to us at the moment. There was no sign of the police, or their helicopters. Time stood still.

The wind picked up speed, swaying the treetops around the pond, pushing at us from all sides. Another roar of pain reverberated from the pond, monstrous in magnitude. Margie squeezed me so tight, it was hard to breathe.

"Look!" Percy pointed his six-fingered hand toward the pond.

It appeared just above the trees like a gray goliath, smooth and rotating, and I realized it was the water from the pond. Like a huge vortex it spun upward in a massive column, bits of bushes, reeds, tree roots, rotted logs and mud, all trapped inside the wall of energy.

I heard someone gasp.

Four balls of light rose from the trees and circled the column like sentinels as it climbed to a great height, tapering near the bottom. One light dove into the maelstrom and another roar of agony and rage split the air. The light reappeared as another one dove in, disappeared. The howling ensued, turning more into anger than hurt. The second light flew out of the darkness just as the other two were entering. One of the lights faltered and pulled back, hovering just above the trees. A bolt of lightning flashed from the clouds and struck dead center in the vortex, followed by a rolling boom of thunder. Both lights flew from the center, moving erratically in orbit around the wall.

Pete? Do you believe? I heard it in my head, like a whisper. It was Buddy. *Pete...we need one more thing, Pete. You have to believe.*

"I believe," I said under my breath.

Then you know what to do, Pete.

I did. I gently pulled away from Margie and looked at her. She must have read my face, because her eyes filled with tears as she shook her head. *No…*she mouthed at me, no sound coming from her lips. I turned and faced the pond. Another ball of light flew out of the maelstrom and dimmed as it slowly dropped.

I broke into a run.

Through the barn, past the cab.

"Pete! Don't!" It was Dad. I didn't slow down or even look at him. I couldn't stop now.

I ran to beat the devil, pumping my arms, my legs starting to burn. Once I was on the road, I reached down and pulled my radio out, never slowing down. I thumbed the switch and it popped to life. The little red light was fading in the gloom and I knew the battery was dying. "Come on," I coaxed it, giving it a shake. The light brightened. I turned up the volume.

Don McLean was saying farewell to *American Pie*, driving his Chevy to the levy to meet some guys that were drinking and singing about dying. *Was I going to die?*

I hoped not.

I'd been so busy with the radio I didn't notice the horror to my left as I ran until a piece of wet, airborne root slapped against my face. The sight made me stop in my tracks. The vortex of water was hovering, spinning over the open pit that was once Edwards Pond, sounding like a freight train at full speed. It reminded me of the Wall of Death I'd seen at the State Fair, only inside out. A large hole lay at the center of the crater and the tail of the vortex disappeared down into the darkness like a thread in the eye of a needle. The wind coming off it blew water and sludge in my face, making it difficult to see, plastering my clothes against my skin like tape. But that wasn't the worst….

It was the bodies.

All of them.

They lined the bottom of Edwards Pond like a grizzly blanket of death. Dozens of skeletons lay among the rocks and cement blocks, ropes and wire inter-twined throughout. Crushed skulls and broken bones lay scattered in every direction.

Pete! Pete! Now, Pete! Do it now!

The voice drew me out of my shock. Buddy sounded desperate, and I'd never heard desperation in his voice until now. They were in big trouble, and I knew I had to act. I stepped to the very edge where the water level once reached and drew back my arm…

Now, Pete, now!

…and threw my radio like a major league outfielder, right at the center. It traveled in a high arc across the soggy bones of the dead and started a slow decent toward the hole. The wind from the vortex pulled at it, and for an instant my heart almost stopped. *Would it make it?*

It landed on the edge of the hole, bounced up a few feet. For a moment I could have sworn I heard the Rolling Stones break into *Down the Road a Piece* before disappearing into the abyss.

I looked up and four lights were circling the vortex again, pulsing bright and strong. The whole pond started to shake violently and I grabbed a small tree nearby for balance. The hole was growing brighter, light travelling up the tail of the vortex like fire on a fuse. I followed it up with my eyes until the whole thing was enveloped in a brilliant white aura. A loud *crack!* drew my eyes back to the hole. Four or five fissures had developed on the rim and now they moved quickly toward the edges—one directly at me. The freight train noise grew louder and louder.

The vortex exploded, hurling water, roots and dead fish in all directions.

My hands were ripped from the tree, the power of the blast throwing me some thirty feet through the air. The landing knocked the wind from my lungs, my body numb from the impact. I was on my back in the wet leaves again, eyes locked on the sky above, blinking to keep my focus, my vision growing hazy and returning in rhythm with my heartbeat. I couldn't tell if I was dead or dreaming.

Above me, the battle raged. A creature more horrible than I could imagine was shrieking and bellowing with fear and anger, its flesh black, the surface alive and fluid, like oily sludge. Tentacles with claw-like tips whipped out at the lights, fighting for its life. Large, hooded cat-like eyes covered its body, pupils red like blood. The lights circled and plunged into the black flesh as great pools of inky fluid shot out, raining down on the bones.

Then I heard it....

Through the roar of wind and beast I heard it approaching, growing louder as the engine screamed to pick up speed. From the corner of my eye I saw the little plane coming in fast from the direction of Harper's Mill, tiny lights blinking against the dark, wet sky. The wings were tipping crazy-like from side to side, tailwinds pushing it faster as it descended toward the abomination above me.

Just for a second, maybe somewhere in my mind's eye, maybe in a dream, I could see Buddy's bloody face pushed up against the tiny side window, one lens of his glasses cracked, a smile on his lips.

And then the image was gone.

The beast opened its maw to scream, teeth long and razor-like, dripping with hate— just like in my dream— because it *was* hate, hate in all of its vile glory, and that little plane, that plane that I knew was from another time, another place, flew straight into it, and it all exploded into a billion pieces of justice that vaporized in the wind and rain over Edwards Pond.

I lost consciousness.

281

"You did good, Pete." The Singing Man nodded his head, smiling. "Yes'um, you did real good…"

He gazed up at the shadows of the man's face, sunlight creating an aura along the edges like a halo. He felt no sadness, cried no tears. There were no voices in his head. He was at peace.

The Singing Man smiled down at him, a brilliant smile floating in shadows. "But I gots'ta go now, Pete. My work's all done fo' now, ya see? But one day I's come back fo' you. Yes'um, in the blink of a eye, I's be back."

Pulling his guitar around, he turned and started down the road. A small wren landed gently on his shoulder, perched, and Pete could hear him strumming those strings.

"Wait!" Pete yelled. "Who are you, mister? I mean, what's your name?" Somehow this felt important to him.

The Singing Man paused and turned, guitar silent, and opened his black hands wide and high. "I'm just tha' road manager, son. Just tha' ol' road manager." He laughed, a deep, bellowing, musical laugh, and started down the road again until his silhouette dissolved in the soft haze of summer.

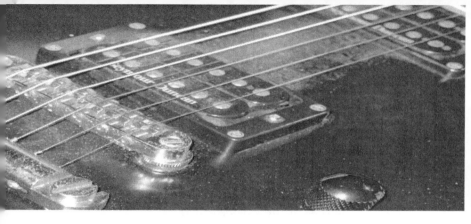

CHAPTER TWENTY-NINE

2011

BILL WAS THE FIRST to notice the doctors and nurses rushing into Peter's room with their smock tails flapping. He stood up and started for the door when the intercom stopped him cold.

"Code blue, code blue!" Two orderlies rushed past Bill, pushing a defibrillator, disappearing into the room.

Clarice let out a wail as she staggered up to Bill and grabbed his arm. Millie and Peter Jr. embraced, both crying as they watched in horror.

It ended as quickly as it started. The four of them embraced, cried and prayed. Four more prayers added to the chorus that sought an answer from heaven.

Arlo was behind the wheel as they barreled off U.S. 70 and headed for Open Bridge Road. Rain hammered the minivan, visibility low. Margie's knuckles were white on the dashboard as she, Martin and Percy held on for dear life. Arlo drove like a man possessed.

"Almost there!" he shouted.

Margie grimaced and doubled over. The pain came sudden and fast. Arlo looked over with a frown.

"You all right, Margie?"

She couldn't answer. All the breath had been pulled from her body. Her eyes watered as she fought against the pain. Percy and Martin risked scooting forward to see what was wrong. After a few seconds, it subsided as quickly as it had come. She sat up, feeling drained, and looked around to see three very concerned faces.

"I'm okay," she said, managing a weak smile.

Arlo reluctantly turned his attention back to the road.

But I'm not, Margie thought. *Not by a long shot.* Something was wrong. It was the baby and she knew it. It was time to come clean.

"I'm pregnant," she said, staring straight ahead.

Arlo hit the brakes, sending the van into a watery fishtail just as they reached the turn off for Edwards Pond. Margie grabbed the dash and held on. When the van stopped, they just sat there, panting. A thousand questions could have been entertained at that moment, a thousand answers given. But there were none. It was just another problem added to the equation, and it pressed down on them like a giant thumb.

Margie felt dampness creep between her legs. The pain started again, slowly, but she held herself up, kept her composure. *What else can I do?*

Arlo backed up a few feet and turned onto the access road. Thunder and lightning pounded the swollen sky above them as rain fell like tears from the heavens.

This was it.

CHAPTER THIRTY

Peter

Blink.

The last thing I remember was the blood red glow that embraced me before I exploded in a brilliant light.

But that was not the end. Oh, no. Death would not come that easy.

Face turned upward, my cheeks feel warm sunlight filtering through the treetops in a place I know as Edwards Pond. I'm lying on my back in the middle of a dirt road. I cannot move. Birds chirp, dragonflies dart across my vision, the air is fragrant with honeysuckle.

But this is not the place I remember.

It has changed. I have changed.

I have no memory beyond my fifteen years, even though I must, for I know this to be a fact.

I'm not cold anymore. I'm really nothing. Just a boy with no life beyond this moment, though I lived one in a beautiful dream once.

I'm just a package waiting to be delivered, a destiny fulfilled.

I can hear him now, his shoes scuttling, along the loose rocks and dirt as he grows nearer, as he comes to collect me, and I tremble.

He's singing, low.

Always singing.

CHAPTER THIRTY-ONE

2011 - Point of No Return

"Looks like the pond's been filled in." Percy spoke to his reflection in the glass.

"Can't blame them for that." Arlo maneuvered the van with caution. "Two-hundred and twenty-seven sets of bones came out of there. Biggest single hate crime in the history of this state."

Martin whistled. "Man, I'd forgotten about that."

A large limb crashed down close to the van, causing Arlo to swerve into the opposite brush before he corrected the wheel.

"Killing ground for a hundred and forty years," Margie muttered under her breath. Her hand absently brushed against the bloody spot on her jeans as she stared through the rivulets of rain coursing down the glass. She was too numb to be scared.

They all thought of this horror from their youth as the van traversed over bumps and gullies in the overgrown dirt road. Headlights cut through the gloom, catching the eye-shine of a wild animal every now and then. Rain continued to pelt the top of the van as it filtered through the trees. They rounded the next bend and their lights fell across something in the road.

"Stop!" yelled Margie.

She opened the door and carefully climbed out. Pain was still racking her body. The blood spot had grown on her jeans down both sides. The other doors opened and she heard them fall in behind her as she approached the lump in the road.

When she reached it, she stopped, weakened and shaking, water dripping from her hair into her eyes. The lightning flashed and she let out a cry of surprise. Peter Travers lay in the mud at their feet. Not the man who owned the record company. Not the father of her two children. But the fifteen-year-old boy she fell in love with.

They all thought it at once. It was like he never left Edwards Pond that day, thirty-seven years ago. It was like they left him here to face his fate.

Margie broke into a wail that echoed through the surrounding woods and fell to Peter's side, her knees sinking in the muck.

"Oh Peter, sweetheart!" She covered him, sobbing, clinching her stomach as waves of nausea washed over her.

Arlo bent down, placing his hand on her shoulder. The others stared down the road into the gloom.

"Margie," Arlo said urgently. She didn't move. "Margie, there's someone here with...with Peter." His voice was shaky.

She raised her head just as the Singing Man materialized from the mist. He walked slowly through the puddles and mud, luminous teeth floating in the shadows of his face, singing low under his breath. The three men took a step back.

"I sees you folks is keeping Peter company while he waits. That's a good thing, yes'um, that's a good thing." He stopped fifteen feet away, water dripping from his hat, guitar slung over his shoulder.

Margie raised her head, face grimaced in pain. "You can't have him!" she screamed. "You stay away from him!"

The Singing Man's smile disappeared. "He's mine, missy!" He

spit on the ground. "We has a deal." His eyes rolled upward. "We has a deal!" he shouted.

Thunder rumbled the heavens, lightning flashed from the sky. Four bolts hit the ground behind the van at the same time, scorching the earth, sending shock waves and debris in all directions. From the smoke emerged the rockers, side by side, boots kicking up sparks on the damp soil. Trailing behind them, Fang growled low in his throat, hair standing straight out like porcupine quills, ears pinned back.

The Singing Man laughed. Laughed high and wild as rain fell in his face. He leveled his eyes at Margie.

"Okay," he said, licking his lips. "Maybe we's can strike anotha' deal. I's knowed you'd probably put up a fight, so I been prepping that baby in you for it. Give the baby for Peter. Give me his soul… now." Darkness flickered across his face, fluid and fast. "Is that what you want?"

"No!" Margie managed to scream, rolling over beside Peter's body as pain seared through her with a death grip.

"Then Peter's mine!" roared the Singing Man.

Margie never heard his last words. She succumbed to the pain, losing consciousness as rain fell hard and cold across her face.

She was lying spread-eagled in a field of wildflowers, somewhere on a hillside. The clouds moved across her vision at alarming speed.

"Margie?"

She lifted her head, looking to her right, then left.

"Margie, my child." The sound of the voice felt like the weight of the earth pressing on her.

"Yes?"

"You must decide, Margie. I know he has blasphemous thoughts in his heart, but you must decide. Peter or your unborn."

Peter or your unborn. Peter or your unborn. The words collided in her head. Emotions welled up like a tidal wave from her heart. She felt pinned down, held in place. Her hand slid down to the curve of her belly. She was surprised at how large it was. How large her baby was. Tears flowed freely down her face, into her hair.

"Why?" It was all she could think of to ask. She didn't want to choose.

Lightning came from the clear blue sky and struck the hillside, sending flowers and dirt in all directions, igniting the dry grass. Smoke billowed across the field.

"Oh God, why?" she screamed, panic filling her.

But God had given His answer. The moment had passed.

In that moment, she had decided, too. And she would suffer the wrath of God if that was His final decision.

"Take me!" she called out defiantly. "Take me and spare my husband and baby, Lord!"

God was silent.

The smoke blew low to the ground, and enveloped her in darkness.

Total darkness.

Percy rolled Margie over and propped her up against his legs. "Margie?" He popped her cheeks a few times, softly, trying to wake her. Arlo and Martin had moved in closer, both keeping their eye on the dark figure. The rockers stood silently in the shadows, Fang heeling at their feet.

The Singing Man raised his arms skyward and shouted, "It's

time! Step away from her!"

"No!" Percy yelled. He drug Margie back a few feet, his heels slipping in the mud.

Lightning flashed and thunder vibrated the ground.

Martin was the first to notice it. "What's that smell?"

Arlo stood up slowly, arms limp at his side. He was looking beyond the Singing Man. Percy and Martin followed his gaze.

The light approaching grew brighter by the second, then movement, then form. Another man walked toward them in the gray light. His gait was slow and steady. When he was twenty feet from the Singing Man, he stopped.

Martin, Arlo and Percy wiped the rain from their eyes with their sleeves, not sure of what they were seeing.

"Mr. Davis?" Arlo asked.

The form didn't answer Arlo. Instead, he addressed the Singing Man. "You will have neither of them!"

The Singing Man smiled at Arlo and turned to face Freeman Davis. "Who is *you*, old man? You bes' be keeping to yo' business."

"You have no more business here, Lewis." Freeman looked over at the four shadows by the van. "He fell from Grace, just so you know."

"Well, that's a game changer, honey." It was Pearl. She moved from the shadows with the other three at her side.

The Singing Man laughed. "Don't tell them lies, Son. I's just here to collect what's mine."

"No one will pay Satan his dues today," Freeman said, low and threatening.

The Singing Man lowered his head, raised his arms, a sound starting deep in his throat. It grew in intensity until he threw his head back with a roar that shook the ground. From the heavens, lightning reached down and embraced him. His clothes exploded off his body. Black leathery wings unfolded across the width of the road. Skin fell off in sheets around his feet, revealing scales. He turned his horned reptilian head and locked liquid, marbled eyes with Percy's.

"Leave her be. I'll be back for the baby," he hissed.

"We'll not do battle on Earth!" Freeman shouted as brilliant white light cocooned his body.

Arlo covered his eyes with his arm and saw the puddle at his feet bubbling. Percy bent over Margie, head low. Martin was on his stomach, both arms over his head. The four rockers stood their ground; boas, dusters, tassels and hair blown back by the force.

Freeman hovered out from the light. His white robe glowed like a thousand suns and reflected off the twelve-foot golden sword in his hands. White wings extending, he pointed at the Singing Man.

"We'll battle in your dominion, Nephilim!"

With a roar, they both shot skyward, wings creating wind that bent trees low and rocked the van on its axles. The sky exploded, fiery fingers of lightning shooting from the midst of the battle as Freeman's sword clanged like God's hammer.

Fang was standing now, barking frantically at the sky.

Arlo and Percy lifted Margie up and placed her inside the cargo door of the van. Martin knelt down beside Peter and removed his windbreaker.

"Here, old friend," he said, covering Peter's smaller frame. His finger felt Peter's neck for a pulse and found one. A very faint one. "I'm not sure all this is real, Peter. If *you're* real. You're…not suppose to be this young." He laughed to himself. A sad, half-hearted laugh that caught in his throat.

Suddenly, the dog was standing next to Peter. He whimpered and lowered his head, licking Peter's face, nudging his master's chin with his nose. Martin watched but remained silent, a single tear forming in one eye and getting lost in the wetness on his face.

Arlo walked over to the ethereal rockers. "Can't you do anything," he pleaded. The hair stood up on his neck, goosebumps on his arms. Their legacy seemed larger than life out here in this rain, this gloom. They were all staring up at the chaos above.

Buddy spoke, but never took his gaze from the sky. "All in good time, Arlo. All in good time."

The sky lit up, turning roiling black clouds into silver. The noise that followed sounded like the earth had cracked open. Arlo grabbed the van's bumper to steady himself.

"There!" shouted Mojo. All heads turned upward as dozens of red lights circled the embattled angels.

Percy joined them. "What are they?"

"They're hell unleashed," Buddy said. He turned toward the others. "You guys ready to rock?" The other three nodded. Fang barked from Peter's side. "Then let's roll."

The four walked beyond Peter's still form and stopped in the road. Fang joined them, his tail high and stiff. Light shot from their eyes and mouths as they all spiraled upward, turning into white fireballs in the gray sky.

"That's so cool," Arlo said. "I think they're the reason I went into show business."

Martin and Percy stared at him a second, then turned their eyes back to the battle.

The rain had stopped. Clouds broke, exposing spans of blue sky. But the war that raged above them remained within a large, white cumulus. White and red flashes of light flared as Good battled Evil. Several rocks struck the road ahead and rolled to a stop. Percy walked over and bent down. They were smoking.

"What is it?" Arlo yelled.

Percy scratched his head and looked up. "Brimstone," he replied.

Arlo gave Martin an incredulous look. "He's kidding, right?"
"No." Martin didn't smile. He looked back at the cloud.

The cloud exploded, sending a light like a nuclear blast across the horizon, as far as the human eye could see. Trees were felled, birds were crushed in mid-flight. The three were pushed face first to the ground by the impact. Arlo lost two front teeth, tore the skin off his chin. Martin's nose was flattened to one side, both eyes blackened. Percy's glasses took out one of his eyes, glass shards tearing and embedding deep in the fibrous white tissue.

But they were conscious when the sky returned to blue and the sounds of the woods crept back.

Arlo stood up and looked around, blood spilling over his lip. The sun broke through the trees, small jewels of light bouncing off the puddles in the road. He saw Percy lying on his side, face bloodied, glasses askew, his chest rising and falling. Martin lay off to his left, gasping for air through his mouth. They were alive, and that was a good thing.

But it wasn't everything.

He looked at the ground below him. He looked down the road. He spun around. Nothing.

Peter was gone.

Arlo dropped to his knees and buried his bloody face in his hands. He cried. He cried for the loss of Peter. He cried for the loss of innocence. He cried for Margie and her baby.

That thought stopped him.

Margie?

Arlo jumped up and ran to the van. Margie was lying in blood. Too much blood. He felt for a pulse and found one, but it was weak. He lifted her up and laid her across the rear seat, buckling her in with both safety belts. He did a visual check of the van when he climbed out. The roof was scrunched down a few inches, but the tires had held.

Thank you, God.

He ran to Martin and helped him up. His breathing was ragged but he was lucid. Arlo hauled him to the van and strapped him in behind the driver's seat.

When he reached Percy, his friend was praying.

"I can't see!" Percy wailed when he felt Arlo's hand on his arm.

"Open the other eye," Arlo said. "And keep praying we make it to the hospital on time."

He did a fireman's carry and hauled Percy back to the van, strapping him into the front passenger's seat. He was running on adrenaline, but the blood he'd swallowed was making him queasy.

"Hold on, folks," he said, cranking the van. He kissed his St. Christopher and said a silent prayer. "This might get a bit bumpy."

CHAPTER THIRTY-TWO

"Yea, though I walk through the valley of the shadow of death..."

ARLO DROVE LIKE THE wind. The van was running rough, but traffic was light and the roads were drying off in the afternoon sun. Martin sat on the middle bench seat, head tilted back, a bloody rag pressed to his mouth to catch the flow from his mangled nose. Percy was ashen, his posture straight, small shards of glass protruding from his left eye, where blood and clear fluid still tricked down his cheek. Arlo's lips were swollen, cut, and felt like two rolls of quarters hanging from his face.

"He's really gone?" It was Percy. "Really gone?" he said to the windshield, to no one in particular.

"But...Mr. Davis, that angel or whatever he was, said that thing...that thing couldn't have him," Martin spat out, laboring between breathing and talking.

Arlo slammed his hands down on the steering wheel. "We don't know what happened up there. Just because the sky cleared and the sun came out...." His voice was full of frustration, fear and anger. He looked in his rear view mirror. "Martin, how's Margie doing?"

Martin reached over the seat. It seemed like eternity passed inside the van before he spoke.

"I don't feel a pulse...." He started breathing deep, ragged breaths. Panic seized him. "I don't feel a pulse, Arlo!"

They were two miles from the hospital. Arlo put the pedal to the floor, blew through red lights, stop signs, horns blaring, cars swerving away from the maniac in the minivan.

"Call 911, Martin!" Arlo shouted over the van's engine. "Tell them we're almost to Mercy General. Tell them her heart stopped!" Then, as an afterthought, "And she's pregnant!"

Martin fumbled with his phone and made the call. Scrambling over the seat, he started CPR on Margie as her arm dangled into the floorboard, the van swerving from side to side. His knees soaked up blood from the seat as he pressed on Margie's chest, half blinded by tears. He tried to give her mouth-to-mouth, but his own breathing was too labored.

Percy undid his seatbelt and crawled to the back. He got down on the floor of the van on his knees and gently grabbed Martin's arm. Martin stopped the compressions and looked at Percy's bloody face. Forty years of friendship spoke through their expressions.

"Trust me," Percy whispered.

Martin moved over and checked Margie's pulse as Percy laid his hand on her stomach.

"Nothing," he said, staring down at Margie's face.

Percy closed his eyes. His finger began to glow, faint at first, then burst into a brilliant light.

"What's going on back there?" Arlo shouted.

Martin opened his mouth, then closed it. The smallest murmur of life vibrated through Margie's neck and into his fingertips. The next beat came stronger.

"We have a pulse!" Martin shouted. "We have a pulse!"

"Good," yelled Arlo. "Hold on!"

The van turned sharp, tossing Percy and Martin around like rag dolls, but Percy kept his hand planted on Margie as they approached the emergency room entrance. The brakes locked, stopping the van in a three-foot skid. The rear door flew open and two medical technicians jumped in, lowering the seat back and unbuckling Margie. They both stopped when they saw Percy's finger.

"What are you looking at?" Percy shouted. "Haven't you ever seen a gift from God before?"

They looked at each other, puzzled, then slid Margie out to the gurney with Percy still attached. Martin was right behind him.

"Move, move, move!" Martin yelled.

The techs took off running with the gurney, Percy keeping pace, Martin at his heels. Arlo caught up with them as they entered the building. A PA with a clipboard was waiting.

"OR 2!" he yelled, and took off running with them. They rounded a corner and shot straight for the operating suite at the end of the hall. The gurney hit the swinging doors just as the PA grabbed Percy's arm and Margie disappeared inside, leaving them standing there.

"You have to wait out here, sir." He let go, glancing at Percy's hand as it fell.

"But—"

"It's hospital policy," he said, looking at Percy's face more closely. Then he looked at Martin and Arlo. "Plus, you all need to get back down to the ER and get those injuries taken care of."

He turned and dashed inside, the big doors swinging closed behind him.

The three of them stepped up to the glass and peered at the big, windowless stainless steel doors at the end of the hallway.

Seconds turned to minutes.

Percy looked down at his hand, at the sixth finger—at his gift.

"It wasn't supposed to happen this way," he said under his breath.

The other two looked at him, nodded. They turned their eyes back to the glass, hurried footfalls approaching from behind.

Bill Travers paced the hallway in ICU, wringing his hands and staring at the door to Peter's room. Clarice, Millie and Peter Jr. sat in adjoining seats along the wall.

"What in the blazes are they doing in there?" he asked Clarice for the hundredth time.

She dabbed her eyes and shook her head, wishing he would sit down and shut up. A nurse exited the room, her face shell-shocked, and scurried down the hall before Bill could stop her.

"That's my boy in there!" he yelled after her, his whole body shaking.

"Bill, please," Clarice said, patting the seat next to her. "Sit down. They're doing what they can."

Bill glared at her and continued pacing. After a few minutes the door to Peter's room opened and his doctor stepped out. He stood there a moment, jaw hanging open, eyes fixed on some point unknown.

Bill was on him in a flash. "What's wrong, doctor. What's going on with my boy?" he demanded.

The doctor gently pushed Bill aside and plopped down in the seat next to Clarice. He looked up at Bill, over at Clarice and the kids. He stared at his hands, then dropped them in his lap and shook his head.

"I did all I could," he said, voice cracking as he studied the tiles between his feet. "But it wasn't enough."

Millie let out a cry and buried her head in Peter Jr.'s shoulder. Bill's eyes teared up, his old arms gone limp at his sides. Clarice slumped in shock, cried dry for the first time in her life.

"I've never seen anything like that in my thirty-five years of medicine. He was dead," the doctor continued, in a daze. "He was dead…I called him. He was dead for twenty minutes."

Clarice sat up straight. Millie stopped crying, processing his words. Bill didn't wait around to hear more. He bolted for the door and pushed it open. Six people of medicine stood around the bed, silent and reverent over the man now propped up against the pillows.

"Dad?"

Margie sat on a blanket spread across green grass, the sun warming her skin through her summer dress. She was at peace as she watched children play and listened to their laughter fill the air.

Freeman Davis strolled up and sat down beside her. He glanced at her, saw the innocence and faith shine from her skin.

"Is this what you want," he asked, turning to take in the merriment of a summer day, to see what she saw.

"Yes." She didn't look at him. There was no need. She'd given herself for those she loved. She had no regrets.

He looked over at her and knew she spoke from the heart. "Good. So be it."

"Clear!" Everyone stood back. Eyes watched anxiously over

surgical masks, gloved hands at their sides or held out and covered with the blood of the woman that now lifted inches off the bed as current surged through her body.

The head surgeon looked down at her with a heavy heart. *Two lives.* He shook his head. The odds were against them. Way against them. It was time to call this one.

Rising, Freeman meandered back the way he came, whistling a tune as he adjusted his guitar strap on his shoulder. He stopped after a ways and turned to look back at her. *He was going to like this gig, yes he was. The Lord gives to those that give their hearts unconditional, amen.*

He walked on, singing a song he'd heard a group of young men sing in his garage back in a time that was almost lost in memory.

When he glanced back again, she was gone.

Amen.

Escorted away from the doors by hospital staff, Martin, Percy and Arlo were being tended to separately in the emergency room. They never heard the doctor call status in the OR. Never heard the talk among the OR staff. Never saw the gurney wheeled out.

Sometimes faith is not a singular act.

Sometimes its power is the sum of the collective.

Sometimes....

EPILOGUE

THE FOOTBALL ARCED HIGH across a perfect blue sky. A man nearing his sixties, but still in good shape, tried to leap and grab it, but it glanced off his fingertips and rolled toward a towering elm tree.

"Good one, Dad!" a younger man called out.

The wife hugged her youngest son and laughed at her husband's antics. "Your daddy's silly, isn't he, Freeman?" The boy giggled and took off in the direction of his older brother, hoping to throw the ball, too.

"He has good balance," her daughter said. "I wish mine did."

They sat on a blanket spread on green grass, the sun warming them through summer dresses.

"Enjoy the gifts they're given, sweetheart. No two are quite the same," she said to her daughter.

The man ran down to the elm, spotting a group of five people seated in a circle in the grass. They were playing cards. An old man raised his head and looked at him. The dog at his side whimpered and thumped his tail in the grass.

"You lose this?" the Singing Man asked, holding the football out to him.

The man approached and smiled. He grabbed the ball from the old man's hand. No words were exchanged. It was forbidden. The other four didn't look up from their cards. They didn't have to. The man could see the stirrings on their backs, beneath their clothing. *Finally*, he thought, remembering a dream from long ago. He smiled at the old man again and nodded.

"Daddy! Daddy!" little Freeman squealed, bounding down the hill.

The man met him halfway, scooping him up with one arm, and looked back.

Just grass surrounding an elm tree.

The boy giggled in his ear. The man smelled his little boy smell, that smell of innocence, and turned his face toward the heavens, toward a place where faith is borne by desperation and hope.

And *Love*.

AUTHOR'S NOTES

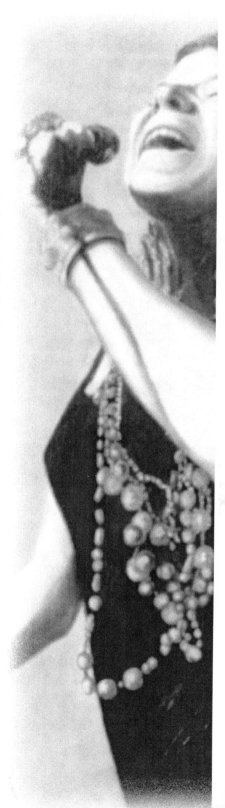

Fact: On December 9, 2010, Jim Morrison was posthumously pardoned by the state of Florida for a 1970 indecent exposure conviction, stemming from a 1969 concert. The author believes that this unfortunate incident was what Mojo was referring to before he leveled the cabin.

Fact: The cab that Pearl was driving in this book was a yellow 1970 Mercedes Benz, in case you were wondering. The Lord works in mysterious ways....

Fact: One of Buddy Holly's favorite past times was fishing. That's why it felt right to have him asking Pete about it from the get-go. Although he had other pressing matters, I would have certainly put Buddy fishing at Miller's Reservoir or Finley's Lake somewhere in this story had time permitted. But not Edwards Pond. No way. Sorry Buddy...

Fact: I don't know if Jimi Hendrix ever owned, much less rode, a motorcycle, but a jacket cover for South Saturn Delta caught my eye one day, and…well, Jimi just seemed natural on that motorcycle.

Fact: For clarification, Chief Lewis was not an intended characterization of the legendary Jerry Lee Lewis. The first time I saw the Chief in my tiny head, he looked like a young Jerry Lee… and it stuck. Similarities, if any, were just my way of having a little fun. If I'm lying, may great balls of fire rain down on me!

Fact: The Rock and Roll "historians" out there will probably scream about my misguided facts on the guitars of Holly and Hendrix. For the record, they both used Gibsons and Fenders throughout their brief careers. They needed distinction, so I flipped a coin. But don't worry. I got their permission to do so during a motel room séance in Florida…back in 2009.

Playlist

Buddy Holly: Peggy Sue
Buddy Holly: That'll Be The Day

Richie Valens: LaBamba

Big Bopper: Chantilly Lace

Jerry Lee Lewis: Great balls of Fire

The Rascals: Groovin'

Aretha Franklin: Respect

Van Morrison: Brown-eyed Girl

Eric Clapton: I Shot the Sheriff

The Temptations: My Girl
The Temptations: Just My Imagination

Jefferson Airplane: White Rabbit

Steppenwolf: Born to Be Wild

The Doors: Riders on the Storm
The Doors: Light My Fire
The Doors: Roadhouse Blues

Jimi Hendrix: Foxy Lady
Jimi Hendrix: Purple Haze
Jimi Hendrix: All Along The Watchtower

Janice Joplin: Piece of My Heart
Janice Joplin: Me and Bobby McGee
Janice Joplin: Mercedes Benz
Janice Joplin: Get It While You Can

Don McLean: American Pie

Norman Greenbaum: Spirit in the Sky

A Personal Note to You, Dear Reader

The inspiration for this book came from an actual place and time that has resided comfortably, and with much love, in the recesses of my heart for many years. The writing of it has taken me down many roads full of adventure, heartache, doubt, inspiration, revisions, edits, and the general angst that all writers experience. And yet, like a man who lays his love of forty-seven years to rest in a wind swept cemetery in the autumn of his life, I have no regrets about the journey. Not a single one.

Life is about Hope. About Wonderment and Fulfillment. About that mysterious place between Dreams and Happiness.

And about Faith.

There is no room for the emptiness of Regret.

I hope you, dear reader, have no regrets about taking this little journey with me.

B.S., October 26, 2011
Colorado Springs, CO.

Byron Suggs

Primarily a writer of southern fiction, Byron Suggs is the author of *Rockapocalypse: Disharmony of Justice* (a novel of youthful dreams, adult peril, and Divine intervention by a few deceased rock icons), and *Cold Currents,* a southern literary mystery/thriller. His third novel, a follow-up to *Cold Currents,* is slowly being downloaded from his brain to digital format and should be completed by Spring 2013. His short works of fiction have appeared in publications such as <u>Aries: A Journal of Arts and Literature</u> and <u>Black Heart Magazine</u> (e-zine).

A child of the 60's, his first viewing of *The Wizard of Oz* shaped his outlook of the world and erased any boundaries that could have stunted his imagination. He believes that a good tale should take you on an exhilarating adventure and leave you a bit more enchanted after you turn the last page.

CPSIA information can be obtained at www.ICGtesting.com
Printed in the USA
LVOW070042061012

301750LV00001B/6/P

9 781938 679018